Loose Id ®

ISBN 1-59632-823-1
ISBN 13: 978-1-59632-823-5
THE BLACKER THE BERRY
Copyright © November 2008 by Lena Matthews
Cover Art by April Martinez
Cover Design by April Martinez

Publisher acknowledges the authors and copyright holders of the individual works, as follows:
FOR LOVE'S SAKE ONLY
Copyright © December 2005 by Lena Matthews
THE BLACKER THE BERRY
Copyright © October 2008 by Lena Matthews

This book is an original publication of Loose Id®. Each individual story herein was previously published in e-book format only by Loose Id® and is a work of fiction. Any similarity to actual persons, events or existing locations is entirely coincidental.

Printed in the U.S.A. by
Lightning Source, Inc.
1246 Heil Quaker Blvd
La Vergne TN 37086
www.lightningsource.com

Contents

FOR LOVE'S SAKE ONLY

Dedication

For my Aunt Charlotte, who will die when she finds out I wrote this book with her in mind. Surprise, enjoy, don't kill me.

Chapter One

"Damn, these people are crazy," muttered Charlotte, looking from the bucking rider to the crowd roaring their approval. "This is insane."

A soft laugh escaped from TJ Maguire, her client from the rodeo company sponsoring the event. Charlotte could tell that the voluptuous redhead loved this sport just as much as the crazed fans hollering in the stands.

"You haven't even seen the half of it," TJ assured her with a smile.

And she wasn't sure if she wanted to. People were shouting, cheering, and drinking more here than at any college football game she'd ever gone to. All over some fool holding on for dear life to a horse that didn't want him on his back. If this was what this town did for fun, they could count her out.

"I can't believe how crazy people are about this." Crazy seemed like the right word, too. To Charlotte, it seemed a bit cruel and inhumane, yet the stands were filled with people who paid twenty-five dollars each to watch some man risk his neck for a stupid gold belt. She didn't know who she felt more sorry for—herself for having to be there, the rider getting jerked all over the place, or the animals being ridden for the crowd's amusement. It was all a bit too much for Charlotte, a Los Angeles native.

Looking back at the field, Charlotte let out a loud sigh of relief as the rider was tossed down to the ground. The people filling the arena jumped to their feet, roaring their approval, as she sat still, praying for divine intervention. The ride had taken less than seven seconds, but to her it felt like a lifetime. And to think she thought hockey was a rough sport. "I'm going to grab something to drink," she shouted to TJ, who was on her feet with the crowd.

Sure that she wouldn't be missed, Charlotte scooted her way out of the stands and down the steep steps. She couldn't believe Nathan, her boss and friend, was considering giving up Los Angeles—the Mecca of the business world, in her humble opinion—for this place. As much as Charlotte adored him and enjoyed working for him, she really was beginning to question his judgment.

And he was giving it all up for a woman—his entire life! For a woman who dressed up like a clown and willingly jumped in front of a bull. Something just wasn't right about that.

Walking around the stadium, Charlotte people-watched, observing the many different faces of people who loved rodeos. Her job required that she figure out how to draw in more people, but her brain didn't get the appeal to begin with. It wasn't like it catered to only the Caucasian population. There were Hispanics, Asians, and even a few African Americans wandering the grounds. More people were into rodeo than she would have ever imagined, and that straight baffled the hell out of her.

When she walked as far as she could and the noisy crowd finally dissipated, Charlotte found herself a bit lost. Wandering around, she headed down a corridor and followed the bright light looming up ahead, like the North Star in the dead of night. Hurrying her steps, she turned a corner and came to a dead stop in front of a wall of muscles, covered in plaid.

"Sorry, miss. I'm afraid you can't go back there," a firm voice stated, pulling her out of her silent reverie.

Startled, Charlotte glanced around, trying to get her bearings. *Go back there?* Hell, she didn't know where *there* was. Looking around the large beast of a man, Charlotte's eyes ran across wooden fences filled with animals calmly grazing in the sun.

"Ma'am." A giant of a man, dressed in jeans and a plaid shirt with the sleeves cut off, stood in front of the gate, staring down at her, with his massive arms crossed over his enormous chest. "You have to leave."

Well, that was beyond obvious. The last place she wanted to be was where they kept the smelly animals. Give her a dark alley filled with bums any day. "I'm sorry, I was only…"

"Only owners and riders allowed back here," he interrupted, frowning down at her as if he was guarding the Holy Grail instead of livestock.

"That's fine, if you could just tell me…"

"Look, lady…"

Lady! For some reason, Charlotte seriously doubted he meant "lady" in a good way. "If you would stop interrupting me, this would go a lot faster."

The rhinestone-cowboy-in-training looked startled at her angry words. It was a look Charlotte was accustomed to seeing on a man's face, especially on the face of a man who thought he could walk over her because she was petite. "Where is the…"

A loud whinnying drew her attention, as she darted around the hardheaded cowboy to get a better look. Something was wrong. Ignoring the menacing glare aimed at her, Charlotte side-stepped around the human barrier, but before she could get a step closer to the sound, beefy arms reached out and grabbed her, picking her up in the air.

"No reporters."

No, he didn't just grab her like that. "Put me down, you ass."

"Gladly," was the only warning she received before she was released as quickly as she'd been grabbed, and dropped onto the dusty ground. "No reporters."

Charlotte was able to keep herself from falling to the ground—but just barely. Never in her life had she been grabbed like that, and he wasn't going to live much longer to brag about it. "Why? You got something to hide?"

"A body in a few minutes," he growled, stepping closer to her.

Eyes widening, Charlotte took his words for the threat he intended, but instead of running as he might have hoped, she stepped closer. Charlotte had never given into bullies, whether they were the corporate kind or the cowboy kind. Dicks came in every color, shape, and size, literally and figuratively, and she was more than able to handle them. "You are *so* dead, rump ranger."

"What is going on here?" bellowed a voice from behind her. Turning with every intention of blasting the new intruder, Charlotte was cut short by the size of the man. If she thought Tiny here was huge, then this man had to be enormous. He towered over her five-four frame by yards, and looked like the very definition of a cowboy.

He wore a t-shirt that seemed as if it was stretched beyond belief across his massive chest, and his long, lean legs were covered in denim. A cowboy hat adorned his head, worn low over his brow, with dark brown hair trickling down his tanned neck. He looked like the Marlboro man on steroids.

"We got a reporter trying to sneak back in the corrals," Dick Number One answered, staring at her.

"Reporters are allowed back here only after the tournament."

"Well, that's nice to know." Narrowing her eyes, Charlotte faced the larger man head on. Maybe he was able to understand English. "But since I'm not a reporter, it doesn't exactly pertain to me, now does it?"

"Sure you're not," her nemesis muttered behind her.

Charlotte twisted around quickly and shoved her finger in his face. "Listen carefully, cattle boy. I am not a reporter. NOT A REPORTER." The blank look on his face only further inflamed her. "Am I talking too fast for you?"

"You little…"

"Ernest," the intruder said, stepping between them. "I think we can take her word for it."

Ernest. Charlotte snickered. No wonder he was so disgruntled. Turning back to her, the intruder looked down pointedly at her finger, which was still aimed menacingly at Ernest, and smiled. "I think you can put that away now. I wouldn't want you to hurt anyone with that thing."

Looking down at her index finger, Charlotte quickly yanked her hand back down to her side, slightly embarrassed. She couldn't believe she'd allowed the sun-damaged cowboy to ruffle her feathers. "If someone could just direct me toward the main office, I'll gladly leave." Charlotte resisted the childish urge to roll her eyes at Ernest, who was still staring at her as if he was waiting for her to rip out a notepad at anytime.

"I'll be glad to show you."

Finally, someone who wasn't suffering from sunstroke. "Thank you. I was beginning to think there was a cowboy-to-city-folk language breakdown here."

The brim of his hat didn't shield the laughter sparkling in his azure-colored eyes. "I took a correspondence course."

Charlotte couldn't resist the humor of the situation. The one good thing about arguing with Ernest was that it had taken her mind off of the horror show she had witnessed. "You mean, you get mail out there on the range?"

"Only as far as the crow flies."

The cowboy stuck his hand out to her and smiled. "Name's Tyson Wilcox, but you can call me Ty."

Charlotte returned his smile and took his work worn hand into hers. "Charlotte Sane."

"Shall we, Ms. Sane?" Gesturing out in front of him, with a sense of chivalry centuries too far gone, Ty shocked Charlotte, something that wasn't easily done.

"Thank you," she said softly, all thoughts of her surroundings now completely gone from her mind.

As they passed an irritated Ernest, Charlotte heard him say faintly, "Reporter."

"Cattle dung," she threw back over her shoulder, without losing her pace, feeling better than she had all day.

She had to be the cutest little thing Ty had seen in a really long time. It wasn't often he was caught off guard, but when he stumbled across the pint-size imp giving Ernest, a man who injured more men than a bucking bull, a hard time, Ty was impressed. He had actually seen Ernest make hardened men cry, but something about Charlotte's stance had said she wouldn't go down without a fight. And there was nothing Ty admired more than a filly with spirit.

At first he'd interceded on her behalf, thinking he was going to be saving her hide, but one look at her finger pointing threateningly at Ernest, and Ty quickly realized the wrangler was the person in trouble. Ty was willing to bet his daddy's land that Charlotte would have had Ernest roped and branded before the man knew what was coming.

"So what brings you to our little town?"

Charlotte glanced up at him, amused. "What makes you think I'm not a local?"

Okay, she must be kidding. Ty didn't know what Charlotte thought the locals looked liked in Santa Estrella, but they damn straight didn't look like her. No one who'd been raised around cattle would ever have attended a rodeo in black slacks and a cream-colored, button-up, long-sleeved shirt. And although the color suited her mocha-tinged skin, and she looked as tempting as sleeping in on Sundays, it was entirely the wrong thing to wear. It was almost ninety-eight degrees in the shade, and she looked like she was about to attend a board meeting. A local she wasn't, but Ty wasn't going to hold it against her. "Let's call it a hunch," he simply said.

"Well, you're right, Cowboy Ty. I'm a long way from Kansas."

So, that's where they were growing sexy little she-devils these days. Ty made a mental note to visit Kansas more often. "Are you having a good time?"

Charlotte shot him a quick glance before looking away again. "Not really."

"Why not?"

"This isn't really...my thing."

That was obvious. "So what *is* your thing?"

"Not torturing animals, that's for sure."

Ty stopped short, amazed at what he'd heard her say. Torture! Was she for real? "I don't know what you've been told, but I can promise you the horses aren't hurt, let alone tortured."

Sighing, Charlotte brushed her ebony bangs from her eyes and faced him. "Look, I know you more than likely make your living following the rodeo and wrestling bulls or whatnot, and I truly mean no disrespect to your chosen profession, but there's no way on God's green earth you're going to convince me it's not torture."

Well, hell. Only in a stadium full of single, beautiful women would Ty find the one PETA-pledging member. "It's nice to see you're open-minded about it."

"There's nothing to be open-minded about. You have your version…"

"And what?" he questioned with a small smile. "You have the truth?"

"I wasn't going to say that."

Yeah, but something about the tilt of her chin assured him she was thinking it. "Is this your first rodeo?"

"And last, God willing."

"Enjoyed it that much, did you?" he teased as they begin to head back up the corridor.

"Am I bowling you over with my excitement, or what?"

"Definitely *or what.*" The circuit wasn't for everyone, but it wasn't what Charlotte was making it out to be, either. "What brought you here, if you don't mind me asking?"

"Work."

"You're not with PETA or anything, are you?"

"No, but I have a mind to drop them a line."

Ty reached out and touched Charlotte's arm, stopping her in her tracks. "How much of the rodeo did you actually see?"

"I saw enough."

Somehow Ty seriously doubted that. "Through your fingered-covered eyes? Or were you actually watching the show?"

There was a war going on behind her pretty brown eyes, as if she was battling with herself about how much she wanted to admit. "A little bit of both."

"And did you get to see the animals afterwards?"

"The Lone Ranger didn't let me anywhere near the animals."

Her reference to Ernest brought a smile to his face. She had a quick wit and a spunky attitude. They were going to get along just fine.

"And besides, I'll be back in Los Angeles in less than a week. With work and all, I won't have time to visit the animals."

"Darlin', you're breaking my heart." The last thing Ty wanted to hear from this dark beauty was that she was leaving and wasn't coming back.

"Why's that?"

"Because your first memory of me isn't going to be as pleasant as mine is of you."

Eyeing him, Charlotte crossed her arms over her plush chest and eyed him amusedly. "Are all cowboys this smooth?"

Hooking his thumbs in the belt loops of his pants, Ty rocked back on his booted heels. "It's in the genes."

Looking down at the crotch of his jeans, which were getting tighter by the second, Charlotte looked back up at him and winked. "I'd say it's in the jeans."

Good Lord, the little devil was flirting. "Charlotte, I think I like you."

Laughing, she shook her head in mirth and started up the path again. Ty followed behind her shaking his head as well. She'd done it again. Just when he thought he had her in a little box, she surprised him. He could get used to that. That, and the way her plump little ass filled out her pants.

She was no bigger than a minute, but too cute for words. Her short dark hair was cute in a boy-like haircut, longer on top and tapered in the back, but Ty liked it. It was short and sassy, just like her. And her body—good Lord, that body—was what wet dreams were all about.

"Are you going to stare long?" she chided, raising a brow.

"Just long enough, I reckon."

"You're so silly," she laughed, tapping him on his arm.

"Thank you."

They talked as they walked through the stadium, seemingly of unimportant things, but Ty took every single piece of information she shared, and stored it in the back of his mind. He'd seen more in her in the five minutes since they met than he had in women he'd known for years, and it made him want to get to know her better.

He'd purposely taken the longer route to the main building so he could spend a few more minutes getting to know her. And although he had livestock to look after and riders to check on, Ty found himself dragging out their stroll, just for a little more time with Charlotte.

"Not that I don't appreciate this first class treatment," she said with a smile, "but shouldn't you be out there digging your spurs into a horse?"

"First of all, spurs, despite their bad rap, aren't sharp, especially the ones used in rodeos. They're mainly for show. The riders are trying to show the judges they have control of their feet and aren't just sitting there like a lump of clay trying to hang on."

"It takes skill not to fall off?"

"Apparently you've never had much power or speed between your legs."

"Not the four-legged variety, that's for sure," Charlotte quipped back.

Ty couldn't help but laugh. She was like a refreshing breath of air. And although all of her ideas about rodeos and ranchers in general were outdated, there was a kindness he recognized in her, which seemed out-of-date in most people today. She was misguided, but her heart was in the right place, and that alone was worth the time. "Seriously though, would you like to?"

"Ride a bucking horse? I don't think so."

"What about any horse? I have a small spread about forty miles away, and some of the sweetest horses God ever created."

"So you don't follow the circuit?"

"No, I don't." In fact, Ty hadn't entered a rodeo in years. He was only there because two of his horses were, and if everything went right, by the end of the tournament they wouldn't even be his horses anymore. But he wasn't sure what Charlotte would find more repulsive—the rider of the horse, or the owner allowing the horse to be ridden. Normally what others thought wouldn't mean a hill of beans to him, but for some reason what Charlotte thought, did.

"Are you going to be here all weekend?"

"I'd planned on it, what about you?"

"I haven't made up my mind just yet."

Pausing at a little booth, Charlotte looked over the trinkets, eyeing the Indian jewelry being sold. Ty came up behind her and picked up a silver bracelet with tiny turquoise stones delicately entwined in it and held it up next to her arm. "This would look lovely on you."

Charlotte took it from him and slid it over her hand. Ty was right. The silver looked amazing against her bronzed skin, sending images of her wearing nothing but the bracelet racing through his head. "It is pretty."

"Let me get it for you." His words surprised them both. Yet he didn't want to take it back. Ty wanted her to have it, and more importantly he wanted to be the one who gave it to her.

"No, I couldn't," she said, setting it back down on the table. Charlotte turned to walk away, but was brought up short by Ty's hand on her wrist.

"Why?"

"Because I don't know you, for one."

"Do you want to?"

Eyes widening, Charlotte seemed at a loss for words. Ty was sure it was something that did not happen to her often.

"Do you always move this fast?"

"I don't believe in wasting time."

"Charlotte." A loud, booming voice called her name from behind them, causing Charlotte to turn quickly in the direction the sound came from.

"Shit, what time is it?" she muttered, trying to pull her arm from Ty's grasp. "I have to go."

Ty didn't budge. "Who's that?" he questioned with a frown. Ty didn't like the way the man was glaring at them, or calling down to her as if he had prior claims.

"My boss." Nodding her head to the frowning man in silent communication, Charlotte turned back to Ty with a disappointed smile. "I have to go. Thank you so much for the walk. You really took my minds off of things."

"I'm serious about the ride." Ty wasn't ready for her to go. Especially not ready to relinquish her to another man.

"Maybe another time." She gave him a parting smile, and went to leave, but still Ty didn't let go. Turning to him, she mockingly frowned, "Listen, cowboy, I'm going to need my arm back."

"When can I see you again?"

"Charlotte!"

"I'm coming!" she yelled back over her shoulder, yanking her arm free. "Infuriating pain in the…"

"I want to see you again," Ty persisted.

Charlotte ran her free hand through her hair in frustration. "We're going to the little party tonight, will you be there?"

He hadn't planned on going, but there was no way he was going to miss seeing her again. "Yes."

"Okay, I'll see you then. I really have to go now."

With a parting smile, Charlotte hurried over to the other man leaving Ty standing in her wake, staring after with a smile. "Damn, she's something."

Chapter Two

It was just like a scene out of *Urban Cowboy*. Cowboy hats adorned the majority of the heads in the bar, and people were wearing jeans tight enough to cut off the circulation in their nether regions. If Charlotte weren't afraid of drawing more attention to herself than she already did by being one of the only black faces in the crowd, she would have sat down and taken a few pictures. None of her girls back home would ever believe where she was.

Not that she was into the club scene back in LA, but still, here she was more like a fish out of water. And it didn't help that she was a tad overdressed for the evening. Where most of the women were in tight jeans and tiny shirts that barely covered their bosom, Charlotte was in a short black dress. It wasn't fancy, but it wasn't jeans. She'd wanted to look nice for the evening, and instead she just looked out of place.

But being different was something Charlotte was used to. Because of her profession, she was used to being the only African American, and sometimes the only woman, in the boardroom. Looks and comments were things she overlooked on a daily basis, so she knew she could overlook it for tonight. Especially if it meant she got to see her cowboy again.

And that was the way she'd begun to think of Ty, as her cowboy. Although they'd only talked for a little while, Charlotte found herself intrigued by the imposing man. There was just something about the way he looked at her from beneath the brim of his sexy tan Stetson, that made her knees wobble and her pulse dance.

She'd thought about him all afternoon long. Normally, when it came to business, Charlotte was able to tune everything out and focus on the project at hand. It was how she had gotten so far in her career by the age of thirty-two, further than men who were more than double her age. But today, Ty had taken her mind off her game.

Even Nathan noticed her distraction, which was a bit odd, seeing how he was having attention issues of his own. For two lifelong workaholics, they were both having a hard time thinking about work. Must be something in the dusty air.

"If you say one word, I'll fire you on the spot."

Confused, Charlotte twisted around in her chair to see what had Nathan riled, and almost dropped dead on the spot. Her normally conservative boss was dressed like a country music singer.

"Oh, my God!" Eyes widening in shock, Charlotte couldn't have closed her mouth if her life depended on it.

"I'm not joking, Charlotte," he growled, pulling out a chair at the table and dropping into it.

"Who's laughing?" Charlotte wasn't amused. She was amazed. He looked damn good. Either her taste in men was changing, or there was something in the Southern California air that made men in cowboy boots and Stetsons suddenly look unbelievably great. Charlotte finally understood what the fuss was all about when it came to cowboys.

Nathan shot her a quick look, as if to judge her sincerity, and what he saw must have appeased him. "This doesn't get out."

His discomfort was amusing and endearing, all at the same time. "I'm not going to breathe a word, but damn, you could have given a girl warning. An ass that great deserves a heads-up."

"You're enjoying this a bit too much."

"As if you wouldn't if the situation were reversed," she teased, nudging him gently with her shoulder. "In the seven years I've known you I haven't been able to get you to change suit colors, and in one week, Calamity Jane has you wearing her brand."

"Her form of persuasion was a mite more tempting."

"It's like that, is it?" Damn, it was in the air. Charlotte was going to have to start taking shallow breaths if she was going to get out of Santa Estrella with her heart in one piece.

Nathan didn't answer her, which was answer enough. The intense look on his face spoke volumes, as did the way he perked up when Loren walked into his view.

He turned to Charlotte as he rose. "I'll be..."

"It's all right, Nathan. I can take care of myself, you know."

With a nod, he was gone, and Charlotte was more amused than she'd been in eons. Nathan was a goner. Charlotte only wondered how long it would take him to admit it.

Sitting back in her chair, Charlotte sipped her wine as she watched the dance floor with a look on her face akin to amusement. The shuffling and buffling looked difficult, but in no way resembled the grinding she saw back home. Although some of the moves guaranteed that you knew all of your partner's body dimensions, it still wasn't the dancing she was used to. Neither was the music, if that was what they called this whining, blaring from the overhead speakers.

"So, is this more your thing?" said a smooth voice from behind her.

Charlotte smiled, but didn't turn around. She knew exactly who it was. His voice had been rolling around in her head all day long. "Not exactly, but close enough, I guess."

Ty chuckled and dropped a black hat on the table next to her drink, as he slid smoothly into the seat next to her. It was so slick, Charlotte wondered if it was a honed skill that he practiced over and over again on the local bar bunnies.

Charlotte had rehearsed how she was going to act, but when she turned to look at him, all thoughts of pretense flew out of the window. The man was fucking hot! There went her cowboy hat theory, because without it, Ty was still gorgeous.

Dark brown, curly hair brushed his temples and his nape, short enough not to appear too girlish, and long enough that she would have something to pull on in bed. His eyes were a brilliant shade of blue, with long lashes that almost seemed too feminine. On any other man they would have been, but on Ty, they just looked mouthwatering. His eyelashes were the only thing feminine on him, though. Ty had a strong jaw line, a nose that seemed as if it might have been broken once or twice, and the beginning hint of stubble on his cheeks, though Charlotte could tell he'd already shaved tonight.

Gathering her wits, Charlotte stumbled for something to say. Ty's effect on her was disconcerting, to say the least. Charlotte wasn't one to let men get the upper hand in her relationships. She liked to feel in control of everything, and the last thing she was feeling around Ty was in control.

"So," she said, mentally grasping at straws. "Is this your fancy hat? The one you wear for 'special occasions'?"

Ty's eyes crinkled at the corner. "Yes ma'am," he drawled in a fake southern accent. "I even have one for Sundays."

"Is this how you normally spend your Saturday nights?" she asked, taking a sip of her drink to steady her nerves.

"No, actually I don't come into town very often, unless I have business to attend to. The ranch keeps me pretty busy."

"So you made an extra trip to town just to see little ol' me," Charlotte teased.

"Yes." The way he said it was completely serious, and devoid of any humor, causing Charlotte to stare in surprise. She hadn't been expecting that.

"Oh."

"You seem surprised."

"Ty, I have to say there isn't much about you that doesn't surprise me." Charlotte was too blown away to try and play any games. She didn't know how to deal with him. He wasn't anything like she'd been expecting or used to.

His long, graceful fingers toyed with the rim of his hat, as he watched with an expression akin to amusement. "Don't you like surprises?"

"Normally, no." Charlotte hated not knowing what was coming next. She liked everything to be in nice, safe little boxes, especially her men.

"Then I guess you're going to have to get used to it."

Charlotte snorted instead of replying. Ty was too cocky for his own good. He reminded her of a male version of herself.

"Care to shine my belt buckle?" Ty asked, changing the subject.

Shine his what? "Excuse me?"

Ty smiled at her confusion and nodded his head toward the dance floor. "It's slang for dancing. See the way she's rubbing against him?"

It better have been slang. "See, where I come from, we call that grinding."

"A little culture shock, huh?"

Charlotte wouldn't necessarily call this culture, but whatever floated his boat. "Let's just say, when I hear the expression 'hoedown,' I think of something entirely different."

"And honky-tonk?" he asked, amusement gleaming from his eyes.

"You don't even want to know."

"You're probably right," he agreed with a smile. Holding his hand out, Ty tried again. "Well..."

"I don't think so," Charlotte said, eyeing the people moving on the floor. Knowing her luck, she'd fall flat on her ass. She'd been blessed with rhythm from birth, but the moves they were making required a bit more than the ability to find the beat.

"Come on, it'll be fun." Ty stood up and moved to pull her chair back, but Charlotte shook her head no. Once again, he was going outside of her comfort zone.

When all else fails, pick a fight. "What, you want to take me out there so everyone can see what a fool I'm going to make of myself?"

His smile slowly slid off of his face, making Charlotte feel as low as an ant's belly. She hits, she scores. "Sorry," she muttered, wondering if her dress was loose enough for her to kick her own ass.

Ty leaned down until he was a hair's breath away from her ear, his words tickling her senses as he spoke to her. "No. I want to take you out there so every man in here can see what a beautiful woman I have on my arm. I want to twirl you around, dip you, spin you, show you a different way to have a good time. But most importantly, I want a reason to be able to hold you in my arms, besides the fact that I can't get you out of my head. Is that all right with you?"

Charlotte nodded her head like an idiot, too shocked to speak. Was he kidding? She wasn't going to be able to stand, let alone dance, after his sexy little speech. She was weak-kneed, lightheaded, and completely aroused, and Ty hadn't touched her with anything but his words.

Ty pulled back and tipped her chin up with his fingers so she was looking directly in his eyes. "Ms. Charlotte, you're looking all kinds of good tonight. " Dropping his fingers from her chin, Ty picked his hat up off of the table, and slipped it on his head. "May I have this dance?"

As if there was any doubt. "Yes."

* * *

It had taken a bit of work to get Charlotte on the dance floor, but Ty could tell she was having a good time now that she was out there. A few boot scuffs and a smashed toe later, she was dancing like a natural, following his lead as if they'd been partners for life. Ty was a big believer that chemistry on the dance floor was parallel to the chemistry a couple had in the bedroom, and by the way she was moving next to him, they would be combustible.

Ty hadn't been kidding when he said he wanted to feel her in his arms. From the moment he'd spotted her in the bar tonight, he knew that the attraction he'd felt earlier in the day wasn't all in his head. She was a sexy little package, especially when she was decked out like she was tonight.

The little black number she was wearing was stunning, particularly the way it molded to her curves the way his hands itched to. Ty missed a step or two because he'd been paying more attention to the way her ass filled out the back of her dress than he was to the flow of the song. But he couldn't help it. He was an ass man, and she had been blessed with a fine cut.

He wasn't the only man to notice the contours of her body. Ty was on the receiving end of several envious stares tonight, but he took it in stride. Charlotte was a beautiful, desirable woman, and any man alive would be a fool if they didn't notice.

Laughing as she missed a step and almost knocked into someone, Charlotte rolled herself into his arms and gave him a little bump with her bottom against his crotch. Ty's body, stimulated already from just being close to her, kicked into overdrive at the mere touch of her ass against him.

Charlotte looked up at him smiling, no doubt unaware of the havoc she was causing inside of him. Her pretty brown face was damp with perspiration and her eyes were lit with joy. It was a look he could get used to seeing on her face. She gestured for him to move in close, and leaned up to speak in his ear. "We better get off this floor before someone penalizes me for full body contact."

Ty nodded and led her off the floor. He'd had enough of the musical foreplay for one night. Ty was ready to move on to the next stage. The table she'd been sitting at was occupied now, so they squeezed up next to the bar.

"What would you like to drink?" he asked, nodding to the busy bartender, who was waiting to take their order.

"Water is fine." Grabbing a napkin off the bar, Charlotte dabbed at her forehead, as he paid for their drinks. Ty handed her the tall glass of ice water and watched in amusement as she drank it almost completely down in one gulp. His amusement quickly merged into arousal as he watched her take an ice cube out of the glass and run it over her throat and down her dusky cleavage. Ty would have given his left testicle at that moment to be the ice cube, or better yet, be the slip of water running down between her breasts. When the hell did his jeans get so tight?

"That was more fun than I'll ever admit," Charlotte said, dropping the lucky ice cube back into her glass. "But, like Cinderella, I should be heading home."

"*Home* home?" God wouldn't be that cruel!

"Oh, no, I'm here until Monday, then back home to LA."

The fates were kind to his undeserving soul. "Monday is a lifetime away. There are so many things that can happen between now and then."

Charlotte tilted her head and raised an eyebrow slowly. It was probably one of the sexiest things Ty had seen in a long time. "Sounds...tempting."

God, he hoped so.

Easing back on the barstool, Charlotte crossed her leg over her knee. "Are you working the arena tomorrow?"

Ty paused with his beer in mid-motion, when she began to gently rock her foot in tune with the music. Her skirt rose up a bit, and he was playing peak-a-boo with her thigh.

"Earth to cowboy. Earth to cowboy," Charlotte teased, snapping her fingers to capture his attention.

Ty was too aroused to be embarrassed. "Listen, little lady," he drawled, watching her eyes light up with humor. "You can't expect me to pay attention to what you're saying up here, when you have my complete attention down there. I'm a man, sugar; I can't multitask."

"You're not even going to deny you've been ogling me and not listening to a word I've said?"

"Honey, I'm hardly listening now." Charlotte roared with laughter as Ty looked on with a smile. She might have thought he was joking, but he was completely serious. It was hard to pay attention to one thing, when his cock was focused on something else.

"You are bad."

"Darlin', you have no idea." But he'd liked for her to.

"You didn't answer my question earlier. Are you in the rodeo tomorrow?"

"Why? Would you come out and watch?"

"No, but I might be tempted to play nurse afterwards." Her words were like arrows shooting straight at his groin. Just when he thought she couldn't get any sexier, she'd up and say or do something else. It was getting to the point where it was hard to sit still.

"I'm not in the rodeo; my horses are."

Charlotte's eyes widened in surprise. "Really? I thought you were a rodeo rider guy."

"No, I haven't done it in years."

"It doesn't bother you to see your horses hurt?"

Good Lord, she was never going to give that up. "Charlotte, I swear to you on my father's soul, they aren't being injured."

"For all I know, you may not like your father."

Ty couldn't help himself, he had to laugh. Never had one person amused and aroused him so much. "I happen to have loved my father very much, and as far as the horses go, you don't have to take my word for it. Come check them out before and after the show tomorrow. I'll give you a grand tour."

"Is this kinda like 'Come up and see my etchings'?"

"Whatever gets you there."

"I don't know. Ernest, the cowboy from hell, might not let me come back."

"Let me worry about Ernest."

"We'll see. I do have to do some work while I'm here."

"Not 'we'll see.' Say yes."

She raised her brow again, in the way he was beginning to love. "Are you always this demanding?"

"Yes." And as far as Ty was concerned, it was best that Charlotte find out now. She was a strong woman, he could tell right away. He could also tell that she was used to men following her lead, and if she thought she was going to play games with him, she seriously had another think coming.

"I'll try my best, but I really should be going."

Ty nodded, allowing Charlotte to think she'd won the battle. There was no doubt in his mind that she would be at the corral tomorrow; she was just trying to get him to squirm. Charlotte obviously didn't know him well. "I'll walk you to your car."

"It's okay, I didn't drive here. I just walked over. I'm staying at the Marriott a few doors down."

Even better. "Not a problem. I don't mind a little stroll."

They hardly talked as they exited the bar, just exchanging small glances and small talk as they got closer to her hotel. Ty could feel the air thicken between them, both of them knowing a choice was going to have to be made about what to do once they arrived at her room. Ty knew what he wanted, and he could tell she wanted the same thing too, he just didn't know if she would admit it.

"I had a really nice time," she said as she walked backwards to her door. Ty didn't say anything, but continued to maintain eye contact with her. He wasn't ready for the evening to end. He wasn't ready to say good-bye.

Tossing him a quick smile, Charlotte had turned to slide the card in the slot when Ty grabbed her free hand and turned her around to face him. She was just going to slip in and disappear. "I can't let you slip away without knowing how you taste."

Ty normally wasn't one for public displays of affection, but he felt an overwhelming need to feel her body against his own, and their location was the least of his worries. Dropping her purse onto the ground, Charlotte moved into his embrace as if she was coming home. All pretense of modesty was gone as they met each other halfway, both eager to taste one another.

Their mouths melted into one, demanding and seeking, urging each other on, as they rose together. Ty easily picked Charlotte up and leaned her back against the wall, all without breaking free of her tempting mouth.

She was such a tiny thing, no bigger than a minute, yet Ty didn't doubt they would fit well together. When it came down to it, everyone was the right size when they were lying down.

"Why don't you invite me in?" he whispered against her lips, not wanting to move away from her intoxicating mouth for a single moment.

"That's not a good idea," she moaned, as she slid her hands down his back, pulling him closer to her.

"Oh, but I disagree." Moving his hand from around her back, Ty slid it down her small waist and down to the lush bottom that had been tempting him all night.

Charlotte's grip tightened for a moment before she released him, and turned her mouth away from his, giving him another tempting place to graze. "This is crazy. We just met today."

"I'll respect you in the morning," he promised, nudging her neck with his lips. Ty felt like he'd been waiting a lifetime just to get her in his arms, and now that she was there, he didn't want to let her go. It felt so right.

"But I might not respect you," she said with a soft laugh, gently pushing him back.

Ty groaned, as he sensed her conviction. He was as hard as steel, and the last thing he was worried about was her respecting him. "Just for the record, I'm okay with you thinking I'm cheap."

Charlotte slid her hand between them and used it as a restraint to hold him back. "Tomorrow isn't that far away."

"Right now it feels like eons."

Chuckling, Charlotte stood up on her tiptoes and brushed her mouth against his again. Before he could deepen the kiss, Charlotte pulled back. "You're hell on my senses, cowboy. "

"Trust me, darlin', it's mutual."

"Tomorrow," she said, sliding her hand down his stomach slowly, before allowing it to drop back down to her side. "Tomorrow."

Charlotte turned quickly and unlocked her door, slipping in before Ty could stop her. Hard as hell and twice as horny, Ty gave a deep groan before dropping back against her door in frustration. She wanted him and Lord knew he wanted her, too. Who gave a rat's ass about the rules?

Looking down at his watch, he gave a little chuckle before turning and knocking on her door. There was a shuffle of noise, before Charlotte opened the door again and looked up at him unsurprised.

"Yes, cowboy?" she asked, her voice as ruffled as he felt.

Ty put his hand on the door and pushed it open. "It is tomorrow."

Chapter Three

If it were any other night, in any other city, with any other man, Charlotte would have been able to resist temptation. But it was hard as hell, tonight, with Ty. Never before had she even contemplated having a one-night stand, let alone sleeping with a man she'd just met, but once again, it was something in the air, and just something about *this* cowboy that was making her break all of her rules.

It was almost as if he had read her mind and knocked on the door just as she was kicking herself for not having the courage to go the extra step. The same courage that was escaping her again, now that he was standing right in front of her.

"This isn't exactly what I had in mind." *Liar!* her conscience screamed at her, as she held firmly to the door. It was the only thing of substance holding her up.

Ty just smiled and stepped in her room, nudging her back with a hand on her waist. "It's what I've had in mind, all night."

"Oh…" Words escaped her, as her pulse sped up. Cowboys should come with a warning label.

"If you don't want this, say so now."

"Lock the door," she whispered, tired of fighting herself. It was a losing battle, especially when she didn't even want to win.

Satisfaction appeared in his blue eyes as he released her and locked the door behind him. Nervously, Charlotte turned away from him and walked to the edge of her bed. It had been a long time since she'd made love, and this would be the first time she had ever made love with a man of another race. What was he expecting? What was she expecting? What if all of the stereotypes were true?

All of her questions flew out of her head as she felt Ty step up behind her and slide his arms around her waist, pulling Charlotte back against his hard body.

The hard, cylindrical shape of his penis against her back put aside all doubts about whether or not the size thing was a myth. Ty felt more than capable of handling all of her wants. "I don't know what to think about this."

Ty leaned forward, and nuzzled the back of her neck, sending shivers down her entire body. "You think too much," he whispered softly, tightening his grip on her.

"I've never done this before."

"I don't care about yesterday or tomorrow. All I care about is tonight."

"But..." Ty spun her around and took her mouth under his. Charlotte's protest dissipated as she was swallowed whole by his passion. Their tongues entwined, stroking each other to a feverish pitch. They kissed as if they were desperate for each other, and for Charlotte, at least, it was true.

It was a difficult position to maintain, with her being as short as she was, but it allowed her to feel every inch of his body against hers. Every hard, long, full inch of his body.

Breaking away from the kiss, Ty grabbed onto her waist and hoisted her up onto the bed until she was standing up. Charlotte laughed as she held onto his shoulders, trying to gain her balance.

"Lift up your leg," Ty ordered, pulling the shoe off her foot when she obeyed. He did the same to her other shoe and slowly lowered her leg back to the bed. Cupping his hands around her calves, Ty watched her face as he ran his hands slowly up her thighs, to the hem of her dress.

Charlotte felt faint as Ty lifted the dress and pulled it over her head. Dropping down to her trembling knees, she was finally, thanks to the height of the bed, face-to-face with the towering man, and enjoyed the view of his eyes darkening with passion as he took in her provocative stance on the bed.

"You're not small everywhere, I see."

Narrowing her eyes, Charlotte tugged on his t-shirt and pulled him in closer to her. "You better be talking about my breasts, buster."

"Oh, I am, baby, those and this…" Ty pulled her closer and smacked her on her full ass. "…sweet, sweet behind. From the first moment I saw you, I wanted to sink my teeth into you."

Smirking, Charlotte shook her head. "Sorry, cowboy, but no biting allowed."

Ty took both of Charlotte's hands and pulled them back behind her, capturing them in one of his. "I think there might be a breakdown in communication, princess, but you're not in control in here. I am."

Charlotte's eyes widened as her heart skipped several beats. Licking her lips, she baited. "Who said?"

"I did." Moving his hands softly over her ass, Ty raised it again and delivered another stinging tap. "You have a problem with that?"

Was he joking? Charlotte couldn't think straight. Talk like that wasn't supposed to be sexy. She was a liberated, no-nonsense woman, who…who was melting at his take-charge attitude. It was a good thing she was never going to see him again after tonight, because if anyone ever heard about how wet he got her with just a smack of his hand, she'd die. "No."

"Good." Stepping away from the bed, Ty pulled his t-shirt over his head. "Reach around you and release those beauties. Do it slowly. I want to enjoy the show."

She was going to die. Just flat out die. Ty was expecting her to follow orders when all she wanted to do was to follow his hands down his flat, rippling stomach to the zipper that was holding back the one thing she couldn't wait to see. But he paused, with an amused smile on his face. "I'm waiting Charlotte. Don't make me tell you twice."

Her muscles quivered as she hurried to obey. *When did the situation reverse and he become the one in control?* Charlotte never let anyone get the upper hand with her, it wasn't how she worked. Yet with Ty, all she wanted to do was to cater to his every want and desire. Charlotte didn't want to waste time fighting, when she was just delaying what they both wanted. Unhooking her bra, she tossed it casually to the side, and sat back down on her heels, waiting for him to make a move.

It was Ty's turn to stumble. His eyes narrowed on her breasts, as her mahogany nipples tightened with arousal from watching him stroke himself through his jeans. Charlotte had never felt so decadent.

"Sit back," he ordered as he dropped to his knees in front of her. Charlotte's rear end barely touched the bed before Ty's hand wrapped around her hips and pulled her until her legs were dangling off the edge of the mattress. Grabbing the band of her lace black panties, Ty slowly pulled them off, ordering her to lift her hips as he pulled them down her body.

Her legs were spread lewdly before him, her wet sex aching for him. Pushing her thighs further apart, Ty brought her moist center up to his waiting mouth, and finally put his devilish lips to some good use.

Charlotte gasped when Ty's tongue found her aching center. It had been so long since she'd felt the touch of a man, and damn, did it feel good! His lithe tongue tasted and teased her latten-tinged labia, before zeroing in on her aroused clit, as Charlotte writhed on the bed in ecstasy. It seemed as if his mouth discovered every secret of her sensitive folds, bringing her body quickly to orgasm from his tongue alone.

"You're so responsive, baby. I could devour you all night." Ty blew gently on her sensitive nub, bringing forth new sensations to her already aroused body.

"Stop," she practically mewed, pushing on the top of his head to ease him away from her tender clit.

"I've only just begun." Ty pushed up from between her legs, standing up in front of her, naked and proud.

Charlotte didn't know when he had taken off the rest of his clothes, and she didn't care. All she wanted was his cock in her. And she wanted it now. Sitting up, she reached between his legs and grasped his hard member in her greedy hands. Ty was just as large in the penis department as he was everywhere else, and she couldn't wait to be filled by him.

Slipping his cock between her hungry lips, Charlotte slid his smooth length as far into her mouth as she could. What she couldn't fit, she pumped gently with her hands, enjoying the feel of him finally in her body. But Ty had other plans. He wrapped his hands in her dark hair and used it as a handle to pump her up and down his thick cock.

There was something very powerful and vulnerable about Ty controlling the rhythm and speed. Her safety was in his hands, as his most prized possession was in hers. With the blowjob under his control, Charlotte was able to concentrate on the taste and feel of her new lover and virtually leave the driving to him.

A hoarse chuckle filled the air, as he released his hold on her hair and slowly pulled his cock out of her mouth. "Damn, darlin'."

Licking her parched lips, Charlotte stifled the urge to pull him back in and finish him off. His taste was addictive, much like the man himself. "Why did you stop?"

Ty leaned down and picked her up, pushing her further back on the bed. "Because as wonderful as your hot mouth felt, I'm willing to bet your sweet pussy will feel ten times better."

Good Lord, Charlotte thought. She had officially died and gone to heaven.

She was so damn sexy it hurt. A body made for loving, and a mouth made for sin, Charlotte was like birthdays and Christmas all rolled into one. The thought that, in just a few short seconds, he was going to be able to slide into her tight little body, was making his balls hurt.

As if the feel of her mouth sucking him in hadn't been hot enough, Ty had to settle his erratically beating heart down when he watched his pale cock disappear into the dark beauty's mouth. It was an erotic scene he'd never imagined before, and it made him harder than he would have ever thought. Finally, Ty understood why God had made people of different races. The beauty of the mingling colors was enough to take his breath away.

Reaching onto the floor, he pulled his wallet out and grabbed the three condoms he'd stashed in there earlier in the evening. With a flick of his hand, Ty tossed two onto the bed as he ripped open the remaining one.

Perched up on a bent arm, Charlotte glanced down at the condoms and then back up at him with a slight smirk on her pretty face. "Only three, cowboy?"

"Don't worry, darlin', us cowboys always have a back up plan." Like coming in her mouth, her ass, her hand. Ty wasn't going to let the lack of condoms spoil the many opportunities her willing body had to offer.

Ty slid the condom on, all the while staring at Charlotte's body displayed wantonly in front of him. He could sense her desires and taste the lingering essence of her pussy in his mouth.

Reaching back to the floor, Ty picked up his pants and pulled his belt free from the loops. Charlotte's big brown eyes widened as she pushed up to a sitting position. "What do you think you're doing with that, cowboy?"

Her voice quivered as she spoke, but Ty noted what else happened. Her nipples hardened, and she licked her lips as if in anticipation. It was those telltale signs that convinced him to revisit the belt idea later. His cock jerked in agreement.

"I want you to hold onto it, above your head."

"Why?"

Climbing into bed next to her, Ty laid the belt above her head. Taking her hands firmly into his, he raised them as well, watching in satisfaction as she grasped the belt like he'd instructed.

"Because the headrest on the bed sucks, and I want you to let yourself go for me. To let me make you come over and over again, knowing that I, and only I, am in control of your passion." Ty slid between her parted legs, feeling the hot, moist heat from her center brush against his abs. Charlotte was just as turned on as he was. Her pebble-hard nipples and the moisture gathering between her satin legs spoke volumes to him. "I want to make you come."

"Again," she whispered hoarsely.

"Again and again and again." Reaching between them, Ty grasped his aching cock, and centered it against her wet entrance.

Ty slowly pushed inside of Charlotte's waiting body, biting down on the side of his mouth so as not to cry out. He was larger, larger than most, and Ty knew if he wasn't careful he could hurt her. But it was killing him to restrain himself and not drive deep into her waiting body like he wanted. Her pussy was that good.

Hot, luscious, and tight, the warmth from her body damn near seared the condom to his skin. For the first time in a long time, Ty wanted to feel a woman's body without the added benefit of latex. He wanted to feel her warmth firsthand as he powered into her. The only thing holding him back was the knowledge that this time wouldn't be the last time he was with her. They had plenty of time for bareback when she knew him better—and she *would* know him better.

"You're burning me alive, darlin'," he growled, pulling back before powering in again.

Charlotte arched her hips up to his for more. Her arms held tautly above her head by sheer willpower alone, were trembling with her effort. Ty could tell she wanted to move them, but like a good girl she didn't. "Ohhh…" Charlotte closed her eyes as she arched up to him, biting down on her lip to stifle her moans.

"Fuck, fuck, fuck…" she muttered over and over again, singing her own little song of ecstasy, and Ty couldn't agree more. He wanted to fuck, fuck, fuck her all night long. "Harder please…harder."

A woman after his own heart. "Anything you say, darlin'."

Steadying himself on his knees, Ty pistoned in and out of Charlotte. Her pussy grasped at the length of his cock, gripping it tightly as he undulated deep inside her hot tunnel. Ty wanted more. He couldn't get deep enough. Moving his hands, he placed them by her head so he could move deeper. Turning her head, Charlotte bit into his forearm, crying out her pleasure around him. Her sharp teeth dragged a fierce growl from Ty as the added slice of pain slid like a lover's caress down his soul.

"That's it, baby, give me everything. Give it all to me."

Charlotte ripped her mouth away from his arm and cried out with passion. Jerking her hands from above her head, she moved them, belt and all, over Ty's shoulders, gripping his pumping ass with the leather of the belt, pulling him tighter into her. "Don't stop. Don't stop," she begged as she met him thrust for thrust.

The cold, abrasive leather bit into his taut buttocks as Charlotte used the belt as leverage to force him deeper into her body, but Ty didn't mind. In fact, he loved that he had brought her to that feverish pitch.

"Come on, darlin'," Ty growled, picking up speed, "take more."

Charlotte whimpered his name as she gyrated on the bed. Her body shivered as she took more and more of his hard cock. "Ty...Ty, please..."

"Right there, honey, right there," he urged as he felt his own orgasm creeping up his spine. She felt so fucking good. Ty didn't think he could ever get enough of her tight body.

"Oh, God, oh, God..." Charlotte cried out as she came, pulling him deeper into her body.

The walls of her vagina pulsated with her release as she milked his cock plunging into her depths. Ty bit back a masculine groan as he pumped in rapid succession, coming into her grasping body. His entire body ached with his release, and his tense muscles quivered as he pulled out of Charlotte slowly.

Spent, Charlotte released her grasp on the belt and dropped her arms down to the sides of her lethargic body. Her body glistened with sweat as she lay dazed on top of the quilt. A lazy chuckle escaped her as she rolled her head over to look at him. "Damn."

Laughing, Ty couldn't have said it better. They had fucked like it was an Olympic sport, as if they were going for the gold. His body was a trembling mass of nerves, everything still tingling from their release, and yet, despite the massive release they had both just experienced, his hunger for her was not sated.

Ty eased out of the bed and disappeared into the bathroom, coming back tidied up and with a cool washcloth for Charlotte.

Sitting down on the bed, he slid the cloth between her legs, startling her into opening her eyes. "If I were a cat, I would purrrrr..." she teased.

"I could have sworn I heard a purr somewhere in there."

"Are you sure that didn't come from you, cowboy?"

"Cowboys don't purr." He growled playfully.

Her warm brown eyes were alight with mischief as she rolled onto her side, running her delicate hand down the length of the belt. "You get points for creativity, that's for sure."

"And you get points for taking orders."

A slow smile spread across her face. Running her hand up his thigh, she brushed her fingers against his cock. "I follow orders well."

His sleeping cock aroused from its vegetative state. He'd give her an order, all right. "Let's put it to a test, shall we?" Dropping the towel onto the ground, Ty crawled over, cradling her body under his.

He wasn't in the mood for foreplay; he just wanted her hard, fast, and as often as she could take. Sliding his hand down her thigh, Ty raised her leg over his hip as he settled down between her supple thighs once more.

"Ty," she said, bracing his chest with her hands.

"Yes?

"This time put your hat on."

Chapter Four

Charlotte was a coward. It wasn't something she was proud of, but it was the truth. Too embarrassed to face Ty this morning, she had snuck out of her own hotel room. Her own room, for Pete's sake, and here she was now, roaming the rodeo grounds feeling like a fool. Fool was the other stand-out word that kept rolling around in her mind, because only a fool would willingly leave a man as handsome and virile as Ty asleep and alone in the room.

Last night had been one of the best nights of her life, but this morning, Charlotte had rolled over and seen Ty still in bed, looking as beautiful asleep as he did awake, and she instantly became petrified. For her first and last one-night stand, she had definitely picked a winner, but knowing that Ty would know how easily she had given in to his charms made Charlotte feel horrible.

The old adage was true; no man would buy the cow if he got the milk for free. And Charlotte had been extremely free last night. Free with her wants, free with her desires, and completely free with her body. She had let Ty, a man she'd only known for a day, do things with her that she had never allowed her past lovers to do. There was just something about him that made her give in to him. Something lethal, and she had to run from him, and herself, before she did something stupid, like lose her heart to him.

Pushing the trailer door closed, Charlotte leaned back against the cool wood and banged her head softly repeatedly into the door. She had only come down for the weekend. Two days to do grunt work and then straight back home. And in one night she had put aside all of her morals and beliefs and given in to a handsome man in a Stetson.

"So stupid!" She cursed herself for the hundredth time, but this time, like the last, she wasn't sure if she was cursing herself for leaving his bed, or allowing him into her bed in the first place. The ringing phone cut off her self-loathing. "Sane here."

"That's always good to hear," chuckled her best friend, Tamara. "So how are things on the Ponderosa?"

Charlotte closed her eyes for a second and smiled. Tamara's friend-radar must have gone off. They had always been able to tell when one needed the other. "A bit more exciting than I ever thought possible."

"Really? Do tell?"

"I am such an idiot." There were no two ways about it. Walking across the room, Charlotte set her briefcase on the table before sitting down in a chair.

Tamara's warm laughter filled the line. "I so love when your rants begin this way."

"Then you're going to love this." Taking a deep sigh, Charlotte blurted out what had happened last night, giving as much detail as possible considering her location. By the time she had finished bringing Tamara up-to-date, Charlotte was exhausted, and feeling ten times the fool. "I can't believe I ran out on him."

"I can't believe you're able to walk."

"No shit." She laughed, shaking her head in denial. "I'm such an idiot! Why did I leave him?"

"Because you're an idiot. I thought we already went over that," Tamara concurred, without missing a beat.

"Tamara, you're not supposed to agree with me."

"Please, I'm your friend, if I can't tell you when you're being an idiot, who will?"

"Do you have to say it with so much glee?"

"As a matter of fact, I do."

Charlotte could hear the amusement and love in Tamara's voice, and it went a long way to sooth her rumbling nerves. Standing up, she walked across the room to the large windows. "Do you think I'm a skeez?"

"Hell, no. For once in your perfect little life you went out and had a great time, with what sounds like a great man. That doesn't make you a whore, Char, that makes you human."

Leaning against the window, Charlotte looked out at the busy rodeo. Who would have ever thought she would have had to travel three hundred miles to find her humanity? "Being human sucks."

"Who are you telling? Last night you spent the night playing Cowboys and Indians, and I spent it poring over job applications. How is that fair? I was so depressed, I ended up eating a box—yes, you heard me, a box—of brownies. Being unemployed is hell on my diet."

"Tamara…" Charlotte groaned.

"Oh, don't 'Tamara' me. I ate a box of brownies. You slept with a cowboy. I'm thinking we're about even."

"Yeah, but I bet I enjoyed Ty a hell of a lot more than you enjoyed your brownies." Charlotte couldn't help but tease.

"Well, that's good to know," said a hard voice from behind her. Charlotte whirled around from the window and almost dropped the phone as Ty slammed the door shut behind him.

"Because for a moment there, I was beginning to wonder. Hang up the phone."

Shaken by the fierce look in Ty's eyes, Charlotte quickly pulled the phone back up to her ear. "I'll talk to you later."

"Later?" Tamara jumped on the one word like it was the last lifeboat off the Titanic. "Why later?"

"Because I have company."

"The kind of company that spends the night?"

"Yes."

"Ooh...I want details."

Ty stalked toward her, looking angry as hell. "Hang up the phone *now.*"

"Later," Charlotte promised, hanging up without saying goodbye. "Ty, I'm surprised to see you."

"I bet you are." His tone was as fierce as his expression, but Charlotte refused to cower.

"Is there a problem?"

"You could say that." Ty pressed a hand against the window and leaned in close to her. "I'm really disappointed in you, Charlotte."

Crossing her arms over her chest, Charlotte returned Ty's glare with one of her own. "Sorry, cowboy, I gave it my best shot. If last night didn't do it for you, I don't know what will."

"Last night was wonderful, as you well know. It's your morning-after attitude that needs some adjusting."

"Lucky for you, you won't have to worry about it any longer." Ducking under his arm, Charlotte walked a few steps away. She needed to clear her head, and fast.

"Charlotte, Charlotte, Charlotte," Ty tsked, walking up behind her. Brushing gently past her, he took off his hat and dropped it down on the table, casually sitting down next to it. "I never took you for a coward."

It was one thing for Charlotte to call herself a coward, but quite another thing for Ty to do it—no matter how right he was. Walking around him, Charlotte grabbed her briefcase off the table. "This meeting is over."

Reaching out, Ty grabbed her arm and halted her exit, ruining her perfect parting line in the process. Bastard.

"Far from it, darlin'."

"Listen, cowboy…"

"No, you listen. I've met some stubborn women in my time, but you, my dear, take the cake. Leaving like you did, Charlotte, was cowardly and low."

"You're just mad because I left before you had the opportunity to." That didn't even make sense to her, but it was better than saying, *I'm scared.*

Ty released her arm and stood back up. "Is that what you really think?"

"Look, I'm sorry if I broke some morning-after courtesy. I figured it would be easier all the way around if I just left when I did."

"Easier for whom?"

Finally, the million-dollar question. "For both of us. I just don't want to make this into a big deal. We had a good time last night."

A soft smile passed across his face, causing Charlotte's heart to kick it up a notch. "Just good?"

"Okay," she admitted, with a smile of her own. Who was she kidding anyway? "A very good time, but that's all it was."

"It doesn't have to be."

Was he crazy? Hell, was she? Because Charlotte was more than tempted. "Ty, we're from two completely different worlds."

Chuckling, Ty brushed his callused hand against her cheek. "Last time I checked, Charlotte, Los Angeles was still on Earth."

"Are you being obtuse on purpose?" Why couldn't he have been like every other man on God's green earth, and be happy that she'd snuck out? Without even thinking, Charlotte leaned her head into his hand. It felt so right. "You know what I'm saying."

"I hear everything you're saying. I just don't buy it."

"You don't have to. All that matters is that I do." She was going to remain firm on this. He was so capable of breaking her heart. After one night she was already in pieces because of this man.

"Why?"

"What do you mean, *why?*"

"I mean, why are you trying so hard to push me away?"

There was something very, very dangerous about this man. If he wanted, Ty could have her eating out of his hand, and Charlotte was afraid he knew it. "It was a one-night stand."

"It doesn't have to be. Last night was one of the best nights of my life. Sex aside, I really like you, Charlotte."

"You don't even know me."

"I know enough."

Rolling her eyes, she stepped away from his caress. "Like what?"

"Like I want more."

Ty watched the doubt flitter across Charlotte's face, partially frustrated and partially amused. She was as stubborn as she was beautiful, and that was really saying a lot. And she was hell-bent on driving him insane.

"This will never work," she repeated, as if he didn't understand her the other times she said it. He understood her, all right, and part of him, be it ever so small, even agreed. But just being in the same room with her again was causing his gut to clench. Charlotte had a pull over him, and she was worth it.

"How do you know?"

"Because…"

"Not good enough," Ty interrupted. He had never had to beg a woman in his life, and he wasn't going to start now, but he'd be damned if he let her walk out of his life without even giving them a chance.

"What do you want from me?" Charlotte's fear was as apparent as her need.

Everything, but Ty knew if he said that, she would hightail it out of the room so fast his head would spin. "Come with me. Now."

"Where?"

"To my home. Give me tonight."

"I'm leaving for home tomorrow."

"That's tomorrow. I want tonight."

Charlotte eyed him warily, as if she still didn't quite trust him. She was like a skittish mare, in need of a firm yet tender touch, and Ty was just the man to provide both.

"This is crazy."

"I'm willing to concede that," he admitted with grin. Despite how persistent he was being, Ty knew that this was fast. Hell, he was even amazed at the speed in which he was going, but he couldn't help himself. Call it strange, call it fate, call it insanity, Charlotte was the one for him.

"I have to leave in the morning." Charlotte repeated, stressing the word *morning.*

Holding out his hand to her, Ty asked, "Is that a yes?"

Sighing, Charlotte placed her hand in his. "Yes."

* * *

After two phone calls and a quick meeting with her boss, Charlotte was strapped in his truck and on the way to his ranch. Normally Ty would have stayed to the very end of the rodeo, but for once, he had his own bucking beauty to ride.

They had to make another quick stop at her hotel room, where he insisted she check out. There was no way in the world he was going to let her go back there tonight, especially if this was to be their last night together. He insisted that she leave her car, but only because he didn't want her to sneak off in the dead of night. Ty wasn't going to put anything past Charlotte.

Ty's spread had always been his pride and joy. The Dollar Ranch had been in his family for three generations, and if God was willing, it would be in his family for another three to come. He loved his land and he wanted Charlotte to love it, too.

Pulling up in front of his home, Ty hopped out of the truck and walked around to open the door for Charlotte. Smiling her thanks, Charlotte took his hand and stepped out. Stepping away from the truck, Charlotte stared at her surroundings with a look of amazement and awe on her face. "Ty, it's lovely."

"Thank you." Ty had always thought so, but he was probably biased. The Dollar was set back on one hundred and fifty of the best acres God had ever created. His brick house was flanked by several outbuildings, and pastures stretched as far as the eye could see. It was his home and he loved it.

"You're a lucky man to have all this." Turning around in a semi-circle, Charlotte put her hands up to her eyes, framing them from the sun's fading rays.

"I've always thought so." Grabbing her bag from the back of the truck, Ty placed his hand on the small of her back, and led Charlotte up the walk to his home.

Ida, his housekeeper, met them at the door with a smile on her face. "I see we're having company," she said as she opened the door for them.

"That we are, Ida, I'd like to introduce you to Charlotte."

The older lady stuck out her hand to Charlotte, with a warm welcoming smile on her face. "It's very nice to meet you."

"Nice to meet you as well." Charlotte's voice held a hint of surprise in it, as if she was shocked by the warm welcome.

"Shall I ready the guest room?"

"No," Ty said, ignoring the glare Charlotte sent him. "She'll be staying in my room."

"Very well," Ida replied, with a twinkle in her eyes. She might have been from a different generation, but she was familiar with Ty's ways.

Charlotte's fuse was a lot longer than Ty gave her credit for. She actually lasted until Ida left the room before she turned on him. "I can't believe you said that."

"Said what?" Ty asked, setting her bag down by the stairs.

"That I'd be staying in your room. She's going to think…"

"…That I'm a very lucky man," Ty interrupted, placing his finger against her full lips. "We don't stand on ceremony around here. Ida and her husband, Sly, who you'll meet later, have been on this land longer than I've been alive. They're not the judging type."

"Still…"

"Still what?" Pulling her into his arms, Ty smiled down into her upturned face. "Something tells me you're just looking for a fight."

"What if I am?"

The challenge in her smile almost made him laugh out loud. Charlotte was a handful, and he loved it. "Then I'm just the man for it."

"Ty," Ida said, coming back into the hall. "Mr. Zellerman called. He wants you to call him back ASAP."

"Damn, honey, I have to take this call."

"I can show her to your room, while you make your call."

"Is that okay?" Ty asked, not wanting to put Charlotte on the spot.

Charlotte rolled her eyes at him. "I think I'm capable of being alone in your house for five minutes."

Ida's laughter sounded like a roar of approval. She had been known to be quite feisty in her day, as well. "I think I like your lady."

"Behave," Ty warned, looking at the two apples of his eye.

"Who are you talking to?" Charlotte asked.

"Both of you." With a wink, Ty headed down the hall to his office, with the sound of Ida's laughter in his ear.

By the time he finished his phone call more than five minutes had passed. Following the smell of dinner down the hall, Ty skipped his bedroom in lieu of the kitchen. The mouthwatering smell of pot roast wasn't the only reason he headed in that direction. Ty could hear Ida and Charlotte's laughter all the way down the hall. It was a sound that brought a smile to his face, and a warm sensation to his heart.

Ty would have never believed he would have fallen so quickly, but here he was, standing outside his kitchen with a stupid grin on face, all because of Charlotte's laughter. If the guys could see him now...

He could hear Ida speaking as he entered the room, "And by the time his father made it over the fence, Ty was chin-deep in mud, squealing like a little pig."

Wincing, Ty wished he had been a few seconds earlier, he might have saved himself some embarrassment. "You're fired," he teased, walking all the way into the room.

Ida waved her hand at him. "Well, if you're going to fire me, then I'm going to have to tell her about the time Sly caught you and little Ann..."

Rounding the island, Ty placed his hands over Ida's mouth, silencing the laughing woman. "Forget it. You're rehired and with a raise."

Ida winked at Charlotte as she pulled Ty's hand down from her mouth. "That's what I thought. Dinner is ready. Let me set you two up, and I'll take Sly's and my dinner out to our house."

"What? No!" Charlotte cried, looking at Ty to intervene. "Please don't do that on my account."

"You guys don't want to be saddled with us old folks."

Charlotte scurried down from her stool and around the counter. "Please join us."

Ida looked to Ty, who nodded his head in agreement. He was a bit shocked that Charlotte insisted, but glad just the same. Ida and Sly were more family than employees, and they had been eating with him since his parents passed away ten years ago. "Just think of all the embarrassing stories you can tell her over dinner."

With a faint blush, Ida conceded, "And what I can't remember, I'm sure Sly will fill in."

"Wonderful." Charlotte turned to look up at Ty with a huge smile she couldn't hold back any longer. Bending forward, Ty took her sweet lips under his, much to Ida's amusement and Charlotte's embarrassment.

Sitting out on the porch later that evening, Ty held Charlotte in his arms as they rocked on the swing.

"It's so very peaceful out here. I can see why you love it. And Ida and Sly have to be two of the nicest people I've ever met."

"They really like you." Leaning down, Ty kissed the top of Charlotte's head, feeling happier and more content than he had felt in awhile.

"You know this is never going to work." Charlotte voice broke the comfortable silence.

"It already is."

Her soft laughter made him smile. "It doesn't work because you say it does. We have too many differences to make this work."

"But we also have something more." Ty tilted her chin up so they were looking eye to eye. "Tell me you don't feel it."

"I feel it, all right," she teased, running her hand up his thigh. "But I'm still going to drive home tomorrow."

"And maybe you won't. Maybe you'll give me another day." And another. And another.

"It was just a one-night stand."

"Then why are you still here?" Ty asked, loving the way her brown eyes narrowed at the corners. She was going to fight this all the way.

"Because," she replied stubbornly, looking back out into the distance.

Ignoring her lack of reason, Ty pushed off the ground with his foot, sending the swing rocking again. "That's what I thought. Now sit back and enjoy the view."

"Sit back." Charlotte's eyebrows drew together. "Did I miss the part where you became the boss of me?"

Chuckling, Ty pulled Charlotte over onto his lap until she was straddling him. His cock hardened under his jeans instantly at the feel of her on top of him. "You must have, darlin', but let me refresh your memory."

Chapter Five

"I'm leaving today, and I mean it, Ty," Charlotte warned, wagging her butter-coated toast at him.

"Sure you are," he teased. Grabbing her hand, he brought the toast to his mouth and took a bite. "That's what you said two days ago."

"I know, but I really mean it this time." Like she'd meant it the other dozen times she'd said it over the last week. "I really have to get back to the office. If Nathan wasn't so far gone himself, he'd have fired me days ago."

Now that Nathan was relocating to Santa Estrella, Charlotte's excuse for not going home was becoming weaker and weaker, as was her desire to return. Somewhere along the line, she had lost her taste for the hustle and bustle of city life and was fast becoming a convert to ranch life. She loved it there almost as much as she was beginning to love Ty.

"If he fires you, I'll hire you."

"You couldn't afford me, cowboy."

Ty waggled his brows teasingly. "I'm sure we could work out a payment plan."

Giggling, Charlotte bet they could. Ty was a very, very naughty boy, and fast becoming the best mistake she'd ever made. "How much longer are you planning to hold me hostage, cowboy?"

Snorting, Ty eyed Charlotte over his coffee cup. "I loosened the cuffs this morning, didn't I?"

"Shut up." Zinging the remaining piece of toast at him, Charlotte bopped Ty in the head. Blushing she glanced quickly over his shoulder to see if Ida had heard anything, but if she did, the housekeeper was keeping it to herself.

"You liked it, you know you did."

She had, but she would never admit it to him. Ty was too cocky by far. "I have no idea what you're referring to."

"Liar."

"Pest," Charlotte replied, sticking her tongue out at him.

"I can think of better things for you to do with your tongue." His gaze was on her mouth, his stare intense and sensual.

"I bet you could." A simple look, a single phrase, and she was becoming aroused.

"Don't make me separate you two," Ida threatened, as she gathered up her purse from the mudroom. "I'm off to the store. Do you need anything that isn't on the list?"

Ty looked at Charlotte and mouthed, *condoms and lube,* causing her to break out in another fit of laughter. They were fast running out of both, much to her embarrassment and amusement, just one more reason why Charlotte was finding it harder and harder to go home.

Sure there were reasons to go home, like her family, friends, and job, but there were even more tempting reasons here. Reasons that ensured she was smiling nonstop and coming up with every reason under the sun to stay a day or two longer.

"I should be back in about two hours." Stopping by Charlotte's chair, Ida asked with a smile, "Will you be here when I get back?"

"No." Charlotte really needed to get going.

But before the word had left her mouth, Ty interjected with, "Yes."

Laughing, Ida shook her head. "That's what I thought. I'll be back."

Charlotte waited until Ida left, before she reached out across the table and took Ty's callused hand in hers. "I'm going to have to leave one day, Ty."

"It doesn't have to be today," he replied stubbornly, refusing as always, to listen to reason.

Ty had made it clear, over the last few days, that if it were up to him, he would have all of her things shipped to his house, and her upstairs, chained to the bed. Okay, the "chained to the bed" part didn't sound so bad, but Charlotte did have a life to get back to, no matter how unappealing it was becoming. "You say that everyday."

"And I mean it everyday."

"I'm leaving today, Ty," Charlotte said firmly.

"No."

"This isn't up for debate."

Sitting back in his chair he regarded her stonily. "Don't you like it here?"

"You know I love it here, but I have plants to water, food to throw out, people to see."

"And then you'll be back?" It might have been a question, but it came off like a demand, causing steel to shoot straight up her spine.

"Eventually."

"Next weekend," he ordered calmly.

"Oh, is *that* when eventually is? I always wondered about that." If he was going to be stubborn about this, then she was going to be stubborn right back. Charlotte had every intention of coming back next weekend, she just wasn't going to let Ty think he could boss her into it. Her hardheaded cowboy had a lot to learn when it came to women.

Charlotte stood, pushing her chair back, and took her plate and cup to the sink. With a few feet of distance between them, Charlotte turned back around to face him, with her resolve firmly in place, but instead of facing an angry Ty, she faced an amused one.

"You're cute, you know?" he said, as he stood up with his dishes and walked over to where she was.

Narrowing her eyes, Charlotte waited for the punch line, and when none came, she become even more suspicious. Ty didn't add a comment, didn't try to manhandle her, he simply went to the sink and rinsed out his coffee cup. Something was up. "Is that it?"

Shooting her an amused look, Ty walked back to the breakfast table and picked up his hat. "What do you mean?"

"No argument from you?"

"Do you want me to argue with you?"

Yes. No. Hell. Charlotte was more confused than when she started this conversation. "So you're okay with me going home today?"

"I'm not okay with it, Charlotte, but short of locking you in my bedroom, I can't stop you. I don't want you to think of the ranch as a prison. More like a haven."

Walking to him, Charlotte laid her head against his chest, loving the sound of his strong heartbeat against her ear. "You're making it very hard to leave."

A low chuckle rose from beneath her ear. "I hope so."

Ty held her to him for a second, and Charlotte, a person who wasn't used to leaning on another human being, let her heart open for him. She was finally beginning to understand the concept of love at first sight, even if she was too blind to recognize it at first.

Brushing his hand against her hair, Ty broke the comfortable silence. "I have to go check on my baby."

Startled, Charlotte pulled abruptly away from his chest. "Your what?"

"Chiana, my mare. We had to separate her from the other horses."

"Is she okay?" Now that Charlotte knew she didn't have any baby's momma's drama to worry about, she was filled with concern. She knew how much the Dollar meant to Ty, and anything that was important to him was fast becoming very important to her.

"Yeah, she..." Pausing, Ty stepped back. "Do you want to come meet her?"

There was no law that said Charlotte needed to leave *right* now. "Of course."

With a lazy smile, Ty took her hand in his and headed outside. Charlotte would never get over the vast amounts of open space Ty called home. Even though there were stables, barns, and pastures everywhere, it still seemed as if Ty's property went on for days. Bypassing the large stable, they headed to a small red building resembling a mini barn, with the Dollar Bill monarch logo on the door, prompting a question Charlotte had been meaning to ask. "So where does the Dollar Ranch get its name?"

Pushing back the door, Ty led her down a small hallway to a single stall next to a tack room filled with hay. "My great-grandfather started this ranch with four quarter horses—three mares and a stallion."

"So?" Charlotte questioned, not getting the correlation.

Unlatching the gate, Ty entered the stall with the russet mare. Looking over his shoulder at her with a devilish sparkle in his blue eyes, he answered her question. "What do four quarters equal?"

"A dollar...oh, duh." Charlotte laughed. "The Dollar Ranch. I like it."

"I'm sure my grandfather would be pleased." Bending down, he picked up the horse's leg and checked it over. "Whoa, baby. I'm just here to check you out."

Leaning on the wooden gate, Charlotte watched Ty lovingly caress the mare. There was so much tenderness in his touch, and gentleness about him, that it was sometimes hard to see her passionate, dominating lover as the same man before her. "What happened?"

"A combination of things," Ty said standing back up. "A hired hand not paying attention, a mare in heat, but not in the mood, and a randy stallion who wouldn't take no for an answer."

"Kinda like his owner, huh?" Charlotte teased. Reaching slowly across the gate as Ty had shown her, Charlotte allowed the horse to get accustomed to her scent before delicately stroking her muzzle. "What's wrong, honey? Not in the mood for some loving?"

"Horses generally don't mate in the winter," Ty said, coming out of the stall.

"Why not?"

"Because they're pregnant for about eleven months. So for racing and showing it's best to have the mare foal early, say January or February. Hence we normally breed them between February and March."

Ty slid up behind Charlotte, trapping her between his body and the gate. Her pulse began to race as it normally did when Ty was near, but the feel of him, heavy and aroused, was causing her heart to work overtime. "So did someone forget to tell the stallion?"

Nuzzling her neck, Ty teased her senses causing her nipples to harden beneath her blouse. "Like his owner, Slate doesn't always care what's right or wrong. He only knows what he wants, and he'll do anything to get it."

"Sounds just like you," Charlotte murmured, burrowing into Ty's warmth. It seemed as if a lifetime had passed since they'd last made love instead of mere hours, and Charlotte was aching to have him inside of her again. "Temptation will get you every time."

She was driving him wild. And it wasn't as if she was actually doing anything. Just knowing she was within his reach, ready and willing, was all it took to keep Ty hard all week long. They'd made love more times than he could count, and each time was better than the time before. She was sweet, insatiable, and the keeper of his heart, but she was also hell-bent on going home.

Every time she mentioned going home, Ty found a way to distract her, but this time he could tell she was serious and it was driving him insane. He was only seconds away from tossing her over his shoulder and carting her off to the nearest minister he could find, but Ty knew he needed to be patient and give her time to make the decision for herself. Even if it was killing him.

Slipping his hand around her lithe waist, Ty pulled her body closer to his own. It was getting ridiculously obscene the way his body reacted to hers. Just thinking her name caused his cock to stir. "It's been too long," he whispered into her downy brown hair.

Charlotte moaned her agreement, passionately pushing back into him. Nudging her legs wider apart, he pressed his hand against her mons, cupping her sex through her jeans. "Time to give in to a bit of temptation of our own."

"Here?" Her question came out as more of a moan, causing his erection to pulsate. He loved the sound of her voice, especially when it held a hint of passion in it as it did now.

"I won't be satisfied until I've fucked you everywhere." Backing away, Ty led Charlotte around the corner to the hay holding area, next to Chiana's stall. The area wasn't a complete room with doors, but it was a bit further back from the door and away from prying eyes.

"Get out of those pants." Yanking his shirt over his head, Ty reached into his back pocket and pulled out a condom, one of the many he'd taken to carting around the ranch since her arrival.

Looking around at their surroundings, Charlotte shook her head in mirth. "We are not doing this here."

"Aren't we?" He was so hard right now, he couldn't see straight. The woman he adored, in a room with rope, leather, and hay, was wreaking havoc on his libido. The horse wrangler in him wanted to mount her like a stallion takes a mare, strong, demanding, and in complete control.

"I'm not getting freaky in the hay." Her voice sounded appalled, yet the passion was still in simmering in her big brown eyes. "I'll be sneezing and coughing, instead of screaming and coming."

"Don't worry." If a little hay fever was what she was worried about, he could fix that really quick. "You won't have to."

Picking his shirt up off of the ground, Ty laid it against the bale, spreading it out like a blanket until the majority of the hay was covered.

"That's not long enough for me to lie on."

"Who said anything about laying?" Dropping the condom on his shirt, Ty did what his heart was craving and pulled Charlotte in for a kiss.

His mouth covered hers as he slipped his tongue between her full lips. Swaying into him, Charlotte parted her mouth, flooding his senses with her sweet taste. It was a flavor Ty was fast becoming addicted to.

Pulling reluctantly away, Ty reached between them, making quick work of her pants, unbuckling and pushing them down her lovely brown legs. Quickly followed by her shirt and underclothes, Charlotte was aroused and naked, awaiting his touch. She shivered a bit in the cool air, but Ty was confident he could have them warm in seconds.

"This is crazy," Charlotte murmured, clinging to his body as he sat her up on his shirt. "Someone could come in."

She talked as she unbuttoned his pants, freeing his member into her waiting hands. Her touch was like firm silk, and he couldn't help but grin at her actions. Ty would never have to wonder if their passion was just one-sided; Charlotte was almost as greedy for him as he was for her.

"I guarantee you no one will interrupt us." If they did, they'd risk more than his wrath. Everyone on the Dollar Ranch knew better than to interrupt Ty for any reasons short of a colic epidemic when he was with Charlotte. He'd hate to lose a man, but he'd hate for them to see his woman naked even more.

Reaching in his back pocket, Ty pulled out his yellow bandana and began to unfold it, watching Charlotte's face the entire time. The closer he stepped to her, the deeper she began to breathe. Her arousal filled the air, teasing his mind like mad.

"Give me your hands, Charlotte," he ordered, sounding a lot calmer than he felt.

Without a moment of hesitation or a word of protest, Charlotte jutted out her hands, surrendering her willpower to his command. It never ceased to amaze him how she gave her trust so completely, yet was still afraid to give her heart the same way.

Quickly binding her hands together, Ty lifted her off the shirt and spun her around, until she was facing the wall, bent over the bale of hay. Her pert brown ass was positioned for the perfect fucking, but he wanted inside her pussy more. Ty needed to remind both of them just who she belonged to.

Grabbing the condom from his shirt, Ty ripped through the foil, impatiently sliding the ribbed condom onto his hard shaft. "I can't get over how beautiful you are," Ty murmured as he moved toward her, aroused and eager. "And this ass..."

Bending down, he nipped at her firm cheek, rousing a hoarse chuckle from her before standing up again and positioning himself at her moist entrance. Grasping her hip, Ty angled her body for a smooth entrance. Her height was a bit of a disadvantage, but he knew once he was inside her tight sheath, he'd be able to maneuver her into a position they both would love.

Before pushing in, Ty slid his cock through the cream-coated lips of her sex. Teasing her engorged clit with the ribbed edges of the condom, Ty could feel the tremors quaking through her body.

"Don't tease me," she demanded, as she pushed backwards trying to get him to slip in. Her warm center called to him, beseeching him to enter, but Ty wanted Charlotte to be as far gone as he was.

He also wanted her to know who was in charge. Lightly smacking her ass with one hand, Ty pushed down on the center of her smooth back, holding her in place with the other. He liked her tied up and docile at his command. "How badly do you want it?"

"Damn it, Ty, don't fuck with me," she growled, looking over her shoulder at him like the fierce kitten she was. Ty loved it.

"You know what I want, sugar?" he asked, tormenting her clit with his cock. "Beg me. Tell me what you need."

"You. Inside of me, now!"

Raising her ass higher, Ty gripped her hips and drove into her moist center, almost stopping his heart in the process. It was always like that, the first surge into her body was all-consuming. The hot swath of her sex made Ty feel like his entire body was on fire.

Charlotte gripped the hay to steady herself, as he powered into her from behind. In this position, he was in complete control of the rhythm and motion, just the way he liked it. Moaning, she cried out, "God, yes. Fuck me harder. Fuck...me."

"Harder, sweet baby? Is this what you want?" He panted, speeding up his rhythm per her request.

Charlotte's guttural moans of appreciation were all he needed to hear to know she was right there with him. Gripping his fingers into the light brown globes of her ass, he looked down and watched as his pale shaft disappeared into her dark sex. The difference in their skin color provided the perfect contrast to highlight his cock driving in and out of her.

"Mine. Mine. Mine." His brain parroted over and over in his head, beating the words like a drum into his mind.

Pushing harder into her he quickened the pace, until he could no longer tell if he was coming or going. Charlotte had given up on all pretense of decorum and was crying his name with every thrust.

Raising his hand, he brought it down sharply against the curve of her bottom, sending Charlotte screaming over the edge. She came in a loud, orgasmic rush moments ahead of Ty, who rode her until their knees buckled.

Catching himself with his hands on the hay, Ty leaned forward and laid his head on her damp, quaking back as the aftershocks rocked through them. He could feel her lissome body quivering underneath him, and it made him want to gather her up and place her on the tallest shelf, to keep her safe from all harm.

This was his woman—*his woman*—and what they had was too good to give up. It wasn't just sex. Sex he could get anywhere at any time. It was something more. Charlotte aroused his mind and his heart, as well as his cock, and she wasn't something he was willing to do without.

Distance be damned. Ty wasn't going to let Charlotte mosey her way out of his life, no matter what.

Chapter Six

Despite every single one of her misgivings and doubts, somehow Charlotte and Ty were making it work. With the right motivation, the three-hour drive seemed to take mere minutes, especially when she knew Ty was waiting for her back at the ranch. Charlotte did most of the commuting, but she didn't mind. The mileage was worth it to be back in his arms.

But today, today he was coming to her turf, and Charlotte had to admit she was a bit nervous. On the ranch they could pretend like the world didn't exist, but here in Los Angeles they wouldn't have such a luxury. It wasn't the city she was worried about, so much as his reaction to her life.

Things in Charlotte's part of the world worked a bit differently than they did in Santa Estrella. Her work and life was an important part of her, or it used to be, and she wanted Ty to see it firsthand. Maybe then he would understand why she still kept coming back. Although Charlotte had to admit, even to herself, that it was becoming increasingly difficult to find a reason to come back home. So much so that Charlotte was at the point where she didn't even understand why she was fighting her feelings for Ty any longer.

"He'll get here when he gets here," Tamara teased slipping out onto the balcony, where Charlotte had snuck out from the office party for a few minutes of peace and quiet. "Geez Louise, woman, get off the man's jock. You act like you haven't seen him in years."

The cool night air drifted over her bare shoulders, causing her to shiver a bit. California was a warm state, but even here it got cold in December, especially in an after-five party dress, a dress that Charlotte had bought specifically with Ty in mind.

The black, knee-length, strapless dress was as simple to take off as it was to put on, and that was something she thought Ty would really appreciate. Rubbing her arms, she turned to her friend and smiled. "Five days can be a very, very long time."

Snorting, Tamara's lovely face showed her disbelief. As Charlotte's unofficial back-up date, she was decked out in her evening finery as well, her pleasantly plump figure accentuated in a two-piece forest-green pantsuit. "He must be king ding-a-ling, because you're all kinds of sprung."

"I'm not..." Pausing in mid-sentence Charlotte gave Tamara's comment a bit of thought. "Well, maybe I am, but you just don't know..."

"Know what?"

Know what it was like to be in his arms. Know what it was like to be loved and made love to by one of the best men she'd ever known. There was so much Tamara didn't know, and there wasn't enough time in either of their lifetimes for Charlotte to fill her in. "He's just great. Just wait, you'll see."

"Hell, I've been waiting to see since the end of November, and if he's not worth it, trust me, you'll hear about it," Tamara promised with a wink.

Charlotte wasn't worried about whether or not Tamara and Ty would get along. They were both such easygoing people that it would be hard for them not to like each other. "He should have been here twenty minutes ago. I wonder if something happened at the ranch."

A large grin spread across Tamara's face, prompting Charlotte ask, "What's so funny?"

"You are." Leaning back against the rail, Tamara crossed her arms over her large chest. "You're wondering if your boyfriend had problems on the ranch. The ranch, for Christ's sake. That's funny as hell."

"Shut up." Charlotte was thankful for the low lighting that was hiding her flush. Saying it like that did seem sort of funny.

"I mean, did you ever see a horse close up, before your visit with the Ingalls?" Tamara ribbed with a grin. "You're the woman who won't go camping unless you're sleeping in a cabin."

"It's not like we're roughing it on his ranch, Tamara. He does have indoor plumbing, smartass."

"But can you see yourself staying out there, like forever?"

Yes, her heart and mind answered at the same time, shocking Charlotte into silence. Looking over at Tamara who had lost all trace of her smile, Charlotte could only stare dumbfounded. She was in love with him, and she wanted to be with him forever. When the hell did that happen?

"Charlotte," Tamara's voice held amazement and disbelief. "You're not in love with him, are you?"

"Charlotte," a voice called from the open doorway, saving Charlotte from answering. Turning, she raised a questioning brow to her co-worker, Val, who was smiling broadly at her. "I think your guest is here."

Looking past Val's shoulder, Charlotte saw Ty standing in the center of the room and almost swallowed her tongue. He was dressed in a dark suit like the majority of the men in the room, but unlike everyone else, he was wearing his black Stetson. Charlotte thought it was damn impossible for him to look any better than the way she had seen him in the past. She had been wrong. Dead wrong.

He didn't just wear the suit. He *wore* the suit. His suit accentuated his large frame, making it seem as if it were molded for his body alone. And the hat that adorned his head, made him appear dashing and debonair. Ty looked fucking great.

Tamara pushed up behind her, staring across the room. "Is that...is that him?" The awe in her voice broke Charlotte's hypnotic stare.

"Yes," Charlotte's voice sounded almost as bad as Tamara's did. "That's my cowboy."

"Oh...my...God."

"You can say that again," Val agreed, fanning herself with her hand. The blonde woman was eyeing Ty like he was a Prada bag on clearance. "I didn't know they made men like that anymore."

"They don't," Charlotte said, pushing past the fawning woman and into the crowded room. "He's a dying breed."

Ty was searching the room for her, giving Charlotte ample time to study him as she approached. Watching him with new eyes, eyes of love, Charlotte wondered what had taken her so long to realize what he meant to her. It wasn't like she'd ever made such an effort with any other man in her life. That alone should have told her of her feelings, but now that she knew, now that she really knew, she just wanted to bask in the glow.

She was in love.

Charlotte was almost to his side before he spotted her, but when he did, his entire face lit up with joy. It was the most beautiful sight Charlotte had ever seen. Her man, happy to see her. Coming to his side, Charlotte stood up on her tiptoes and placed a warm kiss against his firm lips. Although she wanted to strip him bare and have her wicked way with him right there where they stood, she knew she couldn't, so she kept her kiss quick, not wanting to tempt herself more than she already was.

Pulling back, she smiled up at him. "Hi, stranger."

Ty encircled her waist, holding her to him, and smiled back at her. "Sorry I'm late."

"I didn't even notice," she lied, no longer caring how long it took him to get there, just thankful that he was.

"You look beautiful."

"As do you. I didn't know you owned a suit," she kidded stepping back to admire him up close.

"My good jeans were at the cleaners."

"I bet. You know…" Charlotte took his hand in hers, about to say something else, when she noticed the boisterous party had seemed to die down a bit. Glancing around she saw several people avert their eyes quickly, as if they hadn't been staring. Smiling mischievously, Charlotte couldn't help but to agitate the situation a little. "Good thing I like being center of attention."

"I think we should give them something to really stare at." Ty leaned forward and covered her mouth with his own before she could utter a word, and the second his lips touched hers, Charlotte lost all will to.

All thoughts of their surroundings, of the people staring, all fell to the wayside as she gave in to Ty's demanding kiss. She was becoming an addict to his kisses. It had only been five days, as Tamara noted, since she had last seen him and yet she couldn't stop kissing him. She didn't want to.

Ty was the first to break away, which was a good thing, because Charlotte could have kissed him all night. "I think we got their attention."

"I'd say," Tamara called from behind her.

Flushed, Charlotte backed up a step, desperate to get some air to her burning lungs. "We were just trying to prove a point."

"What, that you two need to either go to a hotel or charge a fee?" Winking at Charlotte, Tamara held her hand out to Ty.

"Hello, I'm the best friend, confidante, and one of the many women who are gnashing their teeth in envy."

Roaring with laughter, Ty took her hand in his own. "It's very nice to meet you at long last, Tamara. I've heard many good things about you."

"Not as good as some of things I've heard about you, I bet."

"Really?" Turning his smiling blue eyes toward Charlotte, Ty asked, "What has she said?"

"She's said—" interjected Charlotte, refusing to allow Tamara to get started, "— that if my so-called friend says anything, she will die a slow death. A very slow and painful death."

"You never let me have any fun," Tamara pouted. Sighing, she turned back to Ty. "Would you care to dance?"

"It would be an honor," Ty said, taking her hand and placing it in the crook of his arm. "I'll be back."

"I'll be here." Charlotte smiled, glad to see that the two of them were getting along.

The two of them no sooner made it to the dance floor, than Charlotte was suddenly surrounded by several of her female co-workers. "Who is he?" one of them asked boldly.

Charlotte turned to the lusting women and said the one thing she thought they needed to know. "He's mine."

There were too many men staring at Charlotte's ass for Ty's peace of mind. Not that he couldn't take any or all of them at any given time; he'd just hate to spoil her little party with a blood bath. A party that was becoming increasingly closed in by the second, thanks to the women who wouldn't leave him alone. Too many people, not enough space, and way too many hands accidentally brushing his ass were beginning to wear on his nerves.

Once was a mistake. Twice he could chalk up to an accident. But the third time, the third time would be considered molestation in any court of law. It was almost as if the damn women had never seen a cowboy hat before. Things were so bad, he was leaning against the wall just to preserve the little dignity he had left. Ty now officially knew what a side of beef felt like.

"Having fun?" Tamara asked, handing him a bottle of beer. Where she had gotten a bottle of Coors at this party was beyond him, but Ty was really thankful that she had.

"Of course. I always like to be pawed on Saturdays." Taking a deep swig, Ty moved over on the wall, allowing the sassy lady to join his wall-holding party.

From the short conversations he'd had with Tamara over the last hour or so, Ty was sure he was in for a treat. She had a funny way of looking at things, and seemed utterly incapable of keeping a thought to herself. And everything she'd said so far had made him laugh, and he was sure this time wouldn't be much different. Thankfully, she didn't make him wait too long.

"Well I'm here to protect you, until Charlotte's done with the deal. Anybody who reaches for your ass again will draw back a nub." Her big brown eyes squinted in what Ty assumed was supposed to be a fierce glare.

"Then I thank you beforehand for protecting my virtue."

"Virtue." She laughed in her soft husky way. "From the tales Charlotte's been sharing with me, there's not much left to your virtue. I'm just making my sure my girl's property is protected."

"Are you willing to fight to the death?"

"Of course." As if God was testing her word, a statuesque redhead who'd been eyeing him all night flitted her way over to them. Before she could get a word out though, Tamara growled, "Back off, Ariel," shocking the woman and Ty, who immediately roared with laughter.

The woman's intake of breath was damn near audible, causing Ty to laugh harder as she backed up and stormed away. Everyone seemed to turn in their direction, which was even more amusing now that Tamara was wearing an angelic smile.

"I think I like you," he finally got out as he calmed down, and tears of amusement shimmered in his eyes. He could see why Charlotte liked Tamara. She was good people. Open, honest, and funny as hell, she reminded him a lot of Charlotte.

"Keep Charlotte happy, and I'll like you right back." Slipping him a sly glance, Tamara probed further. "Speaking of Charlotte, what are your intentions toward her?"

"To make her happy for as long as I live," Ty stated with all honesty. There was no doubt in his mind where their relationship was heading. He wanted, needed Charlotte in his life for the long run. She was his. Just as much as he was hers.

"Wow." Tamara stared at him with shock on her face. "I think I like you already."

"I hope so. Can't have you spending weekends on the ranch if you don't."

Tamara just snickered. "I so don't think so. You're not converting me to the dark side."

"What dark side?" Charlotte asked, joining them.

"Your boy here is on a mission to bring all the black folks to the other side."

"Not all, just two," Ty said with grin. Pulling Charlotte into him, he rested his head on top of her hair, breathing in her tropical scent. "Can we blow this pop stand, or are we here for the long run?"

"We can definitely leave. I've schmoozed enough for one night, and all I want to do is to go home and climb into bed."

Squeezing her to him, Ty murmured, "I like that idea."

"Okay, that's enough, you two. Unless you really want the women slicing their wrists in envy, you need to take that shit home. Have some sympathy for us celibate, horny women."

Charlotte's soft laughter filtered up toward Ty, filling his senses with her being. All he wanted to do was to undress her and make love—hell, as short as her dress was, he didn't even have to undress her to make love, but he'd do it anyway, just for the added pleasure.

They quickly said their goodbyes to everyone, and after walking Tamara to her car, Ty and Charlotte climbed into his black sedan. The car had barely started before Charlotte slipped off her shoes and made herself comfortable in her seat. Sighing prettily, she turned in the seat until she was facing him.

"Thank you for coming tonight. I'm sorry I spent most of the evening talking to clients. I know it couldn't have been much fun for you."

"I had a really good time. Tamara is a lot of fun."

"Isn't she though?" Charlotte's voice held a hint of laughter in it, and after meeting Tamara, Ty completely understood. "You weren't too bored, then, huh?"

"Not too bored, no. Definitely not any less bored than you'll be when the situation is reversed and we're at a party for the ranch."

"I don't know. If all the men look as good as you did tonight, I'm sure I can find something to do to occupy my time."

"Brat," he teased. Reaching over, Ty placed his hands on her thigh and lovingly caressed her.

When Ty pulled up to the exit of the parking lot, he paused, turning to look at Charlotte, whose eyes were closed. "Baby," he whispered, nudging her thigh with his hand. "I'm going to need directions to where we're going."

"Hmmm..." she yawned, opening her eyes for a few seconds before shutting them again. "We're going home."

Rubbing his hand back and forth over her thigh, Ty smiled down at his own personal sleeping beauty. "I haven't been to your house before," he reminded her gently.

"Not my house," she murmured, snuggling deeper in her seat. "I want to go home. To your house."

Ty froze, startled to hear Charlotte refer to his house as home. It was pleasing, but surprising nonetheless. "To the ranch, darlin'?" Ty wanted to make sure he heard her correctly.

"Yes. Home."

Home. The words sounded like poetry on her lips. "Home, it is."

The dashboard clock flashed the time at Ty, and despite the late hour, he was feeling wide-awake. Awake and strangely exhilarated. Ty didn't know what kind of epiphany Charlotte had come to, but whatever was making his brown-eyed beauty sing her new little tune, he was all for it. It was about damn time, too.

He wanted her to think of the Dollar as home, as their home, because he had already begun to think of it that way. All they needed to do now, in his opinion, was to wrangle up a judge and make it legal. The sooner the better, too, as far as he was concerned.

These little jaunts of hers back and forth to LA were beginning to cause wear and tear on his well-being. Sometimes it felt as if he wasn't whole until she was back home with him.

The three-hour trip seemed to pass by in the blink of an eye, and before he knew it, Ty was driving through the gates of the ranch. Parking the car, Ty took a minute to watch Charlotte sleep, her ample chest rising and falling with each breath, a soft sawing noise drifting up from between her lips. She was just as adorable asleep as she was awake.

Leaning over, Ty brushed the back of his knuckles against her soft cheek, tenderly calling her name. "Wake up, sleepyhead. We're here."

Charlotte rolled opened her eyes and looked over at him sleepily. "Where are we?"

"We're home."

Chapter Seven

Charlotte awoke to Ty's teasing tongue tormenting her aroused clit. Closing her eyes again, she reached between her splayed thighs and tugged on his thick hair, bringing him closer to her aching center. What a way to start the day.

Ty chuckled against her, sending chills coursing throughout her sensitive mound. Shivering she dug her toes into the warm sheet, pushing up into his torturing mouth, as she rolled her head back and forth against the pillow in pleasure.

Her body trembled in ecstasy as Ty feasted on her. He dallied around her aroused bud before traveling down her hot center and slipping into her soaked sex. He toyed with her. Keeping her on edge, giving her pleasure, giving her pain, never giving her all at the same time, practically forcing the orgasm to rip from her body. And when it came, it came like a crashing wave, washing over her fiercely yet thoroughly, encasing her entire body with pleasure. Languishing in the aftermath, Charlotte felt weak, which was funny since she hadn't done anything but lie there and receive pleasure. Life was good.

"Good morning," she whispered opening her eyes, watching Ty stare up at her from between her spread thighs. His mouth glazed with her juices, his eyes were alight with love.

"I'd say," he teased, before blowing gently on her clit.

"Stop," she mumbled, pushing at him. There was only so much a woman could take in a span of a single minute.

"I don't think so. I'm never going to stop." Moving up her body, between her legs, Ty leaned over her. "You're mine. Forever."

"I think I'm okay with that." Smiling, Charlotte wrapped her legs around his lean hips. "Does that mean you're going to wake me up every morning like this?"

"I think I can arrange that." Ty nudged the head of his cock against her slick opening, and pushed forward. Their groans filled the air as he filled her snug depths with his hard member, and for a moment, neither of them spoke, both lost in the sensation of the other.

It had been a week and a half since her Christmas party and two days before the holiday itself, and Charlotte couldn't be happier. They had finally come to an agreement about the living arrangements, and after New Year's, she was going to close up shop on her LA lifestyle and give ranch living a go.

With Nathan relocating to Santa Estrella it was the perfect time for Charlotte to make the move. She would be able to keep her job and be with Ty, the best of both worlds, all within her grasp. Life just didn't get much better than that.

They were even talking about marriage, or rather, Ty was talking about it, but Charlotte hadn't said yes yet. She wanted to take things slower. A bit too slow for Ty's liking, but he was dealing...or his version of dealing, anyway.

Gripping both of her hands in one of his massive ones, Ty held her hands over her head, holding her down to the bed. "You know, if you marry me, I can promise you wonderful orgasms like that on a daily basis."

Leaning down, he took her elongated nipple in his mouth, teasing the aroused peak with his lips. His teeth nibbled at her aching tip, before suckling it to a feverish peak, then releasing it to move to its twin. Moaning, Charlotte arched up to him, testing his grip on her wrists. She loved it when he held her down like this. It made her feel so vulnerable, but safe at the same time. Ty would never hurt her…unless she begged him to.

"I'm getting them anyway," she groaned, clenching her muscles around his throbbing cock. The heat building in the nadir of her pussy was threatening to take over her entire body.

"You know, you're just making this harder on yourself. You're going to give in soon. I can feel it in my bones," he panted, speeding up his rhythm.

"I don't think that's your bone you're feeling."

"I love you," he murmured, staring into her eyes. His grip on her wrists tightened, but Charlotte didn't mind. He loved her.

"I love you, too," she replied, looking up into his adoring blue eyes.

His eyes narrowed as he focused on what she'd whispered. "Tell me," he demanding, pushing into her again. "Tell me again."

Charlotte complied, moaning, "I love you," over and over as he plunged into her. She was unable to deny Ty the words he longed to hear. Everything of hers was his. Her body, her soul, her mind belonged to Ty, a few words wouldn't make that much of a difference.

Tightening her legs around his waist, Charlotte met him thrust for thrust, milking his cock with the walls of her pussy. Each stroke brought her closer to the passion she had only truly experienced in Ty's arms.

"So fucking good," he muttered. "So good."

Charlotte couldn't agree more. She trembled at his words, taking every inch of his cock her hot little box could handle. "Harder," she pleaded, waiting to take him as deep and as hard as he could give.

Ty gave her what she craved, and Charlotte came, exploding beneath him as he exploded in her. Clenching his teeth, Ty shuddered as he pressed into her once more, her name a cry on his lips.

He collapsed besides her, looking as tired as she felt. "You're going to marry me," Ty demanded, his voice not daring her to disagree.

"I know," Charlotte admitted with a secret smile of her own. "I just wanted you to work for my yes, first."

After great sex and a long, relaxing shower, Charlotte was ready to climb right back into her bed and pass out again, but duty called. Strolling down the hall, Charlotte stopped in front of Ty's office, knocking on the door before she entered.

"Ah, there she is." Ty and his lawyer, Russell Crichton, stood, smiling at her as she walked in the door. He was too busy looking at her to notice the look of shock on the faces of his business associates, but Charlotte didn't miss it. "Gentlemen, I'd like to introduce you to my fiancée, Charlotte. Charlotte, this is Dean Zellerman and his father, Beaumont. And Russell you've already met."

Charlotte nodded to Russell, but her gaze never left the Zellermans. Recovering quickly, the older of the two men hid his shock behind a mask of disdain. It was a look that Charlotte had seen a million times in her lifetime, but one she hadn't been prepared for here. It was earth-shattering. A real wake-up call on the eve of the beautiful dream Ty had inspired inside of her. Hiding her hurt beneath a cool façade, Charlotte stuck out her hand, forcing the man to either shake it or look like an ass.

"Good afternoon." Take that, you narrow-minded prick. She'd kill him with kindness and watch him choke on it, with a smile.

He shook her hand quickly, barely holding on to her hand for a second. His companion, though, was different. He looked like a younger version of the first man, and he smiled warmly at her as he shook her hand. His behavior almost made up for the older gentleman's...almost.

Walking over to Ty, Charlotte could see that he sensed something was wrong. She didn't want to worry him though. So, instead, she put on a brave front and smiled, loosely wrapping her arm around his waist.

"The Zellermans are interested in investing in the Dollar."

"Well, we're still in talks," the elder Zellerman interrupted, shocking Ty and his son both. But Charlotte wasn't shocked. There was nothing about his behavior that was surprising at all.

"In talks?" Russell questioned, his confusion shared with two of the other men in the room. "I was under the impression that we were done with talks."

Flushing, the man looked over at Charlotte before glancing away. "Papers haven't been signed yet. I might need a bit more time."

"Time, huh?" Ty's words were as sharp as a blow, his gaze cutting through the older man like a fiery torch. "Seconds before my fiancée walked into the room, you were creaming to sign on, but now, now you need more time."

"I...I..." Stumbling over his words, Beaumont looked from Charlotte to Ty as if trying to come up with his story.

"We do want to sign," Dean interjected, looking at his father with distaste in his eyes. "As you know, Tyson, I'm in charge of the company these days; my father is a mere...figurehead." He added the last word as if it were repugnant.

"Then perhaps you need a new figurehead." Enclosing Charlotte's icy hand with his own, Ty faced the Zellermans head-on, sealing his fate and hers. "But I think I'll have to decline your offer. I'm not sure if you're the right company for the Dollar."

"Wait…"

Charlotte had heard enough. "Excuse me," she whispered, before bolting out of the room, to the surprise of everyone.

What had she been thinking? Things were never going to change, not even in the middle of nowhere on a ranch. And now their love was costing Ty money, money she knew he needed to expand the land like he wanted. Running up the stairs, Charlotte was in the room before she knew it, staring at nothing and everything all at the same time.

Tears ran down her face as she glanced at the bed where they had just professed their love, where she had less than an hour ago accepted his proposal, and Charlotte wanted to die. The pain was so intense it almost brought her to her knees. Opening the closet door, she gathered her clothes, intent on packing and going home, when she heard the bedroom door shut behind her.

"What the hell are you doing?"

Turning around slowly, she faced the man she loved and did the only thing she could think of to salvage his life. "I'm leaving."

Ty couldn't remember the last time he'd been so upset. What had started out as a great day was quickly heading down the shitter, one flush at a time. He had really been counting on the money from the investors to branch out a bit more. It would have been well spent on staff and horses, but he would never stoop so low as to work with a closed-minded prig like Beaumont. Not for any amount of money.

His ranch meant the world to him, but Charlotte meant the galaxy, and Ty would rather lose everything than be without her.

The deal with the Zellermans was over, as far as Ty was concerned. He really liked Dean. Ty knew he had the gift of making money hand over fist, but Beaumont was one sorry son-of-a-bitch whose name Ty wouldn't have his ranch associated with.

The moment he had seen the look of distaste on Beaumont's face was the moment the deal went south. And despite Dean's protest, Ty wasn't going to change his mind. He'd get the backing from someone else, or not expand at all. It was just that simple.

Or at least he thought it was. Now looking at Charlotte's tear-soaked face, Ty was lost. How could she think of leaving, when he'd willingly give up everything for her? "What is this all about?"

Charlotte gripped her clothes to her like they were a lifeline. Stepping toward her, Ty stopped in his tracks when she held her hand up to ward him off. What the hell was going on here?

"Talk to me, Charlotte."

Shrugging her shoulders, she looked down at the clothes, refusing to meet his eyes. "What do you want me to say?"

"You can start with why the hell you're gathering your things?" he fumed. He was in no mood to play guessing games.

Charlotte raised her head to look at him. "It's over, Ty."

Ty froze, his body pausing in mid-motion. Even his breathing seemed to still as he stared at her from across the room. "What did you say?"

His words where sharp, like the crack of a whip, bringing a fresh round of tears to Charlotte eyes. He hadn't meant to make her cry, but he was too worked up to comfort her right now. How could she say that? Think that?

"I said, it's over. We're over."

"Never."

"You say that now, but what will you say next month or the month after that when you find doors closing to you everywhere you turn?"

Ty felt the tension leave his body. This he could fix. "I rejected their offer, Charlotte, and kicked them off our land."

"Your land."

"Our land," he reinstated, not willing to let something as stupid as Beaumont's prejudices ruin their relationship. "Nothing's changed."

"Everything's changed. I thought things would be different here. That it wouldn't matter here."

"They don't matter here."

Charlotte gave a sad little smile. "It matters everywhere."

Ty felt as if a cold fist was gripping his heart. She was completely serious, and utterly scared. "He's just one person, Charlotte. One."

Shaking her head, Charlotte watched him with sad look on her face. "That one sale would have helped you bring your dream to life."

"You're the only dream I want to bring to life." Ignoring everything she said, Ty walked over to her and took her in his arms. Pulling her into his embrace, Ty held her to him, trying to stop the terror that was taking hold of his soul. "I love you, Charlotte. Nothing else matters."

"Stop it, Ty," she cried, jerking herself out of his arms.

"Do you really think I care whether or not that deal goes through?" His fear quickly turned to anger. This was fucking ridiculous. "Or, better yet, do you think I want to do business with a man like that? Hell, no."

Charlotte reached out and caressed Ty's cheek as tears trailed down hers. "Do you really think that he's going to be the only one? There's a world full of Zellermans, and you can't afford to tell them all to fuck off."

"This is just an excuse you're using to run." Ty grabbed her hand, and pressed it firmly to his cheek. "It's what you always do when things get rough, Charlotte, you run. But you can't run from me. I won't let you."

"Ty, I'm never going to fit into your world, any more than you would willingly fit into mine. You love this ranch, and it's a part of who you are. If you lost it because of me, you would end up resenting me, and I could never handle that."

"But you can handle leaving me?"

"No, but I have to. For both of our sakes. I love you, Ty."

"Liar," he thundered, pushing her hand away. "If you loved me you'd stay. You'd forget this foolishness and we'd find a way to work this out."

"We can't fight the world. And it's silly of you to think we can."

"Silly. Don't talk to me about silliness. This whole damn conversation, argument, is silly."

"Why won't you listen to reason?"

Ty stared at her in amazement. Reason. What the hell did she know of reason? "Are you even listening to yourself? Less than two hours ago we were lying in that bed making plans for our future, and now you're talking about leaving because people won't like the fact that we're not the same race."

"I could deal with them not liking it, but I can't deal with you suffering because of it."

"Like you give a damn about me suffering." Turning, Ty jerked open the door and stormed out of the bedroom.

To hell with her. To hell with the whole damn thing. If she was going to toss their relationship away because she was scared, then he didn't need her. Life was scary, and Ty wanted a woman who would ride into a storm with him, not cower at the first sign of rain.

In time, he would stop hurting.

Barreling into his office, he slammed the door shut behind him. It was a good thing the office was empty, because if he had seen either of the Zellermans, older or younger, Ty would have put his foot through their asses.

Walking to the bar in his office, Ty poured himself a glass of whiskey, staring down into the russet liquor that reminded him so much of Charlotte's eyes.

"Is everything okay?" Russell asked, coming up behind Ty. So intent on his thought, Ty hadn't heard anyone enter. "You okay, man?"

"Fine." Taking a deep drink, Ty turned to look at his worried friend. "Everything is fine. Did you get them off my land?"

"Yeah, much to the dismay of Dean. He'll be kicking his father's ass all the way back to Sacramento."

"A man after my own heart."

"Is Charlotte okay?" He repeated his question.

"She's just fine. She should be down in a bit, bags in hand."

Russell eyes widened in surprise. "She can't blame you."

Ty chuckled harshly. "Oh, no, she doesn't blame me. See, she's too busy saving me."

"From?"

"The world." Tightening his grip on the glass, Ty could feel himself getting angrier by the second. "Charlotte's under the impression that because of her, my livelihood will go to hell in a handbasket."

"Do you think that?"

"Of course not," Ty thundered, surprised his friend would even ask. Without her his life would be hell. It had only been five minutes and he was already feeling the fires beckoning from below. Charlotte was wrong.

Russell slapped his hand on the bar, breaking the silence. "Ty, are you going to sit in here pouting while she leaves?"

That brought Ty's head up. Was he? Hell, no, he wasn't.

Pushing the glass into Russell's hand, Ty turned on his heel and stormed across the room. He was almost out of the door when Russell called out to him. "Where are you going?"

With his hand on the door, Ty looked over his shoulder at his friend and a devilish smile stretched across his face. If Charlotte thought he was going to lie down and take this, she had another think coming, like the flat of his hand on her luscious ass. "To make that hardheaded woman listen to reason. Even if I have to lasso her ass to me to accomplish it."

Chapter Eight

Charlotte had gotten outside and down the front steps before she realized what a humongous mistake she was making. Why the hell was she allowing a small-minded man to determine the fate of her future? She was never one to let other people influence her decisions, so why was she listening to them now?

Because you're afraid, her mind chided.

Like she didn't know that. But now, instead of just being afraid of what the future would hold, she was afraid she had pushed Ty away. Setting her hastily packed bag on the front porch, Charlotte stared out into the vast green pastures she'd already begun to think of as home and wanted to cry anew.

Her heart was in the right place, but whether Ty would see that or not was a completely different story. She had done it all for his sake, for the ranch's sake, for everything but love's sake.

But she didn't want to lose him. Damn it all to hell.

"Fuck!" She yelled to the heavens, accidentally startling Ida who was walking up the steps.

"Wow. What did I miss?"

Embarrassed about her outburst, Charlotte flushed. "Sorry, I didn't see you there."

Ida merely smiled. "I've had days like those myself, honey. Don't even worry about it. Is the meeting over already?"

"Over, and then some." Sighing, Charlotte ran her hands through her short hair in frustration. What was she going to do? She'd reacted without thinking, and now everything was a giant mess.

Ida stepped up on the porch, her smile slowly sliding from her weathered face when she spied Charlotte's bag on the ground. "Is everything okay?"

There weren't enough words in the English language to explain the cluster-fuck that was her life. "Not by a long shot."

"What…"

Charlotte walked away, not sure what else to say. She didn't mean to be rude, but short of saying *I'm a big stupid loser,* which left a lot to be desired, nothing came to mind.

Walking aimlessly around the grounds, Charlotte went over her options again. There were only two that truly seemed viable. She could either try to kiss and make up, or try to hide and lick her self-inflicted wounds. Although, knowing Ty, he wouldn't let her stay hidden for long.

Troubled, Charlotte headed inside the barn where she and Ty had made love not so long ago. It was one of her favorite places to visit on the ranch, so she wasn't too surprised it was where her aimless wandering had led her.

They'd come here many times over the last few weeks. Sometimes just to talk, others to visit whatever animal Ty was babying at the moment, but whenever they came, he would always tease her about taking her into the tack room. Sometimes he did. This was their place. A musty room filled with hay. It wasn't romantic, but it was theirs.

Charlotte walked to the stall and leaned on the wooden gate. Chiana was no longer standing in the stall. Instead a pretty ebony mare was in her place. Calling softly to the horse, Charlotte stuck her hand over the gate, running her hand down the horse's forehead softly.

Looking into the mare's deep, dark eyes, Charlotte made a decision. Well, not really a decision, since she'd known from the moment she stepped outside that she had made a mistake. More like a choice. A choice to grow up and to stop running away.

Ty was right. From the start, she'd run from him, using her fear as a shield. It was like Charlotte was waiting for him to make a mistake so she could say, "Ah-hah, I knew you weren't perfect." But he wasn't perfect, and Lord knew she wasn't. This morning was proof of that if nothing else was.

Perfect or not, she was his, just as much as he was hers. And Charlotte loved the stubborn fool too much to take one step off this land. Ty was stuck with her, whether it was good for him or not.

"You planning on stealing my horse and making a run for it?" Ty drawled coming up from behind her.

Not daring to breathe for fear of ruining the moment, Charlotte simply turned around to look at him, needing to reassure herself that it wasn't a dream. It wasn't. Ty was there. Letting out a deep breath, Charlotte smiled. Relief filled her soul and tears of joy filled her eyes. He was there. He'd come for her.

"You know what we do to horse thieves around these parts, don't you?" Ty cocked a brow, waiting for her to reply.

"Your horses are safe, cowboy." Charlotte matched his teasing tone with one of her own. She felt lighter, finally able to breathe. Everything was going to be okay. They were going to make it. They had love on their side, how could they not? "We never did get around to the riding lesson."

"There's time."

Smiling, Charlotte agreed, there was time.

She was still here. The residual anger that had been tearing at Ty's soul slowly began to fade away. Charlotte was there, and whatever demons she'd been fighting were conquered. He was still going to tan her hide, though, for putting them through that little drama, but afterwards they were going to make love. Slow, sweet, deep love.

"I don't suppose you'd be willing to overlook my little outburst and blame it on...I don't know...that time of the month?" Charlotte took a step toward Ty, heart in her eyes, as Ty took a step toward her.

"We can if you're willing to overlook my choice in business partners and submit to a punishment worthy of your bratty behavior."

"Punishment, huh?" They were standing toe to toe, and as close to eye to eye as their height difference would permit. "Do you think I need to be punished more than I've already been?"

Ty wanted to burst out laughing. Did she need a punishment, was she kidding? Charlotte had almost killed him when he she said they were over. A spanking was the least she deserved. Of course, it wouldn't just be a spanking. It would lead to other things. Other *nice* things like toys, rope, and orgasms. She'd pay, all right, over and over until they both passed out from pleasure.

Just thinking of taking her over his lap made him hard. "Oh, yeah. You need to be punished."

A slow, sexy smiled slid across her full lips. The same smile that had first caught his eyes. "It's like that, is it?"

"You almost walked away from me. If I don't set an example now, you're liable to try it again, and I'm not going through that hell twice."

"It wasn't easy on my side, either," she pouted, as if that was going to save her fine ass. It was a cute pout and all, but Ty was really getting into the spanking idea.

"Not my problem, darlin'." Ty had run into Ida on his way to search for Charlotte and she'd warned him where Charlotte had been heading. Not before blistering his ears on how to treat a woman though. Like it was his fault Charlotte was as stubborn as she was beautiful.

Come to think of it, *that* should be an extra spanking right there, because he'd had to listen to Ida. Yeah, two spankings. Ty was getting into this punishment idea more and more.

"So what's the plan?" Pressing her breasts into his chest, Charlotte tried to tempt him. Not that he needed any more temptation. But neither did she, if her hard nipples were anything to judge by. "Bend me over your knee until I beg you for forgiveness."

"That's just the beginning. After I tan this delectable ass of yours, I'm going to march you up to the house and call Judge Britton. Tell him he has a wedding to perform."

Startled, Charlotte pulled back. "A wedding! So soon?"

Before all of this nonsense started, Ty had been willing to wait a decent interval, but now decency could be damned, for all he cared. He just wanted Charlotte. And he wanted her forever.

"I was going to take things slow, but you've pushed my hand. The only choice you now have is Christmas morning or Christmas evening."

"I can't plan a wedding that fast."

Once again, she was talking like he cared. "You'd better."

Shaking her head in amazement, Charlotte let out a light laugh. "You're insane."

Her laughter, soft and angelic, was like music for his soul. "I'm willing to take that into consideration, but that's neither here nor there. Two choices, woman. Which will it be?"

"Christmas afternoon."

Growling, Ty pulled her to him. She just had to have her way. Damn, he loved this woman. "That wasn't one of your choices."

"You're so bossy."

"And you love it." Leaning forward, Ty brushed a slow sweet kiss across her pouting lips. "You love me."

"Yes, I do." Sighing, Charlotte rested her head on his chest, holding onto to him with all of her might. "I guess I can plan a quick wedding. We can give this crazy marriage idea of yours a try."

Ty picked her up and carried her back to the tack room. The same room where they'd made love, not so long ago. Setting her down on a bale of hay, Ty stepped between her legs, pulling her close to him. He might have to save that spanking for later. Right now, he just wanted to be inside of her. "There is no try with us, Charlotte. It will work."

Raising a brow, she wrapped her hands in his shirt and pulled him forward until his mouth was just a breath away from her own. "That sure of yourself, cowboy?"

"No, darlin'. I'm just that sure of us."

* * *

For a quickie wedding on a horse ranch in the middle of nowhere, Charlotte and Ty's celebration had been beautiful. Taking another sip of her cool champagne, Tamara watched the lovebirds dance on the makeshift dance floor, with tears of joy in her hazel-brown eyes.

Excited for her best friend, Tamara fought hard to hold back the mixed emotions threatening to bring her down. She was happy for them. So very happy, but at the same time she was sad for herself.

It was selfish and she knew it, but she was going to miss Charlotte. Sighing, Tamara walked toward the bar, intent on snagging something a bit stronger. Champagne was all well and good, but she needed a *drink* drink and something extremely fattening to eat, preferably covered in cheese.

After hijacking a startled waiter's tray, Tamara found a table far away from the skinny women, where she could eat in peace. There was no way she was going to go hungry on Christmas. She'd been good all year, and if Santa didn't count her vibrator, she'd been good for longer than she cared to remember.

"Is this seat taken?"

Startled, Tamara looked up with a mouth full of cheesy-stuffed-something-or-other and almost choked. Inhaling deeply, she reached for her glass. Did she look like she needed company?

"I've never had that reaction before."

Sitting down, the man leaned over and handed her a napkin. Now that her breathing was under control, Tamara's brain resumed its normal function, and she was able to breath. Bad with names, Tamara thought long and hard on his. She knew he was the best man, but she couldn't remember his name.

She'd met him briefly, but hadn't given him more than a passing thought. He was white, wearing a cowboy hat, and she probably weighed more than he did. So, not her type.

"Sorry about that." She gestured to the tray. "I think that was God's way of telling me to back off the cheese do-dads."

"Or maybe he was just telling you to share." Eyeballing the platter, he rubbed his hands together avariciously. "I've been chasing that waiter down all night. Mind if I..."

Well, she did, but Tamara was too polite to say so. "Help yourself."

Sighing, she watched as he did just that. Cute and he ate more than she did. That was just fucked up.

"I'm Russell Chrichton, by the way. We were introduced earlier, but I could tell by the vacant look you just gave me that you didn't have a clue."

"I remembered," Tamara lied. She knew it started with an R...or a letter, or something.

"Right." He grinned, his green eyes twinkling. "So what's with you bogarting all the cheesy puffs, Tamara?"

"A girl's got to eat. And besides, I starved all day yesterday to look good in this hideous dress."

Chuckling Russell tilted his head to side, as if studying her. Something Tamara wished he wouldn't do. The dress wasn't all that bad, but it did show off a bit more of her curves than she would have liked.

"I think you look lovely."

Narrowing her eyes, Tamara snagged a cheese pastry and waved it at him. "Lookie here, cowboy, Charlotte has already warned me about y'all's slick ways. You just stay on that side of the table, and I'll stay on this side. I think Char and Ty have erased enough color lines for one small town."

Russell roared with laughter, turning several heads in their direction. After his laughter subsided to a mere chuckle, he replied, "You are hilarious."

With a mouth full of food, Tamara merely smiled. Making people laugh was her specialty.

"I'm not a *cowboy* cowboy," he continued, taking the black hat off and setting it down on the table next to his glass. "I just look damn good in the hat. And I don't live in Santa Estrella anymore. I have a law office in Los Angeles."

"I live in LA"

"Really?" Interest piqued, Russell went back to studying her. "What do you do?"

"Mainly look for jobs," Tamara admitted with a rueful smile. She had as much luck holding down a job as she had sticking to a diet. But that was life.

"Looking for a job right now?"

"I did say *mainly,* didn't I?" It wasn't a secret. Hell, she spent more time going over the newspaper than birds did. "But something will turn up. It always does."

"What do you do?"

Tamara paused for a moment to study him. She could make small talk with the best of them, but for some strange reason, he seemed genuinely interested. "I'm a photographer."

"Really? How come they didn't hire you to take pictures of the wedding?"

"Because Charlotte wanted to torture me by making me wear this dress instead."

Russell chuckled softly as he downed another appetizer. "Have you ever done surveillance work before?"

"You mean, stalk people with my camera?

"Sorta."

"Do ex-boyfriends count?"

"Did you get away with it?" he countered amusedly.

"Of course."

"Then it counts. I'm looking for someone to take a few pictures for me from time to time. Do you know anything about the law?"

Tamara shrugged her shoulders. This was the strangest job interview she'd ever been on. "Only enough to not break it."

"That's a start," Russell laughed. Reaching into his jacket pocket, he pulled out a wallet and handed her his business card.

"Why don't you call me when you get back home? I'm sure we can work something out."

Glancing down at his card, Tamara wondered if he was serious. "You're a very odd man. Tell me the truth. Was it the cheesy poofs?"

"No," Russell said, shaking his head. "It was your smile. I'm a sucker for nice, full smiles. I think I might have a tooth fetish."

"Well, if the price is right, you can stare at my teeth all day." Tamara tucked the card in the neckline of her dress. It was worth looking into. What did she have to lose?

~ * ~

THE BLACKER THE BERRY

Dedication

This book is dedicated to everyone who e-mailed me, sought me out at conferences, or wrote me a letter requesting this story. When I'd given up on ever writing something for Tamara and Russell, I'd receive a new message asking me about them. You, my readers, never let me forget Tamara and Russell were characters worth plotting for, and The Blacker the Berry *wouldn't exist without all of your dedication to this couple. I hope you enjoy the story and that it was well worth the wait.*

Chapter One

"Tamara, I need a favor."

Tamara Holifield gripped the cordless phone tighter to her ear and rolled over in bed, pulling up her night mask in the process so she could stare wildly at the blaring red numbers on her digital clock. It was only seven a.m. Favors didn't happen until after lunch. "Who are you, and why should I care?"

There was a brief pause before a sharp dash of deep-toned laughter filled the line. Laughter didn't happen before noon, either. "I'm hanging up now," she warned, pulling down her mask to cover her stinging eyes. Last night was the culmination of a series of nights where she had stayed up way too late in her darkroom, with nothing to show for it but smelly, wrinkled fingers.

Photography was her passion, just not her meal ticket. Despite the fact she'd just climbed into bed only two hours earlier, Tamara would soon have to leave the warm haven of her floral goose-down comforter to go clock in at the administrative office of Martin Luther King Jr. High School for another day of file-clerk slavery. She was way too old to be temping, but the man wanted money for electricity and water, and what the man wanted, the man got. Hopefully, though, she'd be able to rely on her pictures soon as a way to make money. She had a show coming up in two months, so she was working overtime to get her ass in gear.

"It's Ty."

"Is that supposed to mean something?"

"To Charlotte, it does." The laughter in his voice, as well as the name he dropped, was like a douse of cold water on her face. Tyson Wilcox was the cowboy married to her best friend, Charlotte, and her soon-to-be baby daddy. Soon. Very soon.

Sleep forgotten, Tamara sat up and yanked the mask off her face. "Is it the baby? Oh my God, it can't be the baby. It's too early."

Jumping out of the bed, Tamara stumbled to her closet, desperate to find something to wear. It wasn't every day a woman became a godmother.

What was she going to wear?

Did she have enough film?

Did she have to time to brush her grill?

"Tell Charlotte I'll be there as soon as possible." Tamara grabbed a pair of jeans off a plastic hanger, breaking the hook in the process. *Motherfucker.* Didn't it just figure?

"Tamara, calm down."

"Calm. I am calm." With the phone held between her ear and shoulder, Tamara shoved her legs into her jeans, hoping to hell they'd fit. She couldn't tell if these were her size if-I-only-lose-ten-more-pounds-I'll-be-able-to-breathe-in-these-jeans jeans, or her double-digit, tag-removed-out-of-shame jeans. "How far apart are the contractions?"

"Tamara..."

Sucking in her never-shrinking gut, Tamara panted, "Tell her to breathe slowly." She tried to follow her own advice and button her pants. It wasn't working. These were definitely not the comfy double-digit jeans. "And tell her to wait until I get there. Oh crap, how am I going to get there?" Her car was as dead as her last diet. "What am I going to do?"

"Tamara, calm—"

Frustrated, Tamara gave up the fight with her button and yelled into the phone, "Ty, if you tell me to calm down one more time, I'm going to lose what little religion I have left and kick your—"

"She's not in labor."

"She's not in labor!" Exhausted and upset, Tamara gripped the phone tighter and dropped onto the bed. "Then why didn't you say so?"

"Maybe it's because you were too busy having a panic attack to listen to reason."

"Ty, baby, I love you like a lost cousin, but right now, I could kill you." Ty laughed, apparently not at all threatened by her comment. "Just because you wrestle cows all day, cowboy, doesn't mean I can't take you out. I'm from west LA." Way west in the suburbs, but he didn't have to know that. "And I'm not afraid to go back to jail."

Sure the first and only time had been during orientation at a local prison for a job she'd been hoping to get. Hoping, that is, until she actually realized she'd be coming in contact with criminals. People who might not take her biting sense of humor the right way.

"Duly noted."

Partially satisfied, Tamara hooked a hand in the waist of her snug jeans and began to pry them down her thighs. A size 10 she wasn't, but that was a problem for another day. "So what's going on?"

Ty's voice lost a bit of the cheerfulness that had been swimming in it a mere moment ago. "Have you talked to Charlotte lately?"

"I talked to her last night." And the day before that. And the day before that. Charlotte had been her best friend since grade school. The two women couldn't have been closer if they came from the same womb, and just because Charlotte had gone country and moved three hours away didn't change anything.

"Did she sound…okay to you?"

"A bit down, but nothing that can't be expected." Charlotte was seven months pregnant and confined to her home. Thanks to the bronco bull she'd married, the petite woman was carrying a large baby, and the two just didn't mix. She was scheduled for a C-section in eight weeks and ordered to stay close to home until then. To say Charlotte wasn't happy would have been an understatement, but it was to be expected. "Why, is something wrong?"

"Well, yes and no."

Despite his no, her heart sped up. What the hell was going on? "Spill, cowboy."

There was a long pause before Ty spoke again, but when he did, his voice was filled with determination. "I want to know if you can come out here."

"When?" Confusion caused her brows to furrow.

"Now," he said firmly. "And before you ask, I want you to stay for a while."

"How long is a while?" Frowning, Tamara sat down and kicked the offending pants off her feet and to the floor.

"Until she has the baby."

His reply had her mouth dropping wide open. Was he kidding? She hoped so. "She's not due to have the baby for two months," she reminded him, just in case he didn't remember.

"I know." Ty sighed heavily.

As much as she wanted to laugh at the absurdity of it all, she knew deep down, Ty wouldn't ask something so asinine if there wasn't a reason. "Talk to me."

"She's not doing okay. In fact, she's doing very not-okay. The pregnancy—as you know, it isn't going very smoothly." Ty paused for so long Tamara almost asked if he was still there. "She's stuck at the ranch, unable to work for long or do a lot, and she's bored stiff. No, she's more than bored. She's unhappy."

"Unhappy?"

"Yes."

And Tamara could tell that as far as Ty was concerned, that was the problem. Amused, Tamara lay back on the bed. "Ty, baby, as much as I would love to, I just can't quit my job. I can't afford to."

"I'll pay you."

The words of the desperate man once more had her grinning. Charlotte was a lucky, lucky woman. "You won't pay me to spend time with my best friend," she said patiently.

"I can't have you doing it for free."

"I can't do it at all, Ty." As lovely as it sounded, she just couldn't be Charlotte's cowgirl in waiting. "Jobs that don't involve flipping burgers or saying, 'Would you like your receipt in your hand or your bag?' aren't very easy to come by these days."

"What about the weekend?"

Tamara grimaced. She wanted to. She really, really wanted to. The last time she'd seen Charlotte was over a month ago, when Ty and Charlotte came to LA for business. Even though the two women talked every day, either via phone or e-mail, it just wasn't the same. Tamara missed hanging out with her friend like they used to, back before she'd lost her heart on the Ponderosa. "I want to say yes."

"Then say it." From everything Tamara had heard and seen in regard to Ty, he was a man used to getting his own way. "Just say yes and I'll make it happen."

"It's not that easy," she protested weakly. "I don't have a car."

"It's not a big deal. I'll find you a ride. Hell, I'll buy you a car if necessary."

"Since when did you two have money to burn?"

"We don't, but I can't go another week with seeing her so unhappy."

Tamara couldn't help but feel a bit envious Charlotte had someone who loved her so much, he was willing to make an utter ass of himself. Even though it was a bit extreme, it was kind of sweet too. "You know you're spoiling her, right?"

"And your point is?"

"Nothing." She laughed lightly. "I get off work tomorrow at three-thirty."

"I'll have a car waiting at your place by four."

"Anyone ever tell you you're pushy?"

"Everyone."

"They didn't lie."

As she hung up the phone Tamara realized she'd have a lot to do before tomorrow if she was going to be spending the weekend down on the ranch. Starting with finding her jeans that actually fit.

* * *

Russell Crichton stared at the closed green door and sighed. He didn't know exactly when it happened, but somewhere along the line, he'd morphed into his best friend's chauffeur. Normally he didn't mind doing a favor for a friend, but this was going past the call of duty.

Four o'clock had come and gone half an hour ago. They should have been on the road a while ago. He was giving this Tamara chick five more minutes then he was off like a dirty shirt.

Angry, Russell walked a few feet away from the door, crossed his arms over his chest, and leaned back against the wall. Some friend this lady was turning out to be. Here it was, Ty was worrying a hole in his gut over Charlotte, and her best friend couldn't even be bothered to stick to the agreement she'd made. People just didn't care about other people these days.

Just one more reason he was making the transition from lawyer to rancher. He was sick and tired of dealing with the scum of the Earth. Sad part was, he wasn't even a criminal lawyer. His specialty was corporate law, and still it was nasty. The things people would do for a dollar were frightening, and he refused to pander to the masses anymore.

A few more months and his dream would become reality. He was going to turn an abandoned, run-down ranch into a profitable one. It was taking a lot of time and a lot of money; lucky for him, he had both.

When the door across from Tamara's apartment opened, Russell straightened up from the wall, then frowned. The African-American woman coming out of the apartment with a suitcase in her hand looked familiar. Very familiar.

The full-figured, dark-skinned woman was wearing an expression similar to the one he was sporting and muttering under her breath as she wrestled the gray bag out the doorway, dropping it on the floor as she closed the door behind her.

When she turned around to face him once more, he moved away from the wall, and lowered his arms at the same time as she looked up and met his gaze. A spark of recognition flared in her eyes as she caught sight of him. At the exact same moment, they spoke.

"Hey," she began.

"Don't I know you?" he questioned.

"Are you"—Tamara ran her gaze over him, from the top of his black cowboy hat, worn low on his brow, down past his shirt, battered jeans, and dinged-up brown boots before zooming back up to his eyes—"Ty's friend?"

"Yes, and you're Charlotte's."

"Yeah," she said with much attitude, before placing her hands on her ample hips and frowning. "What the heck took you so long?"

"Me so long?" Her unexpected anger threw him, as did the bag sitting next to her feet. It was much bigger than a weekend required. How long was she staying? "I've been here since a little bit before four."

"Did it never occur to you to ring or knock?"

"I did," he shot back.

"Excuse me?"

"I did," he repeated through clenched teeth, then it hit him. Feeling a bit foolish, he shoved his hands deep inside his jean pockets. "Just not your door. Ty told me G2."

"Ty told you wrong." She gestured to the open door behind her. "He was off by a number."

"So I see. If you didn't know I was out here, where were you going?"

"To catch a bus."

She said it as if it was the obvious answer, which of course, it wasn't. "A bus?"

"Well, I had to get to Santa Estella somehow."

"And you thought you'd take a bus."

"Yes. I thought renting a private plane would be a tad pretentious."

"I guess." He smiled, in spite of himself. All the less than nice things he'd said to himself about her instantly came crashing back. Here he'd been bitching and moaning about half an hour, and she was preparing to board a bus and take a three-hour drive—probably more with stops—just to be with her friend. Man, he was an ass. "It looks like we're getting off on the wrong foot here."

"No, we got off on the wrong foot two years ago when you bogarted in on my cheesy poofs." She softened her words with a smile that damned near took his breath away. Good Lord, she was lovely. She also possessed a good memory.

"You remember that?" Russell wasn't big on weddings. All he could recall was waiting for the damned thing to be over and being hungry as hell.

"I never forget a good cheesy poof." Tamara turned back to the door and jiggled the handle as if testing the lock. When the door didn't budge, she turned back to him and smiled. "So, ready to hit the road?"

"Now is a good enough time as any."

"Cool."

Before she could bend over to pick up the suitcase, he grabbed the handle and gestured with the bag in front of him. "After you."

Instead of arguing or putting on some feminist show, she merely took off in the direction he indicated. The ride down the elevator was slow but quiet, as was the trek outside. She stopped on the stoop and looked around as he pulled out his key ring, pointed it at his car, and clicked off the alarm. He'd just popped the trunk open when she burst out laughing.

Startled, he paused in the middle of setting her suitcase in, to glance back at her. "What?"

"You drive a Lexus?"

He sat her case down and looked at the luxury car in question, waiting for the joke to hit him as well. "Yes," he said as he closed the trunk and came back to her side.

"Man"—she shook her head in amusement—"talk about judging a book. I was expecting a truck or a coach or something. Not this."

"Sorry to disappoint," he teased. "If it makes you feel better, my other car is a horse." He also had a truck on the ranch, but he figured he'd save that little surprise for later.

"Oh yeah, I feel much better." Her grin was infectious, and he felt a smile grace his own lips.

"That's what I'm here for. So, shall we?"

"Let's."

Russell walked with her to the passenger side and opened the door for her. He waited until she buckled up before closing the door and walking around the front to get into the driver's side. After opening his door, he took off his hat, and sat down, tossing the hat on the backseat before closing the door and buckling up.

As usual the car started like a dream, purring to life at a simple twist of his key. The Lexus may not have been part of the cowboy way of life, but it was sweet as sin, and anyone who said differently apparently had never driven one.

He pulled away from the curb and started the three-hour-long trek to Santa Estella. It was a trip he'd been making a lot in the last three months, so much so, he could probably do it in his sleep. He had become so used to making the trip in peace and quiet, he'd come to think of it as his own little downtime away from life.

It was the one main reason he'd only begrudgingly agreed to drive Tamara. As selfish as it was, he didn't want to have to give up the one moment of tranquility he'd come to look forward to by the weekend. But the idle chatter he'd expected to be bombarded with from point A to point B, never occurred. Before he hit the freeway, Tamara pulled her iPod from her jacket pocket. She put the earbuds into her ears and closed her eyes, resting her head on the headrest.

It was a good thing he didn't want to talk. Right...a good thing. About an hour into the drive, the good thing got old. Real old.

Taking one hand off the wheel, he gently tapped her on the thigh, startling her so bad her iPod flew out of her hand. Although it was funny, Russell held back his laughter while he waited for her to take the headphones off. "Sorry," he said halfheartedly when she pulled the white cord, freeing her eardrums. "I didn't mean to scare you."

"As my momma used to say, if I was living right, I wouldn't be jumping, right?"

He wasn't sure if she was right or not. In fact, he wasn't quite sure he understood what the hell she'd just said. He was just happy she was talking. "Right. So how long are you staying? I saw the bag and..."

"Oh." She chuckled. "Just for the weekend. They did tell you I was going to need a ride home, right?"

"Yes, but I come out every weekend. I didn't know if it was this Sunday or next."

"No, this Sunday."

"So, why the big bag?"

"Despite how it might appear, only a few things in there are clothes. The rest are things for Charlotte."

"Baby presents?"

Tamara cocked a brow. "Look at you all up in my business."

"Hey," he said with a shrug of his shoulders. "I'm a lawyer. I cross-examine in my sleep."

"I guess."

When she didn't volunteer any more information, he prodded, "So..."

"So what, nosy boy?" she shot back, completely ignoring his curiosity.

"You're not going to tell me?" His tone showed the disbelief he felt.

"Nope." She shook her head for good measure, smiling all the while. *Brat!*

"Why?"

"Because you want to know."

He didn't think he'd ever met a more contrary woman in his life. Yet instead of her refusal angering him, it amused him. "That's childish."

"I can live with that."

"What if I said, if you don't tell me, I'm going to pull over and drag you out of the car." Since they both knew the threat was meaningless, it didn't hold much weight, but he was interested to see what her response would be.

"I'd say, 'I hope you ate your Wheaties.'"

His lips quirked with humor. "Why? Don't think I can handle you?"

"No, cowboy, I know you can't handle me."

Talk about waving the red flag before the bull. Russell was sorely tempted to pull the car over for the mere sake of proving her wrong. She might think she was too much for him, but she was wrong. Dead wrong. And he couldn't wait until he proved it to her. "We'll see, Ms. Thang. We'll see."

Chapter Two

The three-hour drive to Santa Estella seemed to fly by to Tamara. It had more to do with the company than the lack of traffic. Even though they'd met at the wedding and talked for a very brief time, she really didn't get a chance to know him.

If memory served her, he had offered her a job during the reception, but she never took him up on the opportunity. Back then she'd been afraid of screwing up and getting fired and then having to see him at every function she attended at Charlotte and Ty's. That didn't end up being the case, though. Not just because she didn't take him up on his offer, but also because after the wedding she never saw him again.

Over the course of the last two years, Tamara had visited the Dollar Ranch more times than she could count, but not once, on any of those occasions, had she run into him. She'd heard of him. Ty mentioned him a few times, but that was about it.

Now, looking at Russell, it appeared as if the man who had once told her that he wasn't a *cowboy* cowboy, might have up and changed his mind a bit, if his outfit was anything to go by.

And damn, did he look good in that outfit. She was willing to bet he looked damned good out of it as well. Hmm...what she wouldn't give to get him in her viewfinder. He had black hair, tapered at the nape, and a sexy goatee. His green eyes seemed to delve into her soul when his gaze was on her. She wondered for a moment how she could have forgotten their depth or intensity.

Several times during the drive, she found herself wondering, *Did God really make men that pretty*? No matter how long she looked at him, be it side-eyed or full-on, she couldn't get over how attractive Russell was. No, attractive was almost too tame a word to describe the man. He was *fine*, heavy on the *ine*.

"By the way, thank you for allowing me to tag along with you. I really appreciate it."

"My pleasure." He said pleasure like some women said chocolate.

She was still focused on his sensual voice when she became aware the car had come to a stop. Looking around, she realized they were at the ranch. Wow, where did the time go? "So, we're here."

"Yes, we are. Ready to get out and straighten your legs?"

Not really, but she wasn't going to admit that. "Of course."

"Great. Hold on." He hopped from the car and hustled around to open her door. She couldn't help but appreciate his gentlemanly habits that seemed to have died out in the city. Maybe it was a cowboy thing.

"Thanks," she said as she rose from the car. When she had to look up to meet his gaze, she was once more struck dumb. The man was something to behold. Muscular without being bulky, Russell appeared leaner, like a basketball player, not scary like a football player. He also towered over her, which, since she was five-eight, wasn't an easy thing to do. Good Lord, she was going to have to get a hold of herself, or run off and become acquainted with Charlotte's handheld shower nozzle.

"Once again," he said with a wink. "It's my pleasure. Let me get your ba—"

"Oh my God!"

Tamara looked passed Russell and over to the front door to Charlotte, who was standing on the white porch in the entranceway with one hand over her mouth and the other resting on her enormous belly. Her big brown eyes were wide as she stared at Tamara. Tamara looked her fill as well.

It had been a little over a month since she'd seen the other woman, and other than her tummy pushing her floral smocked tank shirt out to kingdom come, Charlotte still looked the same. As stereotypical as it sounded, her mocha-tinged skin seemed to glow. Even though her sable hair was cut short in a boy-like style, it seemed healthier than it ever had before. Pregnancy, like marriage, appeared to suit her.

"You don't have to worship me," Tamara teased, moving past Russell toward the porch. "Just sacrifice a few calves in my honor, and we'll call it good."

Charlotte dropped her hand from her mouth and took a step forward. "What are you doing here?"

"I came to see you." Tamara climbed the steps until she was standing in front of the pregnant woman. "But if that's the kind of welcome I'm going to get, I'm going home."

"You better not." Charlotte reached out and pulled Tamara into her arms. Or tried to. Her belly, for once bigger than Tamara's, prevented the two women from getting too close. "I'm so happy to see you."

"I missed you too, shrimp." Her words were like a crack in the dam, causing Charlotte's tears to burst forth. "I'm sorry," Tamara instantly said, unsure why her nickname for her friend would cause this reaction. Charlotte had never protested in the past about the term of endearment.

"She's constantly doing that these days," said a deep voice from behind Charlotte. Still locked in the crying woman's embrace, Tamara could only look up in confusion at Charlotte's husband, Ty, who was lounging in the entryway. The handsome man was grinning from ear to ear as he stared down at the two of them. "Don't take it personal."

"Oh shut up, you," Charlotte said, pulling away from Tamara. With her hand on her hip, she turned around and faced Ty. "Did you know about this?"

The huge man, who easily dwarfed both women, raised his hands in mock surrender and took a step back. "Who me?"

"Yes, you." Charlotte waddled over to him and wrapped her arms around his waist. "Thank you, you big lug."

Ty smiled and pulled her tighter into him. "Welcome, baby. Happy?"

"Words cannot express."

"Can I express something, please?"

Tamara turned from the happy couple to glance behind her at Russell, who had her suitcase in one hand and a smaller black bag in the other. "Move. This shit is heavy."

"Ohh. Sorry." Tamara scrambled out of the way, so he could climb the steps. She wasn't the only one. Ty and Charlotte backed into the house, allowing him room to come in.

"Get in here, girl."

She complied, bringing up the rear, which wasn't a bad thing at all. It afforded her the opportunity to get a glimpse of cowboy ass. Nice.

"How long are you staying?" Charlotte asked, staring down at the two bags.

"I'm just staying for the weekend," she said as she eyed the black bag. "Only the gray belongs to me. I'm not sure who the black one belongs to."

"That's mine," Russell said. "I'm checking into the Dollar this weekend as well. Actually, I stay here most weekends while my house is being gutted."

"Oh." Talk about a nice surprise. "Interesting." Very. And she'd be pumping Charlotte for information about that later.

"If you're only staying for the weekend, what's with the large bag?"

Tamara turned back to Charlotte and grinned. "Presents."

"Presents." Charlotte's eyes lit up. "For me or the baby?"

"I don't know that little intruder yet. They're all for you."

"Yay!" Charlotte let out a childlike squeal. "Give 'em to me."

"No, later." Tamara lowered her voice to a mock whisper. "When the stinky boys aren't around."

"Oh, that's easy." Charlotte glanced up at her husband and batted her eyes. "Honey, poof. Be gone."

"Look at the thanks I get," he grumbled good-naturedly. "But don't think I'm not going to make you pay for that little comment later."

"I'm counting on it." He dropped a quick kiss on the top of her head, before releasing her. He grabbed a well-worn black cowboy hat off the hall table and slapped it onto his head, covering his brown locks in the process. "Come on, Russ, grab the bags. Tamara's to the living room and yours to your room."

"Great, so now I'm a butler as well as the driver." He sent Tamara a wink. "I get no respect around here."

"You're a lawyer," Ty said. "You should be used to it."

"Good point." Russell bent down and picked up the bags. "Ladies."

After dropping the gray suitcase into the large room, the men headed back out, shutting the door behind them. Tamara considered the room the epitome of country living. It was casual and not overly pretentious, even though everything in the room was of the highest quality. The walls were a medium brown earthy tone, garnished with photos that went back several generations, Charlotte's now included. The focal area was a large stone fireplace that took up most of one wall. All furniture was arranged around it, giving the room an even homier appeal. From what Tamara recalled, the taupe couches were extremely comfortable, something that Charlotte immediately decided to take advantage of.

"I've got to sit down. My feet are swelling so bad, I can't stand for more than a few minutes. Of course, I can't actually see my feet, which might actually be a good thing, because if I could see how bad they've gotten, I might just start to cry all over again."

"I'm just letting you know, if you keep that up, I'm out of here. You know I'm a sympathy crier."

"I totally forgot about that." Charlotte's laughter bubbled forth. "What a sight we'd make, both crying like we'd lost our minds. Noses running, snot just everywhere."

"We'd look so hot."

"Damn straight." She chuckled as she eased down onto the brown leather recliner. "So what did you bring me?"

"Lots of stuff." Tamara pulled the suitcase next to the chair and sat on the floor in front of it. After unzipping it, she pulled it open, and pushed the top over, displaying her goodies to Charlotte's eager eyes. "Ty said you were bored, so I brought just what you need to ease all your woes." Tamara pulled out three DVD cases. "*Love and Basketball, Dirty Dancing*, and *300*. Young love, hippie love, and hot gay love."

"They weren't gay in *300*." Charlotte tried to protest, but Tamara smirked at her naivety.

"Girl, please, what movie were you watching?"

Laughing, Charlotte shook her head. "You are too much."

"You say that now, but wait to see you what else I have for you." Tamara set the movies down and pulled out a large plastic supermarket bag tied at the end.

"We have food here."

"Shut up." Tamara tore the bag open and pulled out a portable foot spa.

"Is that..." The awe in Charlotte's voice was funny as hell.

"Yes. Movies and pedicures." It was part of their former Saturday night ritual that used to also include chocolate-covered something or other and a recap of the latest Friday night date disaster. "Just like the good ol' days. You know, before you lay with that white man and let him climb on top of you and have his wicked way."

"His wicked way." Charlotte chuckled as she shook her head in amusement. "God, I love you."

"That's what all the pregnant chicks say," she said with a smile and a shrug of her shoulders. "Now point those dogs in my direction and get to spilling. Who is this Russell Crichton guy, really, and what is he doing staying here?"

* * *

"So are you sure it isn't a big deal, me staying here?" Russell asked as he tossed his bag carelessly on the bed in the room he'd stayed in whenever he came out to Santa Estella, which of late, had been quite often. Now that Charlotte's friend was here, he wondered if he was taking Ty's goodwill a bit too far.

"Of course. This is as much your home as it is mine."

Russell was touched his friend felt that way. Lord knew he'd spent as much time in this house during his teenage years as he did his own. But still... "I'd understand. Hell, it's past time for me to get a room at the local inn, or maybe I should look into getting one of those trailers and setting it up on the property." It wouldn't be long until the inside was done. He would only need to stay in a trailer for a month or so, and since he only came out on weekends, the time would fly by.

"A trailer." Ty crossed his arms and leaned against the doorframe as he regarded Russell. There was a look akin to amusement on the other man's face. "Okay, who are you, and what have you done with my best friend?"

"What do you mean?" Russell frowned.

"I don't know who you are, but the Russell 'Rusty' Crichton I know wouldn't be caught dead in a trailer again. What was it you use to say? 'Roughing it isn't fun, it's a flashback.'"

Russell chuckled at the other man's comment. "If you had a father like mine, you'd feel the same way."

"Boyd was a good man. May he rest in peace."

"Yes, he was." Russell would never deny the character of his father. He had been a good man, but he'd also been a piss-poor provider. He'd dragged his family with him from town to town as he followed the rodeo circuit. Boyd had dreams filled with gold belt buckles and big dollar signs, dreams that never came to fruition thanks to a stubborn steed with a wicked buck. Russell's father had spent all of his life chasing a fantasy, only to end up a hand on the Dollar thanks to a busted knee.

Although Russell had loved his father, he didn't love the life the man made for their family. After graduating high school, it had become his life's goal to prove he wasn't his father, but that useless rebellion was over. He was now making it his life's goal to prove he was a good man, and not one led around by the memory and shadow of a ghost. Still, though, it didn't mean he had to sleep in a tin can to do it. "A very good man." Russell smiled. "But I sincerely doubt he's resting in peace. More like he's raising hell and taking names with your dad at his side."

"Amen to that, brother."

"By the way, dingbat, you gave me the wrong apartment address."

"I did?" Ty frowned.

"Yes, and don't think I didn't have to hear about it."

"Tamara's a mouthy little thing, isn't she? Did she talk your ear off?"

"No, not really." Once he put the conversational ball in motion, she held up her end, but at no time did she ever overwhelm him with chatter. "Charlotte seemed happy to see Tamara."

"She did, didn't she?" A grin lit up his friend's face. The same sappy grin the otherwise intimidating man wore every time mention was made of his pint-sized beauty. He was such a goner, something Russell never thought would happen.

The two of them had chased more tail than tomcats, and now Ty was neutered. What a shame. "Yes, I think you'll be in her good graces for a while. And maybe you can stop following her around like a hound dog."

"Say what?"

"I'm saying you're whipped, boy." Russell flicked his hand as if it held a whip. "Wh-tcssh."

"Wanting to see my wife happy makes me whipped?"

"No, that stupid little grin you get anytime you think of her makes you whipped."

"Says the cynical lonely guy."

"Don't confuse single with lonely," he challenged, even though there was a bit of truth to his friend's words.

"Oh don't worry. I wasn't," Ty said with a smug grin. "One day you'll see, pal of mine. One day you'll see."

Russell shuddered at the very idea. "God, I hope not."

"The plans for the new barn came in. Want to check them out?"

"Of course." Russell rose from the bed and joined his friend at the opened door. "How else will I steal the design and make it better if I don't?"

Ty slapped him on the back as he neared him. The heavy blow made him wince. "You should stick to the lawyering, son, and leave the real cowboy work to me."

"We'll see if you're so cocky when my spread outrivals yours in less than a year. My colts will have your horses looking like well-trained mules."

"I welcome the challenge, Rusty. Saddle up, cowboy."

Cowboy. Russell liked the sound of that. It was so much nicer than blood-sucking bastard, just one of the pet names he was referred to by because of his chosen profession.

The two men chatted as they headed downstairs to the office. As they passed the living room, a shout of laughter rang out from behind the closed door.

The sound caused both men to stop in their tracks and glance at the oak door. They stood silent for a moment outside the room and listened in while the women chuckled it up on the other side. After a few seconds, Ty turned his head and looked at Russell and jerked his head in the direction of the door.

The silent question of "What the hell?" didn't need to be voiced aloud. He too was interested in whatever had Tamara laughing so hard. Russell shrugged his shoulder in confused solidarity, and nodded his head, gesturing for the other man to open the door. He was just as curious as Ty was as to what was going on behind the closed doors.

When Ty turned the knob and pushed the door open, both men peered inside. Russell wasn't sure what he expected to see, but it sure wasn't Tamara sitting on the floor in front of a seated Charlotte, with a soaked foot in one hand and with something that looked like a lava rock in the other.

"And then he said…" Tamara's words came to a dead stop at the creaking of the door. She raised a brow and gestured with the rock thingy to the couch. "Welcome to *Tamara's House of Toes*. I'll get to you two gentlemen in a minute."

"I can't speak for Rusty here, but I'm good, thanks."

"Rusty?" Her lips twitched as if she was holding back a laugh. "All right...well, Rusty, do you have a preference in polish color?"

"Whore red," he said, playing along. "And I need my fingernails done too. Plus a Brazilian wax." Russell wasn't quite sure what a Brazilian wax was, but Lord knew, he'd paid for a few while in relationships with women who didn't mind him spending his money on them. "Can you fit us both in?" He nudged Ty with his shoulder. "My friend here is shy, but he could probably use the works."

"Of course. I'm at your service." She turned back to Charlotte who was grinning from ear to ear. "Grab a seat and stay awhile."

Russell looked at Ty, who was watching his wife with a besotted grin on his face, and snorted his amusement. Ty was bewitched by his wife's happiness. So much for looking at plans. Though when he thought hard about it, he realized he was okay with not looking over anything. Like Ty, he was suddenly more interested in what was going on in this room than he was in what was going on elsewhere. And that surprised and intrigued him equally.

Chapter Three

As much as Tamara enjoyed sleeping in, there was no way in the world she was going to do so today. One of the reasons she enjoyed visiting Charlotte was the breathtaking views she bore witness to every day on the Dollar. Her camera became an extension of her arm every time she was here, and today was no exception.

It was barely past six, but she was already up, dressed, and heading out the door. Her camera was loaded and ready, with a spare roll of film in her pocket. As quietly as she could, she walked downstairs, mindful of waking anyone else in the house. Of course, the second she stepped outside and spotted the dozen or so people already hard at work, she instantly felt stupid. Just because six o'clock seemed like an ungodly hour to her, didn't mean the rest of the world felt that way.

Amused by her lack of knowledge, she shook her head and headed down the front porch, stepping into the sheer beauty of the great outdoors. Walking out the front door was like entering another world. She was amazed at the beauty around her. With camera in hand and at the ready, she took off in a southerly direction, heading toward the rear of the house where she knew the horses were sometimes freed to run to their hearts' content in the confinement of the fenced pasture.

Although she would rather eat a horse than admit to having a fascination with the large beasts, she couldn't quite hide her excitement at photographing the animal in its truest form, running with its herd as if it were as free as its ancestors had been. Horses galloping with the wind whipping through their manes were just something she didn't see much of in Los Angeles.

In fact, city life in general didn't often allow her to enjoy an unimpeded view of glorious sunrises or the simple quiet of the country. Nor did it afford her the opportunity to see a god riding a horse.

When she rounded the corner off the house, Tamara came up short and stared in surprise at Russell on a chestnut-colored horse, galloping around the dusty corral. The man and animal moved in perfect harmony, as if they were melded together. The hell he wasn't a cowboy. She'd seen enough Clint Eastwood movies to know the real deal when she saw it.

What surprised her most, though, wasn't the sight of the man on the horse, but the fact that she was able to recognize him, despite the several feet that separated them or the black hat worn low on his brow. He was the type of man whose very persona demanded recognition. And although she continually told herself that he wasn't her type, she still found herself drawn to him.

Damn it, she didn't do cowboys. That was Charlotte's thing, not hers. Tamara was more of a blue-collar, rough-brother kind of girl, not that that had gotten her very far in life. But still, she wasn't looking to take a ride out on the range, with Little Joe and Adam.

Then again, there was no harm in looking, or staring, or drooling, just as long as no one noticed. Not that she'd be the first woman ever caught salivating over a man in tight jeans and a hat. Wait a minute. She wasn't the only one. With a new naughty determination, she headed over to the corral with a purpose in mind. She was going to take his picture. Lots of them. And maybe, just maybe, if she was lucky, she would finally have something worth hanging in a gallery. And if Lilith hung her photos, people would buy them.

Praying the fence would support her weight, she climbed up on it and seated herself on the top rung. With agility she didn't know she possessed, she balanced her big rear end on the fence and took her hand off the wooden beam, wrapping it around the body of her Nikon to support the lightweight camera.

With her eyes on the prize, she took a deep breath, steadied her hand, and aimed, shooting several pictures in rapid succession. The action shots showcased the pure athleticism of the man. Of course, she couldn't help but also capture his rugged good looks.

Russell clicked his heels against the horse's side causing him to switch directions and head toward her. She took a few more pictures of him riding toward her before lowering the camera.

When he stopped a few feet away from her, she spoke, "Hey, cowboy."

With the tip of his index finger, he tilted the brim of his hat up, enabling her to peer deep into the emerald pools of his eyes. "Ansel Adams, my how you've changed."

"Something in the water."

"I'd say." He nodded his head at her camera. "Do you have a license for that thing or merely a learner's permit?"

"Full-fledged license." She raised the camera a bit as she spoke with pride about her baby. "I can parallel park this beauty like nobody's business."

"I bet you can." His upper lip twitched a bit as if he was biting back his laughter. "What are you doing up so early?"

Damn, he was cute. "Taking in the scenery." She brought the camera up more, aligned the viewer with her eye, and took a picture of him, before lowering the camera once more. "What about you?"

"Working my girl out." He ran his hand down the horse's dark brown mane. The loving way he caressed the animal made Tamara want to prance and neigh, just to get a sample of his touch. Wait! What! Did she really just think that? "Since I only get to see her on the weekends, I have to pay her a little attention so she doesn't get it in her head I'm stepping out on her."

"We wouldn't want that, now would we?"

"No, we wouldn't." He smiled in that irresistibly devastating way of his that just made her trigger finger itch. And if she, a dark-skinned, brother-loving, city-dwelling girl, wanted to pull his shirt up and wipe the sweat from his body with her panties…while she was still wearing them, then other women with less crazy notions would simply melt.

The images of money and naked cowboys danced in her head. Inspired, she flashed him what she hoped was a charming grin, and said, "Why don't you do a couple of tricks for me on that pony of yours, so I can take some pictures? I'll immortalize you." She eyed him thoughtfully. "Anyone ever tell you you're too pretty to live?"

From the way his eyes widened, she could tell she'd shocked him. "No, I can honestly say that's never come up in conversation."

And they were the lesser for it in her book. "You should let me photograph you."

"You are," he said drily.

"No, I mean really. Like in my studio." *Under bright lights while you wear nothing but your hat and a smile.*

"Studio, with like cheesy backdrops and wagon wheels?"

"No wheels. No cheesy backdrops."

"Umm…no."

"What are you afraid of?" she challenged. "I thought you mentioned something yesterday about your being able to"—she paused, as if searching for the right word—"handle me."

"I can."

"Then what's there to worry about?"

Russell threw back his head and laughed. He took off his hat and slapped it on his thigh, stirring up the dust before slapping it back on his head.

"What?"

"Do you really think you're going to back me into a corner and make me change my mind? I'm a lawyer, Tamara, or did you forget?"

"You're not a lawyer. You're a cowboy. The sooner you realize it, the better off we both will be." And the sooner she'd get her photos.

"Just when I'm out here."

"I don't think so." There was a lot Tamara didn't know about this lifestyle, but something told her that being a cowboy wasn't something someone just turned on and off at will. It was something inbred in their DNA, like eye color and male pattern baldness. She brought the camera back up to her eye. "Why don't you put that thing in reverse and unbutton a few of those buttons for me?"

"I'm quite sure you're treading the lines of sexual harassment here."

Tamara tilted her head to the side and studied him. "What's your point?"

"Good day, Ms. Tamara."

"Aww, come on," she whined, while with a flick of his wrist he put the horse back in motion and galloped away. "This isn't over, cowboy," she muttered, lowering the camera once more. "Far from it."

Tamara wasn't one to let anything stand in her way once she had her mind made up, and she definitely had her mind made up about him and her cowboy photos. Now all she had to do was convince him and the cuties around the Dollar to pose for her.

It was going to be a piece of cake.

* * *

"Are you sure this is a good idea?"

"Nope." Ty slipped his hands in dark jean pockets and leaned back against the porch railing. "But her doctor okayed the occasional outing as long as she didn't tire herself out or stand for too long. Unfortunately, she mentioned that in front of Charlotte, so short of tying her ass to the bed, I have to actually let her leave the house every now and then."

Russell felt the need to point out the obvious. "But the Watering Hole is rowdy and loud."

"That it is, but we're just having dinner and maybe half a turn on the dance floor, not participating in a hoedown." His nervousness seemed to amuse Ty, but hey, he couldn't help it.

In fact, he couldn't understand how the other man could be so cavalier about the whole thing. Charlotte, adore her as he did, looked like she was a second away from popping like the swollen balloon she was. If she were his wife, he'd have laid down the law a long time ago and forced her to stay home. Then again, his stubbornness was more than likely one of the reasons he wasn't married to this day. "Fine, all I'm saying is, if she goes into labor, I'm out of there."

"What a good uncle you're going to be."

"Hey, my job is to spoil the kid, not mind the momma."

"Good point." Ty laughed. "How're things shaping up at your place?"

Just thinking about his unfinished home had Russell seething. The crew he'd hired to work on his house was a few men short for the weekend shift. For the money he was paying them extra to work on Saturday and Sunday, he would have figured the contractor would have hired more men, especially knowing Russell always showed up on the weekends. But that would have been too much like right. So instead of spending just a few hours at his place, he'd spent the entire day breaking his back helping out to keep everything on schedule. Thus far his weekend away from work had been nothing but work.

"Man, don't get me started. Do you remember that movie *The Money Pit*?" He waited until Ty nodded his head before he continued. "Well, just take Tom Hanks out as male lead and draw me in, and you have my house."

"What's wrong?"

Russell didn't even know where to start. "What isn't wrong is a better question. I spent all freaking day digging holes looking for my septic tank."

"You lost your septic tank?" His voice was filled with confusion.

"*I* didn't lose shit." Russell wanted to get that straight. This whole debacle was not his fault. Just his problem.

"Pun intended?"

Smart-ass. Unamused, Russell shot Ty an aggravated look. "Do you want to hear this story or not?"

"Sorry." Ty's words might have said one thing, but the way his lip was twitching said something entirely different. "Proceed."

So Russell did, filling the other man in on all the details that had taken his weekend from heaven to hell. Just being able to vent his frustrations to his friend made it marginally better, but only slightly.

"Wow."

"Tell me about it."

"Man, if you don't want to go out tonight, I'll understand."

"Nah. I need to get out and clear my head. I need some distractions of the worst sort." And in the worst way. "Speaking of distraction, how's Tamara's visit going? Is Charlotte having a good time?"

"Oh yeah. Every time I turn around, I hear giggling. I have no idea what the hell they're talking about, but it must be funny as hell."

"Speaking of funny. You'll never believe what Tamara said to me today."

"What?"

"She wanted me to pose for her."

"Pose?"

"Yeah." He smiled at the startled looked on his friend's face. "That was about what my reaction was too."

"Well, what did you say?"

"What do you think I said?" Russell replied in a dry tone. "No."

"How come?"

"Do I look like the Marlboro Man to you?"

Ty tilted his head to the side as if he was studying him. "Maybe a bit around the eyes."

"Right."

"I wouldn't go dismissing her outright. Tamara is the real deal. I've seen some of her work. She has talent. In fact, if I recall correctly, Charlotte mentioned something about her having a show coming up soon."

As impressed by that as he was, Russell just couldn't imagine posing for Tamara. The woman saw too much as it was. "If you think it's such a good idea, why don't you pose?"

"She didn't ask me."

Likely story. Russell opened his mouth to speak, but was stopped before a single word edged past his lips by the opening of the front door.

Charlotte and Tamara strolled outside, arm in arm, smiling and laughing. For the first time in a long while, Charlotte didn't look miserable in her pregnancy. She wore a navy blue summer dress that somehow managed to showcase her ever-growing tummy without taking away from the rest of her lovely figure. She appeared more at ease than he'd seen in a good while. In fact, she seemed to glow with inner happiness. The only thing to outshine her, though, was her companion.

Tamara looked utterly and completely jaw-dropping, cock-hardening sexy. Startled by his thoughts, Russell blinked a few times, wondering if this was the same woman who'd ridden in with him just the other day. Her dark, shoulder-length hair was curled in bouncy ringlets that framed her pretty, round face. She was wearing a short black skirt that showed off her long legs and rounded, full rear. And her low-cut red top accentuated her bountiful breasts.

It took an act of God to keep his jaw from dropping open at the mouthwatering sight before him.

"Don't you ladies look lovely!" Ty said, apparently unaffected by the other woman's charms.

Not to be outdone by the other man, Russell spoke as well. "Yes, very lovely."

"Why, thank you." Charlotte preened under her husband's attention, while Tamara looked on with unsuppressed amusement.

He wanted her to say something, anything to prove to himself that the vision in front of him was really the woman he thought she was. But she just shook her head as she watched her friend take Ty's hand before they both headed down the porch steps into the front yard. When she went to follow, Russell called her name softly, causing her to turn back around and face him.

"Yes?"

"You really do look lovely."

"You say that as if you're surprised." There was a hint of laughter in her voice, as if she was making a joke. The only problem was, he couldn't tell at whose expense it was.

The truth be told, though, he was a bit surprised. Not that she could look lovely, but that he found her attractive, and not just in a common, casual there's-something-attractive-about-every-woman-kind-of-way, but in a want-to-get-her-naked-and-do-something-about-it-kind-of-way. Which was an oddity. She certainly wasn't his type, but he couldn't help but react to this gorgeous woman in front of him. She was a sight to behold, and he was doing his damnedest to look. It might not be politically correct, but he wasn't one to pass up an opportunity like this one. "Everything about you surprises me."

"Good."

"Good?" He hadn't been expecting her to say that.

"Yes. If I was so easy to figure out, this would be boring," she said with a wink before turning and heading down the stairs.

Tonight was definitely proving to be an eye-opening experience, in more than one way. He followed her toward the car in anticipation of the evening.

Chapter Four

Tamara considered herself a worldly person. She wasn't a jaded woman, or someone who was easily shocked by the world around her, but this shit here—this do-si-do stuff—was for the freaking birds.

With her mouth gawked wide, she stared at the crowded dance floor of the Watering Hole and wondered what in the world her big butt was doing there. The only other person of color that she could see besides Charlotte was a Latino man in the far corner, looking as at home as every plaid-loving man in the room. This was not a dream. This was *Hee Haw* come to life.

They'd arrived in this otherworldly place twenty minutes ago, and she was still trying to figure out why there was a list of patrons waiting for a table. Ty had seen someone he did business with and had gone over to say hello. When Tamara wondered aloud at the wait, Russell offered to check with the hostess. Although she loved to people watch, this was better than any airport terminal or amusement park. The people here were a sight to behold.

Tamara was hard pressed not to break into laughter. No one would ever believe that she and Charlotte had gotten all dolled up to come to a barn raising in the middle of no-man's-land. Never before had she seen so many rednecks, literally and figuratively, or cowboy hats in one place in her entire life. To her utter surprise, it wasn't just the men wearing hats; the women wore them too. They also wore jeans tight enough to keep Monistat in business for a decade, as well, but that was really neither here nor there.

It wasn't often that Tamara felt out of place, but damn, today was the day. If she hadn't walked in with two of the buffest, tallest men in the room, she would have booked her black ass out of the room as quickly as possible.

"Close your mouth, or you're going to catch flies." The teasing tone of Charlotte's voice reeled Tamara back in. With wide eyes, she turned and faced her friend, amazed her former city-living friend seemed at ease here.

"There are no words," she finally said when nothing else would come. "This is beyond anything I would have ever imagined. Is this much plaid *legal* in the state of California?"

"Apparently." Charlotte leaned in closer to her and lowered her voice. "And the part that's going to slay you is, this is what they would consider their good clubbing clothes."

"Shut up."

"Sorry, girl." Charlotte laughed. "It's the gospel truth."

"And you live here, knowing this? On purpose?"

"Well, it's not like we come in here often, and besides"— Charlotte bumped her hip into Tamara's and pointed toward the filled bar at the denim-covered rears—"there *are* some perks."

Now this they could agree on. The asses she was privy to view were not ones to sit behind a desk for eight hours a day. These were tight, firm buns that got that way through hard outdoor labor, not an hour in a gym. "I guess there is something to be said for sexy men in jeans and cowboy hats. And let's not forget that little twang they have in their voices. I can't discern what it's a mixture of, maybe southern gentlemen with a hint of rake and a dash of good ol' boy, but whatever it is, it gives me a tingly in my tummy and a moistness in my panties."

"Girl, you're preaching to the choir." Charlotte's laughter drew some curious gazes their way.

A sun-bleached blond, his skin tanned a honey bronze, turned at their laughter with a sly look. He caught Tamara's gaze with his own, and with a seductive smile on his lips, he winked.

"Good Lord." Tamara fanned her face with her hand. "Okay, scratch that shirt complaint. I'm beginning to think it will look awful nice on my floor."

"You are so bad."

"Really?" Russell asked, coming up from behind them. "Tell me more."

Before Charlotte did just that, Tamara bumped her friend gently with her elbow. "Just girl talk. It wouldn't interest you in the least."

"I wouldn't be so sure. If girl talk makes your eyes glow like that, then I'm definitely interested."

"Is our table ready?" She batted said glowing eyes and changed the subject, not willing to be pulled into this battle of wills with Russell. Truth be told, she was a bit upset with him for not agreeing to pose. It was stupid, and she refused to pout about it, but it still sucked.

Seriously, Tamara didn't think she was asking too much. These groups of photos could be the artistic break she was looking for. Then again, to be fair, she was well aware there were some people who just didn't like to have their pictures taken. It only blew that Russell was one of those people.

"Yes, but do you really think changing the subject is going to make me any less interested in what you were talking about?"

"No, but your interest won't make me spill my secrets."

"What will?"

It could never be said Tamara was one to miss an opportunity when it was presented to her. "If you pose for me, I'll tell you anything you want to know."

"Anything? No holds barred?"

"Anything."

"Tempting."

That was a start. "I'd give you carte blanche ove—"

"You."

His request sent a shockwave through her system and had her stuttering like a fool. "Na—no."

"Pity." He gave her a knowing look and smiled. Then turned around and walked away, leaving Tamara and Charlotte goggling in his wake.

Oh my. Where the hell had that come from? Tamara could only stare after Russell as he strolled over to Ty and wonder if she had imagined that entire exchange. Was he...flirting with her? No. It couldn't be. Pretty boys like him didn't flirt with girls like her unless they were getting paid obscene amounts of money. And the only thing obscene about her bank account was the bareness of it.

"Ladies," Ty called, gesturing with his hand for them to join them.

"Be right there, honey," Charlotte said with false cheerfulness as she grabbed Tamara's arm in her hand. Lowering her voice, she spoke quickly as they began to walk toward the two men. "What in Rick James's name was that about?"

"You got me." Even though it amused Tamara that Charlotte reverted back to their high school days' repartee, it wasn't enough of a distraction to take away from the anomaly that had just occurred.

"Okay, I got you. But does he?"

"Girl, please." It was as much of an answer as it wasn't, and Charlotte knew it as well as she did.

"And that means?"

"That we're going to have to pray to Father Rick for answers, 'cause I haven't a clue."

Charlotte pulled her to a stop and turned her around so they were facing one another. Staring intently into her eyes, she asked, "Do you and Russell have a thing going on?"

She wondered for a moment if her friend's pregnancy had addled her brains. "I met the man two days ago."

Charlotte shook her head. "Not true, you met him at my wedding."

Tamara pushed down the urge to roll her eyes at the distinction. "Fine, I re-met the man two days ago."

"I slept with Ty the first night we met," Charlotte retorted in a stage whisper.

Tamara chuckled. "I sincerely doubt either of you did any sleeping."

"Oh hush." Charlotte was still a bit embarrassed about her whirlwind courtship with Ty, which of course meant that as her best friend, Tamara was required to tease her about it at every given turn. "And answer my question."

"No, I haven't slept, stroked, sucked, or fucked Russell."

"Yet?"

"Don't go there."

"That wasn't a no."

Tamara didn't need Charlotte to tell her the obvious. She was well aware of everything she'd said and didn't say. "Let's just drop this and eat."

"It's dropped all right. For now."

"I'm starved," Tamara said brightly, hoping to drown out Charlotte's parting words.

"Then let's take our seats," Ty said, gesturing in front of him.

Tamara knew dinner would only be a brief reprieve and had no doubt she wouldn't be able to escape Charlotte's scrutiny forever.

* * *

Russell didn't know why he hadn't seen it before, but Tamara was quickly becoming the most fascinating woman he'd ever known. She was just as lively at dinner as she'd been the previous night while playing beauty shop with Charlotte. It was becoming increasingly apparent there was nothing she didn't have an opinion about or felt unable to express. She did it in a joking way that kept her from sounding like a know-it-all and kept them all laughing throughout the meal.

It was suddenly so apparent why Ty had been desperate to have her come cheer Charlotte up. No one could be around her for long without being infected with her joyous attitude.

She took to her food with the same gusto he was beginning to see she took to life. Instead of repulsing him, though, it appealed to him. It wasn't as if she was overeating or anything. Her meal was smaller than his own by far, but she enjoyed her food in a way he hadn't seen a woman do in years. She savored each bite as if it was a gift. It was refreshing to meet a woman who didn't calorie count or avoid bread like it was the plague.

As they waited for dessert to be served, a cool voice spoke from behind him. "Russell, I didn't know you were in town."

From the tone of the voice and the way Ty frowned, Russell knew without a doubt who was behind him. Sandra Hart was the only woman Ty wouldn't muddy his boots to save from a stampede. She was as bitchy as she was beautiful, but she was damned good in bed, the one and only reason Russell put up with her. Sometimes a man had to let the little head have a say in the decisions the big head made.

He pushed back from the table and stood, as his momma had taught him as boy, and turned to face the blonde woman. "How are you, Sandra?" He leaned forward and kissed her on the cheek, inhaling her overpowering perfume as he did. There was absolutely nothing subtle about Sandra, not her fragrance, not her low-cut blouse and tight jeans, or that ruby red color staining her lips. She was vulgar in the sleaziest of ways, and normally, he adored it.

Normally.

"Other than being a bit peeved you haven't called me, I'm fine." She pouted prettily. That one little look of hers spoke volumes of the retribution Russell would have to pay in order to get back in her good graces. Not that he wanted to. He was a bit over them. "If I knew you were coming here, I could have accompanied you instead of Christian." Sandra gestured to her twin brother, Christian, who was standing next to her, looking as bored as Russell was beginning to feel.

The tall, silent man was a masculine version of Sandra, proving that their shared DNA worked well with two X chromosomes or with just one.

"Christian." Russell didn't offer a hand, knowing from experience that the other man wouldn't take it. Not that Russell blamed him. He didn't imagine he would be overly friendly to a man sleeping with his sister with no thought of marriage in mind.

"Russell." The other man surprisingly managed to sound more cordial than he had in the last two years since they'd moved to town. "In town long?"

Russell was going to have to get used to small town living all over again if he was ever going to make it here. No one gave a second thought to butting headlong into someone's business or asking a question others might consider impolite. But that was the price he'd have to pay to relocate. So, even though he didn't feel as if he owed anyone an explanation to the whys and hows of his life, he answered anyway. "Just the weekend, as usual."

"Is your house done?" The predatory tone in Sandra's voice had him mentally taking a step back. She was a bit too interested for his bachelor peace of mind.

"Close, but not entirely."

"I'm sure you can't wait until it is. I know you must be tired of staying with...friends." She shot a glance over his shoulder in Ty's direction, prompting Russell to wonder, and not for the first time, if there was a shared history between his friend and her.

"More like they're tired of me intruding on them," he said in a teasing tone as he shot a glance over his shoulder. At that moment he spotted Tamara looking on with interest, which brought another reminder from his mother. "How rude of me, let me introduce you to—"

"We've met them already," Sandra interrupted, waving her hand in the air as if dismissing Ty and Charlotte.

Her bad-mannered behavior not only surprised Russell, it angered him, but before he could reprimand her, her brother spoke up.

"Well, maybe not all of them." Christian shared the same glass-clear blue eyes and predatory stare of his sister, only his weren't directed toward Russell as Sandra's were. His were fully on Tamara. A fact that quickly ruffled Russell's feathers.

Even more annoying, though, was her answering smile in the other man's direction.

"Hi, I'm Tamara Holifield, Charlotte's friend from Los Angeles." Before Russell could protest, Christian walked around him, took her proffered hand, and kissed the knuckles in an inane attempt to appear courtly. To Russell, though, all he managed to do was to look like the ass he was. And if he thought Tamara was going to fall for that, he was a fool ten times over.

"Mmm..." Tamara murmured as her grin spread wider.

What the hell! She isn't going to buy that bull, is she?

"Nice to meet you, Tamara; I'm Christian Malt." So nice, apparently he didn't feel a need to release her hand. "And how long are you in town?"

"Just the weekend, the same as Russell."

"Since the weekend is almost up, then, I'd best make do with the time we have left. Care to dance?"

"I'd love to."

Apparently she was. Flabbergasted, Russell stared speechlessly at Tamara as she rose from her chair. She didn't know Christian from Adam, and she was just going to go off and...*dance* with him.

"Dance?" The amused tone in Sandra's voice pulled him back from the brink of madness. "Are you sure you'll be able to keep up? I'd hate for you to tire out the second you get out there."

"Sandra." Russell frowned at her borderline-insulting comment. Either she was really in full bitch mode tonight or he was beginning to notice her bite was a bit more aggravating than her bark.

"Tire out." Tamara snorted with derision. "Sweetheart, I don't know what *y'all* call that dance out there, but back home we call it the Electric Slide. I can do that move in my sleep. Instead of worrying about if I can keep up, you might be worried about your friend here." From the way she drawled "y'all" and the twinkle in her big brown eyes, Russell could tell she was far from cowed by Sandra's callous manner.

"Brother." Christian corrected with a smile on his face. "And for the record, darlin', I have no doubt at all that you can keep up."

"Then come on, cowboy, show me what you're working with." To Russell's disbelief, Tamara hooked her finger in Christian's belt loop and led the grinning man to the dance floor.

The shock on Sandra's face was almost commensurate to the outrage coursing through his system. They both watched in muted disbelief as Christian and Tamara joined the grapevine line and began to step and twist in time with the music.

The grapevine ended, quickly morphing into a two-step. But Tamara had no problem changing musical direction, following Christian's moves as if they'd been dancing together for years. Their bodies swayed back and forth in a pantomime of sensuality.

"Well, isn't she just full of surprises." Sandra sniffed.

"You have no idea," Charlotte said. "I wouldn't be surprised if she taught your brother...a few steps."

"Hmm...now wouldn't that be interesting," Sandra replied.

No. Not at all. A wave of jealousy of disproportionate size hit Russell by surprise. It was a feeling he was unused to dealing with, especially with a woman who wasn't his to claim. No. It wasn't jealousy. It was annoyance and nothing more.

From what he knew of Tamara, she was a nice enough person, definitely way too nice to become involved with a snake like Christian. Besides, a man like Christian couldn't possibly be interested in a woman like Tamara. He would only use her for his own twisted reasons, then leave her high and dry just as he had many other women before.

Russell wouldn't even put it past the man to flirt with her just to get his goat. Christian had made it more than clear on numerous occasions that he didn't want Russell with his sister. Maybe this was his way of getting back at him.

Yes, it was his duty, as a friend of a friend, to warn her before she took Christian's flirting seriously.

Chapter Five

Tamara was tore up from the floor up. Her legs and thighs ached, and her butt felt as if she'd literally dropped it like it was hot. Country dancing wasn't for the weak of heart—or flabby of leg, for that matter. Groaning, she eased down from the breakfast bar stool and walked over to the sink to rinse her cereal bowl out.

Before disappearing in his car last night, Russell had barked at her that they would be leaving first thing in the morning; then he drove off like a bat out of hell. Normally Tamara didn't take orders from anyone, but since he was her only means of transportation back to LA, she was going to let him get away with it. This time.

For a reason only known to God himself, after dinner Russell had turned sullen and snappy. Two qualities Tamara didn't deal well with.

As if her thoughts conjured him from the cosmos, Russell appeared at the doorway to the kitchen. Without a word of greeting, he stomped into the room with a surly expression on his face.

"Morning."

He grumbled instead of replying. Refusing to be annoyed by his less than stellar morning persona, Tamara smiled, turning up the voltage. It was either kill him with kindness or the belt from his very waist. "I've already said my good-byes, so whenever you're ready to go, I am."

"Coffee first."

Was that supposed to be a sentence? Tamara held onto her smile with a death grip, resisting the urge to roll her eyes like mad. "Fine, I'll be out on the porch."

"Fine."

Muttering to herself, she walked out of the room and toward the front door. As she'd told him earlier, she'd already spent some time with Charlotte this morning. She was on bed rest orders from Ty after taking half a turn on the dance floor. Although she could sense her friend's boredom already seeping in, Tamara knew the other woman would do as asked. Since they'd already spoken of her coming down the weekend after next, there was no need for a tearful good-bye. Unfortunately, it left her sitting outside by herself while Rumplestiltskin in there made his morning joe. Still, Tamara wasn't going to complain. A free ride was a free ride. Besides, until last night, he'd been more than pleasant. The only thing she could fathom was that something must have happened while she was dancing.

The screen door squeaked open, and Russell's footsteps rang out over the porch. Once again, he made his way toward her in silence, with a thunderous expression. She could only assume his cup of coffee hadn't been enough to pull him from whatever funk he was in.

"I guess we're ready to go?" She stood from her chair as he picked up her bag and began to clomp down the steps. Following along, she began to chatter. "I hope the traffic isn't too bad on the way home. I think we're leaving early enough, though, so we should be fine. If I can, I'd like to work on a few photos today while the light is still good."

Russell stopped dead in his tracks, causing Tamara to run smack dab into him. "Ummf."

Quickly turning, Russell grabbed a tumbling Tamara, stopping her from falling to the ground. "You all right?"

"Yes," she mumbled as she stepped away. Tilting her head back, Tamara eyed him up and down, as if she was dissecting him. "Somebody erected a mountain in front of me and failed to mention it."

Russell arched a brow. "You're a talkative little thing this morning, aren't you?"

Narrowing her gaze, Tamara placed her hands on her hips and took a threatening step forward. "Did you just call me little?"

"Yes."

Tamara dropped her hands and grinned, all trace of irritation swept away on a dry breeze. "Thanks."

He frowned for a moment, as if his brain couldn't process her response and then shook his head and turned back toward the car. He unlocked the vehicle and then popped the trunk open to stow her suitcase. In the meantime, she situated herself in the passenger's seat. When he opened the door and joined her in the car, she noted his thunderous expression had returned.

After seeing the less than cordial look on his face, Tamara instantly reached for her iPod, but paused when he shot her a look and gave a sharp shake of his head.

"Okay," she said softly to herself as she placed her purse, iPod and all, on the floor between her feet. So much for disappearing into music.

He started the car, and they headed down the driveway. She glanced in the side mirror and watched the ranch slowly diminish in the glass as they drove away. They finally turned the corner, and she turned back toward him.

"Did you have a good time?" Although she'd been expecting some conversation, she hadn't been expecting that particular question.

"This weekend? Yeah, it was a blast."

Frowning, Russell glanced over at her. "I meant last night."

"Yes. What about you?"

"Not particularly."

"Oh, you and…what's her name…Sally, Sarah…" Tamara hedged, even though she knew exactly what the other woman's name was.

"Sandra."

"Yes, Sandra." Distaste instantly peppered her tongue. "Didn't the two of you hook up last night?"

"No. I came home with you three, remember?"

"Yes, but you went out again." Not that she noticed, or waited up to listen for the sound of his engine, which didn't appear until hours later.

"I went by my house."

"Oh." Damn, did that come out happier than she intended? "That explains it, I guess."

"Explains what?"

She didn't exactly mean to say that aloud, but since it was out there. "Your funky attitude."

"My…funky what?"

"Attitude. What happened, she wasn't in the mood or something?"

"Not that it's any of your business, but no. That wasn't the case at all."

Ignoring the "any of your business" line, Tamara forged on. "Then what was it?"

"Nothing."

"Please. I know a case of blue balls when I see it."

"Blue ba— Good Lord, woman, are you always this forward?"

"Yes."

"So I see."

"Life's too short to be phony." It was the creed by which Tamara lived. She believed in honesty and integrity and in living life out loud. Her philosophy on life was one of the reasons she was often fired. She truly didn't know how to keep her big mouth shut. "If I have a question, I ask. It makes no sense to me to wonder and hem and haw around things."

"You have an interesting outlook on life." Gone was the irritated look, and in its place was one of faint amusement.

"I don't know if it's interesting or not, but it's mine," she replied with a shrug of her shoulders. Tamara was used to people not getting her.

"Honesty isn't a foreign language to you, is it?"

"Unfortunately, no."

"I wouldn't say unfortunately. I think it's nice to know where you stand with a person."

"As do I." And with that in mind. "So are you going to tell me or not?"

"Tell you what?"

"What has you in such a foul mood?"

His expression stilled, erasing any hint of humor from his face. "I'm not in a foul mood."

"That's a matter of opinion."

She watched as he attempted to wipe away all expression from his very animated face. Tamara was willing to bet Russell was a terrible poker player. Everything he felt and thought was written there for the world to see. And right now, she saw irritation. "Feel free to listen to your music now."

Oh no he didn't. "Why, thank you, massa. I surely will."

"Stop it." He scowled. "That's not what I meant, and you know it."

"I actually don't know anything of the sort." She might be gearing up for a battle here, but it was one she felt just might be necessary. "You like honesty, well, here's a big healthy dose of it. You're being a butthead, and I don't like it. Which is a shame, because so far I seem to like everything else about you."

Her words seemed to tame the beast roaming restlessly underneath his hard-as-a-shell surface. "You do, huh?"

"Yes, but I'm not afraid to fight a cowboy, so back up off me and just relax."

"I am relaxed. Just a bit..." He rolled his shoulders and sighed.

He wasn't getting away with that. "A bit?"

"Worried," he finished at last as if the words pained him.

"About?"

"You."

Wow, she hadn't been expecting that one. She sat back, momentarily rebuffed. "What about me?"

He grimaced. "I don't know how to put this delicately."

"Say what's on your mind and worry about the niceties later."

"Fine." He took a hand off the steering wheel and ran it through his hair before continuing. "I think you need to stay away from Christian. It's for your own good."

Tamara blinked a few times, willing herself to wake up. What the hell was going on, and when exactly had they entered the *Twilight Zone*? After a few seconds passed and he didn't laugh, she began to realize Russell was dead serious. "Say that one more time."

"Christian," he snapped. His hands tightened on the wheel until his knuckles were white. "You know, the guy you were rubbing against last night. He's not right for you."

"Not right for me what? To dance with? To take pictures of?"

"Take pictures of!" The car swerved to the side of the road as he took his gaze off the highway to stare at her.

"What the hell?" Her hand shot out to grab onto the "oh shit" handle as he quickly righted the vehicle.

"You asked him to pose for my pictures?" The words were clipped as if he was having trouble speaking.

"Uh, no. I asked him to pose for my pictures. Remember? You said no."

He stiffened as if she'd struck him. "I did not."

Tamara couldn't close her struck dumb jaw fast enough. *In what crazy world was he remembering their conversation?* "Right, I think you said, 'Hell, no.'"

"And so you go and ask the next fella that strolls into your sight?"

"Yes. That's exactly what happened." Not exactly. In fact she'd been a bit desperate to find some models, and Christian had seemingly arrived at just the right time. He wasn't the man she wanted, but he would have done in a pinch. Still, if Russell was going to reconsider, she wasn't going to mouth off and fuck it up. He was her first choice, after all.

"Well, I won't have it."

Her eyebrows shot into her hairline. *Okay, boy was losing his mind.* "You won't?"

"Hell, no. No one's posing for your pictures but me." He shot her a quick look that left no doubt about his sincerity or his insanity. "Is that clear?"

"Crystal." It took everything in Tamara to resist smiling. Charlotte was never going to believe this. Hell, she hardly believed it.

"Now when do you want me to show up?"

Tamara quickly did a mental check of her calendar. She wanted to get the pictures taken before whatever roofies Russell was on wore off. "How's Wednesday sound to you?"

"Fine."

Oh man. Tamara didn't have a clue what had changed Russell's mind, but she wasn't going to say a single word to change it back. She'd deal with his high-handed manner later, though. First, it was picture time.

* * *

What in the hell did he get himself into this time? Russell stood outside Tamara's apartment door questioning his sanity for what had to have been the millionth time since Sunday. No matter how he looked back over the drive, he couldn't quite point out exactly where his brain stopped working and his mouth went into overdrive.

This bullshit was all Ty's fault. If he hadn't asked Russell to pick up Tamara to bring her to Santa Estella, he would have never gotten to know her the little bit he did and become protective of her. And a man shouldn't be held accountable for his feelings, or the way the stupid emotions made him act…or act out in this case.

"Idiot," he muttered before raising his fist and knocking on the door. Even though he knew it was highly improbable, he hoped that for some reason Tamara wouldn't answer the door. Then he could leave, with his conscience soothed and his pride intact.

The door swung open before he could dwell on his foolish dreams a second longer. "You made it."

Unfortunately, he said to himself, as he gave a lackluster half smile. "Yep."

"Great." She stepped back with a wide smile and gestured for him to enter. "Come on in."

It was now or never, he thought with an impending sense of doom. This was going to be the last time he ever did a favor for anyone. Sighing, he stepped through the doorway, past an amused Tamara, into the apartment.

"Don't look so thrilled."

"I'll try not to," he said drily as he took in his first look of her place. It wasn't an overly large space, but every square inch seemed to serve a purpose. The area traditionally used as a living room was set up as a studio. A camera was situated on a tripod and pointed toward a curtained area where a single barstool stood. There were lights and other photography equipment he couldn't name situated about. It very apparent this was where Tamara spent her money. Russell didn't know dick about photography, but he knew expensive tools when he saw them.

A sense of respect filled him as he nodded his head in approval and turned to face her. "Color me impressed."

"I decided to leave the cheesy backdrops and wagon wheels for a later date." She winked as she tossed his words ever so pointedly back in his face.

"I guess I deserved that." Russell shoved his hands in his pockets and gave a light shrug of his shoulders. "I've said it before, and I'll say it again: You, Ms. Tamara Holifield, are a constant surprise."

"And you, Mr. Rusty Crichton, are stalling for time." Tamara walked past him to a small island separating her tiny kitchen from the studio. "There's no reason to worry. I promise I won't bite."

"Yeah," he said following her. "That somehow doesn't make me feel any better."

She chuckled lightly as she opened the refrigerator and pulled out a bottle of wine. Russell used the time to study her as she busied herself opening the bottle. She was dressed casually in a pair of jean cutoff shorts and a white spaghetti-strap shirt.

Like Saturday night, he found himself staring at the smooth, dark skin that peeked out at him from the clothing she wore. Her outfit wasn't anything special, but he found himself attracted to the simplicity of it. No, not the clothes, but her. They just highlighted what he was finding attractive. Her smooth skin, large breasts, rounded ass. Somehow it was all working for him. He had to fight back the urge to run his fingers along her arm to see if her skin was as silky as it appeared.

"Done staring?" she asked, all without looking up from her task.

Her humor-laced voice pulled him back into the here and now, forcing Russell to shake his head to clear his wayward, wicked thoughts. "I wasn't staring." He lied with ease.

"No?" She looked up at him and cocked a brow. "What do you call it? Thinking?"

"Yes."

"About?"

Russell glanced down quickly, then back up, looking into her amusement-filled gaze. "What I'm wearing, of course." Well, he had been thinking about clothes…just not his own. "Is this fine?" He gestured to his outfit.

Tamara had asked him to wear something he'd wear to work on the ranch. He'd pulled on a pair of jeans, work cowboy boots, and a black shirt. In his opinion, it was pretty run-of-the-mill, but what did he know about it.

"Sure, it's not like you'll be in it for long."

"Funny." He hoped she was trying to be, at least.

She chuckled. "Would you like a glass of wine?"

"Trying to get me drunk?"

"No." Even as she voiced the denial, there was something in her eyes that said differently. "I want you to look sexy in the photos, not intoxicated."

"You think I need a drink to look sexy?"

"Honey, all you have to do is breathe and you look sexy. I'm just trying to get you to relax."

"Wine won't do it."

"What will?" she asked as she poured herself a drink.

A blowjob. The words popped into his head, but he had the good grace and enough common sense to keep it there and not voice it. "Not sure. Can't we just do this and get it over with?"

"No, and this is why you need a drink." As if he hadn't spoken, she poured the wine, then set the bottle down and picked the glass up and offered it to him. "One glass won't make you loopy, cowboy, but it might help to dislodge that stick from your ass."

"I don't like wine."

"Well, what do you like?"

"Tequila."

"I got it."

"Then get it." Russell decided ongoing protests were useless. As much as he'd like to deny it, he was nervous as hell, and he needed something to calm his nerves. "But if we end up in Vegas, married, you'll have no one to blame but yourself."

She laughed as she retrieved a clear bottle from the cabinet next to the refrigerator. "Consider me duly warned." After setting the bottle on the island she walked to another cabinet filled with dishes and pulled out two shot glasses. Looked as if he wasn't drinking alone.

Feeling loads better about the way things were going, Russell picked up the short, squat-shaped bottle and glanced down at the name. "Patrón."

"Only the best for the best, baby."

"Was that in reference to me or you?"

"Me, of course. I didn't know you were going to need a boost to get you to smile."

She handed him his shot glass and nodded. Before he had a chance to even say "Cheers," she downed her drink and refilled the glass. He quickly followed suit, holding out his glass for a refill.

"If you think it's so easy, why don't you get under the spotlight and let me take pictures of you?"

"I don't take pictures fully clothed."

"All the better." He took a swig from his refilled glass in an attempt to forget the image of her, nude, that continued to pop into his head.

"You talk a good game, cowboy, but you couldn't handle me."

"You know, you keep saying that, yet you've given me no reason to think I can't."

"No reason but the apparent."

"Which is?"

She swirled the clear liquid around in her glass before answering. "Fear."

"Excuse me."

"Fear. You should be afraid, cowboy."

"Of you?" He shook his head and downed his shot. Without waiting for her to complete her hostess duties, he filled the glass himself.

"Yes, of me. Me and the power of the black vagina. Don't you know the saying, 'Once you go black, you never go back'? If you get one taste me of me, it will change your life forever. I'm talking wedding rings, babies, hair grease in your bathroom cabinet, and a silk hair cloth on the bedside table. Life-altering things here. You're just lucky I'm strong of will and mind, buddy, or you'd be in some serious trouble." He couldn't help the chuckle that escaped him. Tamara was certifiable. "What? I'm serious. Just look at your boy, Ty. He's head over heels for Charlotte."

"And that's because she's black, not because she's Charlotte?"

"Well, there's that too, but you know white boys like black girls." Russell was beginning to see why. "It's just fact. Look at your boy, Christian. He wanted me to go for a ride on his horse. I'm not talking about the four-legged one, either."

"First, Christian is not now, nor will he ever be my boy. Second—wait, I don't have a second. He's not my boy." He needed her to understand that point very clearly. There was nothing connecting him and Christian but Sandra, and she didn't really count. "By the way, I wouldn't ride his horse if I were you."

"That's good to know." She laughed.

"That's not what I meant." He flushed.

"Sure it wasn't. Woo." Tamara looked down at the shot glass in her hand for a second before carefully setting it down. "If I keep on drinking like this, I won't be able to take a picture."

"That's okay with me."

"Nice try, cowboy, but I'm not letting go of you that easy."

He was of two minds about her comment, pleased to know she was interested in having him around, although not so happy for the purpose.

"Take a seat on the stool." Tamara gestured to the chair. "I'm going to talk you through the first few shots. We're not going to do anything fancy or too overposed. I just want you. Natural. I'd also like to get some photos of you working around your place"—when he opened his mouth to protest, she held up her hand—"but if you don't feel comfortable with that, Ty's already agreed to let me photograph him. He also said he'd talk to some of his hands to see if they'd be okay with me taking pictures of them."

Well, shit. Now that Ty had agreed, Russell couldn't very well bitch and moan at him. That bastard. "Let's just see how these go."

"Fair enough," she said as she walked around the island and over to the tripod. After bending down to check something, she stood and gestured for him to have a seat. "I'm ready when you are."

A sense of dread filled Russell when he looked at the camera. No matter how much he'd had to drink, he was beginning to realize he was never going to be *ready*. But a deal was a deal. "Where do you want me?"

"Is that a trick question?" Her playful response stopped him in his tracks. She was cruising, all right. And if she kept this up, he was going to feel a strong need to prove her wrong. "Just teasing. Have a seat and we'll work from there."

Before picking up the camera, she reached into her pocket and pulled out a small remote control, then pointed it at a stereo system in the corner. Soft, bluesy music poured out of the speakers and filled the room. The music, although mellow, only managed to make him more nervous, something that, from her low chuckle, must have been more than obvious.

"Relax, cowboy, and tell me about your ranch."

"My ranch?"

"Yeah, what are your plans for it?" As she talked, she began to take pictures. Posing he knew nothing about, but talking about his home, was something he could do. He settled back on the stool, hooking his fingers into his belt loops, and answered her questions.

While they talked, Tamara continued taking pictures. She was casual at first, simply snapping away from different angles, all the while keeping the conversation as smooth as it had been on the ride to Ty's. Her informality put him at ease, and after a few minutes, the alcohol kicked in, and he began to relax. A bit. It was hard to be completely comfortable knowing she was capturing his every move, but it wasn't as bad as he initially made it to be.

He couldn't help but think it was the photographer, though, that made the situation palatable. As he became used to her and the camera, Tamara became more instructional, coaching him through moves and stances.

"Russell, why don't you loosen the top buttons on your shirt?" she asked in a casual way.

Okay. That was a bit surprising. Russell glanced down at his shirt, then back up at her. "How many?"

She moved the camera down so he could see her laughing eyes. From the silly, loose grin that drifted across her lips, Russell began to wonder if he wasn't the only one feeling the effects of the tequila. "All of them. But leave the shirt on. I'm going to turn the fan on low so it will rustle it a bit."

"Why?"

"Because I want to see your sexy chest."

"Sexy?"

"Oh yeah." She walked over to a small fan and turned it on, before turning around to face him once more. "Now don't get shy on me."

"I'm not shy. I just think you're taking an awful big chance that I actually have a nice chest." He unloosed the buttons and slowly pulled his shirt from his jeans. She moved around him, snapping more pictures. Russell felt like a piece of meat on display, yet titillated, all at the same time. "For all you know, I could have manboobs of Meatloaf proportions."

"I'll take my chances."

As she moved back for a moment, the fan caught the edge of his shirt, revealing his muscled chest and abs.

"Meatloaf never looked like this." For the first time this evening, Tamara wasn't smirking. Her gaze ran rampant over his exposed skin. Her eyes had become heavy-lidded as she continued to stare. She licked her lips, and Russell had to push down the urge to lean forward and explore her mouth with his own. He knew when a woman was interested in him, and Tamara was, without a doubt, and he was interested right back.

"You think?" His voice was thick with desire.

"Oh yeah..." Tamara cleared her throat and shook her head for a moment as if trying to wake herself from a daze. "Umm...let's get started, shall we?"

Started, hell, he was already out the gate, and from the hungry way she watched him, Russell was willing to bet his ranch Tamara was too.

"It's getting a bit hot in here," she said as she walked back to the camera. Her hips swayed with every step, drawing his attention to her full, thick ass.

Oh no, it wasn't getting hot. It already was hot.

Chapter Six

Somewhere along the line, Tamara stopped taking pictures for her show and started taking pictures for herself. The original idea she'd conceived was The Cowboy in the New Millennium, but the second Russell opened his shirt, she started shooting Hot, Sexy Man in Her Apartment. It wasn't quite the same, but it was just as sexy.

Moving away from the tripod, she circled him like a lion circled its prey, photographing him at every conceivable angle she could. She got up close, then moved far away, taking time to focus on his entire frame, then edging closer to get just the circled areolas of his nipples. Gone from her mind were images of him as a cowboy; she could only focus on the fact that he was a red-blooded man, with a body built for sin.

After a few minutes of silent movements, her camera clicked loudly, alerting her to the fact she had used all of her memory space. Irritated at being interrupted, Tamara took a deep breath, lowered the camera from her eye, and stepped away from Russell.

"What's wrong?" he asked, as she moved her head from side to side to work out the kinks.

"Nothing. Memory's full. I have to download the pictures I have."

"Are we done, then?"

As if she was going to let him go that easily. "Not even close. Just taking a little break." Tamara walked over to her computer and plugged in her camera. "You want to grab something to drink? It only takes a few minutes."

"No, I'm fine."

Yes, you are. As she watched the screen flicker briefly with every shot she'd taken, she smiled with pride. These were going to turn out wonderful.

"From the way you're smiling, I'd say you like what you see."

"In more than one way." She glanced back at him, trying to put a teasing hint in her voice. This would work out so much better if she kept him off guard. If he was too busy laughing and smiling at her jokes, he wouldn't be able to detect the truth in her words. "The camera loves you."

"I think you're just talented."

"That too."

As she continued to watch the pictures load onto the computer, she was struck with inspiration. "I'll be right back." Before he could respond she sprinted to the bathroom, grabbed her bottle of baby oil, and returned to his side.

"What's that for?"

She smiled and reached up, slipped his shirt from his shoulders with an ease she didn't recognize. "I thought we could oil you up for the next set of shots. Not so much that you look like some stripping beefcake, but just enough to give you a slight glimmer."

Instead of the protest she half expected, he helped her take off his shirt and stood silently before her. Popping open the top, she poured a small amount of oil into her hands and let it warm for a moment before touching him. Her fingers glided over the toned and taut muscles of his chest as she began to rub in the oil. Moving lower, her fingers skated across his abdominal muscles. When his body jerked in reaction, she stepped back in shock. Oh my God, she'd been feeling him up like he was her own personal boy toy.

"Um, let me just wash my hands, and we can start." She rushed into the kitchen to clean her hands and wipe them dry.

"I'm ready whenever you are." She was more than ready. Returning to the living room, she hefted her camera, covering her face from his piercing gaze.

"Could you unbutton your jeans, just like you might have just pulled them on?"

"Unbutton…"

Even as the words left her mouth, she wanted to call them back. Despite all her teasing earlier, she had no intention of asking him to disrobe, mainly because she knew she would like it way too much. Why, then, did she just open her mouth and do the one thing she said she wasn't going to do? She was losing her damned mind, that's why. And it was all Russell's and her libido's fault. The way her hormones were taking over, one might think she'd never photographed a handsome man before. Then again, there was handsome, and there was ride-your-washing machine-until-you-come-screaming-hallelujah handsome, which Russell was. Fuck it. If he was willing, she was going to ask. "Yes. Unbutton."

Russell slowly unbuttoned his pants before lowering the zipper down a tooth or two.

Her mouth went dry as he parted his pants. "Perfect. Stay just like that." Tamara snapped away, trying to capture every emotion flittering across his face. She wondered how far he would be willing to go, and how far she wanted to go, all the while not deviating from clicking away with the camera.

"Lower your zipper a little farther…" Russell did so, but unfortunately rather than seeing more mouthwatering flesh as

she'd hoped, dark material came into view instead. "Well, shit."
Talk about a mood breaker.

"What?" He froze in midact.

"Can you tuck your boxers down a bit in your pants? They're
showing through, and I think it would look a lot hotter if we made
it look as if you weren't wearing any." Hotter for her at least.

"No male in their right mind would go riding in jeans without
any underwear on."

He was trying to be logical. How male of him. "This isn't
about the male mind. It's about the female one. And we like
cowboys commando-style."

"Co—what?"

"Sans boxers."

"This is stupid." He frowned. "I'm telling you, if you're
wrestling a bull or riding for a long time, you want to make sure
your boys are tucked up against you."

"Oh for heaven's sake." She was not going to let him mess up
her fantasy, damn it. Tamara set her camera back on the tripod
and walked over to him. "You don't really have to take them off.
Just tuck them in like this."

"Wait."

"Just look." Without thinking, Tamara pressed her hand down
his pants, trying to move his boxers out of the way. Unfortunately,
soft material wasn't the only thing she touched. Her fingers
brushed against his rigid cock, stilling her movements as nothing
else would have. "Oh."

"Yeah, oh," he said drily.

This was one of those awkward moments she was forever
getting herself into by barreling in first, asking questions later.
Frozen, hand still in his pants, she wondered what to do. At last
check, Emily Post didn't have a rule of etiquette on what to do
after you molest the object of your desires. "Umm…" Nervous

now, she took in a deep breath, inhaling his masculine scent in the process. Damn. This was a really bad time to notice how good he smelled.

"Tamara?" His voice was low and smooth.

"Yes?" she replied, barely able to get the word past her parched lips.

"Do you want to move your hand?"

"Want?" Now that was the question of the hour. "Okay." She turned her hand, but instead of removing it from his pants, brushed her finger back and forth along his ever-hardening cock.

"That wasn't what I meant."

"Oh." Still she didn't remove her hand. She was too close to heaven now to agree to go back to hell.

Russell let out a deep chuckle that had her knees trembling and her pussy flooding with cream. "Let me rephrase. I'm going to count to three, and by the time I get to three, if you haven't removed your hand, I'm going to assume that you know exactly what you're doing."

He could assume right. "One. Two."

"Three," she said, finishing for him. The words had barely passed her lips when she was hauled into Russell's arms. One hand was on her ass as he pulled her tightly against him, pressing his erection, and her trapped hand, into her soft belly. Without any gentle exploration, his mouth descended to hers. Much like the man himself, his kiss was anything but soft and easy. To put it quite simply, he took her breath away. Just when she thought she'd never get enough of his sweet lips, he broke away from her mouth and pulled back a bit. "We on the same page here?"

"Oh yeah, but just to be fair, if you get addicted, don't say I didn't warn you."

"Consider me warned." He drew her close to him once more, this time moving his lips lower to her neck.

She tilted her head to the side as he kissed the sensitive area of her collarbone. Holding on tight to him, she trembled under the feeling of his wind-roughened lips. "I...have...another prop I want you to look...at." Tamara was having a difficult time talking. A first for her.

Russell's teeth grazed her skin before he kissed his way up her neck to the soft shell of her ear. "What's that?" His voice was thick with desire.

"My bed."

"It's about time. Lead the way."

Although she didn't want to leave the circle of his arms, she didn't want to fuck him here in her studio when a comfortable bed was only a few feet away. She stepped back and smiled seductively before taking his hand and leading him down the hall.

Never before had Tamara been grateful for her lack of space, but tonight, the tiny apartment was heaven-sent. She didn't want to wait a second longer than she had to, to get him in her arms. Once they were in the bedroom, her hands picked up where they'd left off earlier, deep inside his open pants. She cupped his erection as best she could, desperate to feel his rigid length sans clothes. When the tight denim didn't budge, she growled low in her throat and pulled her hand out. "Off."

"Greedy much?" he teased as he dropped onto the bed and pulled off his cowboy boots. Once he was barefooted, he stood and moved his hands to his hips, pushing at the waistband of his jeans, until they slid down his lean hips. Tamara took a step back to enjoy the view of the very muscular man standing before her dressed only in his boxers and a wicked seductive smile. Right now, Tamara would have given her right arm for her camera, especially when her gaze ran across the very large bulge in his boxer briefs.

She could feel his heated gaze on her as he kicked off his pants, but hers was fixated on the one area still covered. "Maybe

I'm not the one who should be warned about being ad-dick-ted." His cocky words brought her gaze up.

"You think you have what it takes?"

He cocked a brow as he pushed his underwear down and off. Unable to resist the draw, Tamara lowered her gaze once more, taking in her first view of his thick stalk. "Oh." The word came out more like a whisper than an exclamation.

"I think I might."

She blinked up at him, realizing he was answering her earlier challenge. This war of words was too much for her brain right now. She needed him, now. Grasping the hem of her shirt, she pulled it over her head and stood proudly before him. A size 6 she wasn't—heck, she wasn't even a size 12—but she wasn't going to cower and hide her full frame. If Russell was going to make love with her, then he needed to see exactly what treasure he was about to delve into. From the way his eyes smoldered, she could tell he wasn't disappointed by what he saw, and if she had any doubts, they were quickly squashed by his next words.

"Beautiful." Russell moved closer to her and lowered his head to the full crest of an exposed breast and lightly ran his lips over bared flesh, as he worked his hands quickly behind her back to unbuckle her bra. He paused long enough to mutter, "Let me help."

Under his masterful ministrations the bra quickly came undone and soon hit the floor. Her breasts weren't bare for long, though. Russell wasted no time cupping her full, heavy mounds in his hands. Her nipples hardened under his touch, something he ardently took in as he looked on with pride.

Tamara closed her eyes and leaned into his touch. "Who would have thought you were a breast man?"

Smiling, Russell moved his hands down and around to her ass to give it a good squeeze. "I'm an everything man."

"Then I guess it's good for you that I have a lot of everything to offer you."

"Damn straight and there's no time like the present." As he talked, Russell reached down and unfastened her shorts, lowering her zipper. Hooking his fingers into the cloth, he pulled the denim down her legs, bringing her cotton panties along for the ride. When they puddled around her ankles, she kicked them, along with her panties, off her feet.

Once free of her clothing, she sat on her bed and scooted back until she was leaning against the headboard. She crooked her finger at him and gestured for him to come to her.

"I have a better idea." Russell climbed up on the bed, grabbed her legs, and pulled until she was lying on her back. Laughing, Tamara tried to sit up, but was waylaid by Russell, who pressed her back down. "Where are you going? Stay still."

"Damn, you're bossy."

"And you love it." Before she could utter another comeback, Russell parted her legs, kneeling between them. He moved his hands down her body slowly, caressing her heated flesh as if he was familiarizing himself with every inch of her body. It wasn't a smooth downward motion, because she had curves, but he didn't seem to mind at all. When he came to the apex of her legs, he pressed her thighs farther apart and lowered his mouth to the juncture of her sex. Then slowly began to show her that his mouth wasn't good for just quips.

Much to Tamara's orgasmic delight, he teased and lapped at her pussy as if it was the last supper. His talented tongue quickly had her body trembling and her pussy aching to be filled with his shaft. Tamara arched her back and gasped. Damn, he was good at getting in the last word.

With a guttural groan, she buried her fingers in his silky straight hair and tried to bring him closer to her overheated sex.

She wanted to come so bad, she could taste it. "Please," she begged, out of her body with pleasure. "Please."

And just like that, he answered her prayer, sucking hard on her sensitive clit. She came, screaming his name, from an intense orgasm that wrung her out. Whimpering, she released her death grip on his hair and tried grabbing the quilt instead. She held on with all her might as her body rocked with aftershocks. "That was...amazing."

"Just wait, baby, we're just getting started," he said, as he moved off the bed.

"God." If this was just the appetizer, Tamara wasn't sure if she had room for the whole damned meal.

This wasn't what he'd been expecting when he'd hesitated to knock on her door just an hour or so ago. Not that he was complaining. After the brief taste he had of her, he wasn't willing to leave tonight until he had his full measure. And thankfully, she seemed to feel the same way.

As he slipped his bottoms to the floor, Tamara watched him with hungry eyes. Her intense stare only added fuel to his desire. Russell couldn't remember the last time someone had looked at him with so much naked passion. It fed his ego, making him feel as if he could soar. Russell couldn't wait to sink his cock deep within her pussy. Of course, thinking of fucking her brought home a very real fact. He didn't have a condom. He never had sex without one, so either they were about to be real creative or real unhappy. "I didn't bring anything."

Instead of disappointment marring her face, Tamara sat up with a grin. And opened her nightstand drawer. "No worries. I have some in the drawer." It took only a few seconds to find the box of condoms and dig one out. When she handed it to Russell, he stared down at the shiny black wrapper with a mixture of relief and jealousy. A look that wasn't lost on Tamara. "What?"

"I'm torn here." Russell took the condom from her hand and ripped into the foil. "Don't know whether to be pleased or irked."

Licking her lips, Tamara slipped her hands between her thighs and boldly caressed herself. "You better make up your mind, before I finish without you."

The hell she would. "Oh, I don't think so." His eyes heated with desire as he sheathed his cock and moved onto the bed next to her. "This is my ride, sweetheart; I decide when and how you come."

"Says who?"

"Me." Settling himself between her thighs, Russell took his cock in hand and brushed it against her hot center. As much as he would have liked to sink balls-deep inside her chocolate trove, he needed to make sure she wanted it as much as he did. "Tell me you want me to fuck you."

"Isn't it obvious?" She moaned, squirming beneath him.

"No." And he wasn't going to be satisfied until she answered him. And if he didn't get satisfaction, neither would she. Russell was in charge of this rodeo, and it was about time she knew it. "You want my cock. Ask for it."

"God, I'm going to kill you." Tamara arched underneath him as if trying to seat his cock inside her.

"Probably, but not until I die with pleasure. Say it."

"Damn it, fuck me! Give me your cock. Please."

"My pleasure." Russell didn't let the words slip all the way past his lips before he pushed deep inside her hot, moist passage.

His teeth clenched at the rush of pleasure he felt from being buried within her. Her tight, wet pussy hugged his shaft as he rode her back into the mattress. The way she snugly fit around his cock was pure poetry in motion. In a word, being inside her was exquisite. "God, you feel so good."

"I...was about...to say"—she paused as she fought to catch her breath—"the same thing...about...you."

"Finally, we agree on something."

"Less talking. More fucking."

"Now who's bossy?" Even as he complained, he picked up his pace. Russell didn't have a problem following a good idea when he heard one. Or embellishing on one, either. Rising to his knees, he slipped his hands under her hips, tilting them higher. Then thrusting forward, he sank even deeper into her softness.

She wrapped her legs around him and urged him on with choppy, breathless moans. The erotic sounds were almost as sexy as the feel of her nails digging into his back.

No matter how he pounded her, how he filled her, it wasn't enough for him. He had to get deeper. Drive harder. Fuck her until everything that made him whole was melded into her.

Her heady moans were soon drowned out by the sound of their labored breathing and the squeaking of the well-used bed. She melted in his hands, giving in to the pleasure he gave her. His movements became stronger and more frantic as he drove them higher and higher to the precipice of their beckoning release.

"Harder...God...please..." She gasped as he pulled back then lunged forward, burying himself in her again. Her sweet sheath welcomed him over and over until Russell could no longer tell where she began and he ended. It was a never-ending loop of pleasure that surrounded them both.

Russell didn't want this feeling to ever end, but as Tamara clutched at him, her body trembling under his, he knew she was on the verge of climax. Her body bucked back against his as she fought for her release. Reaching between them, he found her clit and stroked, once, twice. With a silent scream, she stiffened for a moment and then tightened, drawing him in as her body rippled with her orgasm.

It didn't take much more to send Russell careening off the edge right after Tamara. With a few sharp, rapid thrusts of his hips, he came, biting back her name as he did. Blood rushed to his head as the semen rushed out of his cock, making him feel light-headed, but powerful all at the same time.

With a soft groan, Russell released his hold on her hips and gripped the edge of the condom. He slowly pulled from her body, pleased to see that, despite the pounding, the condom had held up. The only cream on it was hers, which added to the delicious aroma of sex filling the air, making his mouth water.

His cock, despite the ball-shrinking orgasm it had just had, jerked in response. "Down, boy," he muttered, as he reached over to her nightstand and grabbed a tissue.

"Talking to me?"

"No, my cock."

"Does he answer back?" She laughed as she moved off the bed.

"No," he said as he removed the used latex. "He doesn't listen, either."

"Don't get freaky now, cowboy." Russell watched her luscious ass as she walked across the room to an open door he could only assume was the bathroom. When she came back out after a few minutes, he himself went into the room, pleased to see it was just what he was in need of.

He quickly disposed of the condom and cleaned up the evidence of their romp before joining her back in the bedroom once more. Instead of being under the covers near sleep as he'd half expected her to be, Tamara had pulled on her shirt and panties and was working on her shorts.

Suddenly Russell felt completely underdressed. Normally he was the one who was quickly dressing to hightail it out the door. "Is this my cue to leave?" he asked, half kidding.

His comment seemed to surprise her. "Did you want to stay?"

"At least until my balls dry off, if that's not too much to ask."

Her lips quivered as if she was biting back a smile. "I guess not. What kind of hostess lets her guest leave with wet balls?" Tamara dropped her shorts back on the floor.

"My thought exactly." Now that was much better. Russell grabbed his boxers and pulled them on.

"Would you like something to drink?"

"Sure, as long as it's not tequila."

"I'll see what I can do."

She headed into the kitchen, and Russell followed, strangely unwilling to have her out of his sight. She reached up to pull a glass from the cupboard, her T-shirt rising to reveal her rounded ass. His cock, which had started to finally deflate, perked up with interest once again.

Good Lord, what was wrong with him? In a vain attempt to focus on something else, anything else other than the bounty in front of him he asked, "So are you going back up to Ty's this weekend?"

She put the glasses on the island, then turned to the refrigerator and pulled out a gallon of orange juice. She brought it back to the table and began to fill the glasses. "I want to, I'm just not sure if I'll be able to."

"I don't mind giving you a *ride*." The pun lingered in the air between them for a second, before Tamara, with all her quick wit, fired back.

"So I see." She chuckled lightly. "But I'm still not sure yet. What about you?"

"Yes. I promised Sandra I would go with her to her parent's house for their annual charity dinner." When Tamara stiffened in midpour, Russell realized how his statement must have sounded to her, especially since they'd just had sex. He quickly added, "It's not a date or anything."

"It wouldn't matter if it was." She finished pouring as if nothing had occurred, and took the bottle back to the refrigerator.

"It wouldn't?"

"No. I'm not the boss of your penis, Russell. You're more than welcome to let him out to visit anyone you want."

He stood in stunned silence for a moment. Had he imagined that brief second of stiffness or what? She didn't care. What the hell! Hadn't they just had some of the best sex ever only moments ago? Now she was almost encouraging him to go screw someone else. It didn't make any sense.

When she cleared her throat, he looked over to notice she was holding out a glass of juice to him. He blindly reached for the glass, still unable to understand this woman who was so unlike any other woman he'd ever met.

And because Russell was Russell, he was incapable of allowing this conversation to just fade away. "What do you mean, exactly?"

She tilted her head and stared at him, as if it was *he* who was slightly mad and not *her*. "Um, I thought it was pretty clear. You don't owe me any explanations. It's none of my business really."

"None of your business? We just fucked not more than five minutes ago." He felt compelled to point out the obvious since she'd apparently missed it.

She crossed her arms over her ample breasts, a frown furrowing her brow. "Yeah, we fucked. So what? We're not married, not dating. Hell, right now I don't even know how much I like you."

He opened his mouth to retort, but she held up a hand, cutting him off. "No, let me finish. I have no right to tell you what to do, and you have no rights to me, either. We had sex. It was good. End of story."

"Not likely. I want to see you again." His words surprised him almost as much as they obviously surprised her. Tamara took in a quick, sharp breath and stared at him wordlessly for a few seconds. A few seconds too long. "Well?"

"We'll probably see each other a lot. I'm still going to visit Charlotte, and I'll still need a ride. You agreed to pose, unless, of course, you're backing out."

Pose. Rides. What did any of that have to do with what he just said? "No, I'm not backing out, but that's not what I meant, either, and you damn well know it."

"Russell, get over yourself. You're in postcoital bliss. Go home, sleep it off, and by the weekend, you'll be thanking me."

"For what?"

"Letting you off the hook. Look, your balls have got to be dry by now. I think it's time you headed home. I'll give you a call if I need a ride, okay?" Tamara turned on her heels and stormed from the room, leaving Russell staring in her wake.

Let him off the hook? What the hell had he missed?

Chapter Seven

"So did you kick him in the balls?"

"I didn't, but I really wanted to." Even though she was on her lunch break, Tamara kept her voice low. She couldn't afford to lose her job, and as pissed off as she still was at Russell, she knew if she started talking too much about what happened last night, she'd just go off and start cursing. Something she probably shouldn't do in the teachers' lounge. "Can you believe him, telling me about his nondate, seconds after leaving my"—she lowered her voice even more—"bed?"

"I like Russell. I really do, but even I'm having a hard time resisting the urge to maim him."

"Don't resist on my account."

"Tell me again, what exactly did he say?"

"Exactly." Tamara switched the phone to her other ear and held it there with her shoulder so she could open her diet soda can. "That he's taking that Sandra woman to her parents' for some dinner, but not to worry, because it's not a date."

"Well—"

"No." Tamara stopped her well-meaning friend. "It's a date. You know it, and I know it."

"But maybe he doesn't consider it a date."

"It's the principle here, Charlotte. I've been in some hit-and-forget type relationships my damn self, and the rules are very clear. It's an 'ask and don't tell' booty policy. I truly could have gone my whole life without knowing he was about to tap her this weekend. My whole life."

"Maybe he isn't going to."

Even though she knew Charlotte couldn't see her face, Tamara made a deadpan expression anyway. "Did you see the same woman I saw?"

"Yes."

"He's going to hit it."

"Ty doesn't think he even likes her."

"Likes her? What are we, in grade school?" Charlotte's rich laughter spilled over the lines. "Besides, what do like and sex have to do with each other?"

"When did you become so cynical?"

"When did you stop being cynical? Wait," Tamara said. "Never mind. I already know my answer. You know, venting to you was a lot more fun when you weren't infected with the love virus."

"Sorry to disappoint."

"Liar." Tamara took a deep drink from her soda, wishing there was a bit of rum mingled in there with her cola.

"Let me ask you this." The tone in Charlotte's voice warned Tamara that she wasn't going to like what her friend had to say. "If this is just a hit it and forget it thing, then why do you care who he hits next?"

The tone never lied; besides, logic had no place in this conversation. "I don't care."

"Who's the liar now?"

"Don't make me hang up on you."

"You better not, heifer."

"And why not?"

"Because if you do, I won't get to tell you about a very interesting phone call you got here today."

Tamara snorted. "If Russell wanted to talk to me, he could have called my house."

"It wasn't Russell."

"Oh." Embarrassment for assuming it was Russell warred with surprise because it wasn't. Tamara had been more than sure he was going to try to get back in her good graces. Showed what she knew. "Then who was it?"

"Christian."

"Who?" The name didn't ring a bell.

"You know, the hot blond you were dirty dancing with the other night."

"Hot blond. What are you...oh. Him? You think he was hot?"

"Oh yeah."

"He was all right." He had seemed nice enough, but he wasn't really her type.

"Just all right?"

The shock in Charlotte's voice had Tamara frowning. "What?" Did Russell and Charlotte see something she didn't? "He doesn't do it for me."

"Not like the dark, handsome cowboy does, huh?"

If she wanted sarcasm, she would have talked to herself. "My lunch is over. I have to go."

"Your lunch is not over. I can tell time, you know."

"Yet you can't tell when it's time to let something go."

"Okay, fine. Be that way. Just don't pretend with me, missy. I know you better than you know yourself."

"I know you better than you know yourself," Tamara mimicked in a lower tone. "Shut it. I need to get back to work."

"Fine. Aren't you interested in why Christian called?"

"Because he had a date when he could pose?" She could always use a few more men to round the pictures for her show.

"No, he wanted to ask you out."

"Me?" Had fat chicks with major attitude come back in style when she wasn't looking or what? "Man, what is it with white men where you live? It's like they have blackitis. See what happens when you move to a town where there are no people of color."

"You shouldn't be so damned sexy," Charlotte teased.

"Don't hate." Tamara shook her head in bewilderment. "Man, that's just crazy."

"No, what's crazy is he wants to invite you to a charity event his parents are throwing. Small world, isn't it?"

"And getting smaller by the second." If she didn't have bad luck, she wouldn't have any luck at all. "So he just happened to mention all of this when he called? You didn't grill him or anything?"

"Would I do that?" Charlotte's voice rose an octave higher, a sure indication she was lying.

"Uh, yeah, you would, nosy."

"Hey, I wasn't going to give out your number to just anyone."

"Give out my—you didn't?"

"Oh, but I did."

"Good-bye, Charlotte." Tamara moved the phone from her ear, intent on hanging up, when a shout had her pulling it back.

"Wait, are you going to go with him?"

"I have to go to Jule's bachelorette party Friday night, remember?"

"The charity party isn't until Saturday," Charlotte smugly informed her.

"If I didn't know any better, I'd say you wanted me to go."

"I do."

Confused she asked the obvious question. "Why?"

"Maybe to show Russell a thing or two."

"You are a troublemaker." Of course, if the situation were reversed, it would be the exact thing she would have suggested Charlotte do.

"And that's why you like me."

"Good-bye, Charlotte." Tamara finished off her soda and stood. "I'll talk to you later."

"Tonight, call me after Christian calls you."

"He's probably not going to call."

"Don't bet on it." Charlotte's laughter carried over the connection.

Tamara shook her head as she closed the top down on her cell phone. He wasn't going to call. Of that, she was sure.

* * *

Once again, fate felt the need to point out to Tamara just how little she knew about men and life in general. As she stood in front of the floor-length mirror inside the door of Charlotte's walk-in closet, she prayed to end the night without having to hear a single "I told you so" from Charlotte.

"Oh, I love that dress on you."

She loved the dress as well. The simple black formal dress complimented her curves, dipping low to highlight her breasts, but had nice thick straps to cover the fact she needed to wear a bra for support. The empire waist allowed the fabric to drape over her not so attractive areas and covered her flaws nicely.

"Thank you."

"I'm sure Christian will too." Charlotte waddled up behind Tamara and pretended to pluck at a nonexistent string on her dress. "You know, Christian, the guy you're going out with tonight, even though you didn't think he was going to call."

So much for prayers. Tamara glanced down at her bare wrist and tapped a nonexistent watch. "Fifteen minutes exactly."

"What's fifteen minutes?"

"The length of time it took you to say I told you so."

"I would never say I told you so."

"Right." She let the sarcasm drip off her words. "By the by, Christian told me he invited you and Ty to the party. I'm surprised you're not going. I thought you might want to see the drama or lack thereof, for yourself."

"First of all, there will be drama." Charlotte held up one finger. Then added another. "Second, I'm on doctor's orders not to travel."

Concerned, Tamara turned around until she was facing her friend. "You had an appointment recently?"

"No, this isn't recent."

"But last weeken—"

"Was last weekend." Charlotte lowered her voice and glanced behind her to the closed bedroom door. "But between you, me, and the bambino, Ty can't stand Sandra or her family. He says she's all about the paper, and I'm not talking about the folding kind."

That didn't surprise Tamara in the least. She'd only met the woman once, and she could already tell she was interested in only how deep Russell's pockets ran. So that answered one question, but it left another. "Why are we whispering?"

"Because Russell pulled up while you were in the shower."

"So?"

"I might have forgotten to mention you were going to be here this weekend."

"You—"

"Ah, ah, ah." Charlotte took a step back and placed her hand on her belly. "Babies can hear, you know."

"We wouldn't want junior there knowing how devious mommy is, now, would we?"

"Nope."

"You are so evil."

"I know." Laughing, Charlotte turned around and headed to the bedroom door with Tamara fast her on her heels. The shorter woman, even despite her increasing size, was still pretty nimble on her feet, and she was out the door before Tamara caught up with her.

"Slow down, woman, before you hurt my godchild, so I can hurt you."

She skittered to a halt as the hallway bathroom door opened, and Russell stepped from the steaming room. He was dressed as formally as she and very obviously wasn't expecting to see her standing there. She watched as his eyes widened and then narrowed as he took in her appearance.

"What are you doing here?"

Vowing to kill Charlotte, Tamara thought, but wisely said differently. "Going to a party, same as you."

"What?"

"Yes," Charlotte butted in. "Apparently Christian was so taken with her, he begged me for her number so he could invite her himself."

That wasn't exactly the way it happened. More like Christian said he had had a good time with her, and he wanted to know if she wanted to attend the party. He even mentioned, in a very kind way, that it would be as friends only, since his parents weren't exactly comfortable just yet with him bringing his boyfriend around. His little confession was the only reason Tamara agreed to go with him, but also one she wasn't going to share with anyone else. So instead, she just smiled and held her tongue.

"Was he now?" The words were clipped and far from pleasant. "And now you're going out with him?"

"Just to the party." Tamara smiled wider, all the while plotting ways to do murder and avoid the death penalty. "So I guess I'll be seeing you there."

"You can count on it." Russell bit out the words before turning on his heel and stomping down the hallway to his room. Instead of slamming the door as she'd expected, though, he closed it with a quiet click. Somehow that seemed all the more dangerous.

"Damn, there are going to be some fireworks tonight."

Tamara rolled her eyes, silently agreeing with her friend. She just hoped she could avoid being in the crossfire.

* * *

If looks could spank, Tamara would be bare-assed and over his lap for her outlandish behavior. It was bad enough Russell was stuck at a party he didn't want to be at, but to make matters ten times worse, Tamara was there as well. The only big difference was she seemed to be having a good time.

How the fuck was that possible? Unlike him, she didn't know a single soul, yet it was she who was standing around talking to people, while he stood solitarily by the wall, staring at her as if he was waiting for her to sprout a second head. Hell, maybe he was. Maybe the other head would belong to the woman he'd spent the weekend with at Ty's or the woman who had come undone in the sexiest of ways beneath him in bed a few days back.

Just thinking of her sweet, earthy scent and the feel of her hot, tight pussy had his cock begging to delve into her once more. Of course, that urge ran a close second to the one he had of spanking her silly.

"If you stare any harder, I might feel the need to call security."

Without looking away from Tamara, Russell replied to Christian's less than amusing comment. "I'm just keeping an eye on a friend."

"Hmm…that's interesting."

"What?"

"That you think the two of you are friends."

The amusement in Christian's voice had Russell seeing red. "We're more than friends, if you must know." Russell turned to stare at Christian, giving the man the weight of his ire to add punch to his words. "Much more."

"So I figured. Aren't you just the popular guy? First my sister, now Tamara. Tell me, Russell"—he cocked his head in thought— "when do you sleep?"

"Is there a purpose to this conversation?"

"Yes."

"Then get to it." Russell wanted to get back to nefarious designs on Tamara and her ass.

"My sister isn't blind. I'd take care if I were you, of who you watch and why. Sandra isn't the kind to take a slight, even a small one, lightly." Didn't he know it. Ever since they'd arrived, she'd been acting perturbed. It probably didn't help that he'd tried to get out of bringing her two days in a row. He didn't want to be here. He wasn't arm candy for the terminally rich and bored. And if it wasn't for the fact that she was shoving his promise down his throat, he would have never showed.

"Don't worry about Sandra. She's a big girl. We both knew what the score was when we started..." Russell didn't want to say dating, because in truth they never did. Theirs was a relationship of physical satisfaction only. Nothing more. Nothing less. "...seeing one another. Neither one of us will walk away brokenhearted."

"Who says I was worried about my sister?" Christian's parting words were like a shot in the dark. It was loud, confusing, and completely out of the blue.

What the hell was that supposed to mean? Russell wondered as he watched the other man walk away and join his sister across the room. Christian leaned down and whispered something in her ear, which caused her to turn around and glare menacingly in his direction. Something that wasn't lost on Christian, who began to grin like a loon.

Irritated, Russell shook his head, and turned his back toward them. *There was something very wrong with that family.*

Dismissing them from his mind, Russell turned his attention back to Tamara. For the first time the entire evening, she was actually standing alone. She seemed to have lost her admirers somewhere along the way. Well, she wasn't going to be that way for long. Russell walked over to her side, his gaze very intent on his prey.

Tamara, unlike him, hadn't been paying attention to his every move, apparently, because she jumped when he lightly touched her arm and spun around. "Oh. It's just you."

Just! Russell didn't like the sound of that at all. "Having fun?"

Tamara rolled her eyes and turned so she was facing toward the open garden doors and away from him. "Oh yeah. Loads. Can't you tell? I'm partying like it's 1999, cowboy style." Sarcasm dripped from every word.

Russell was not amused. "Is that supposed to be a good thing?"

"Yes," she said with a shrug of her shoulders. "That is if you take out the whole Y2K fear. That part was pretty much of a downer."

"Can you look at me when you're talking to me?" He didn't know why it bugged him. He just knew that it did.

"I can; I just choose not to."

"Why?"

"Because I don't like you right now."

He was as far away from like as he could get, but still, he didn't want to be ignored. Her little act of rebellion was just pissing him off more and more. And as bad as Tamara might think she was, she was no match for him. Not at all.

"The feeling is pretty mutual."

That got her attention. Turning to him, Tamara crossed her arms over her bountiful breasts and raised a finely arched brow. "Then keep on stepping. No one asked you to come make nice with me."

"I'm just checking up on you, like I promised Charlotte." Okay, promised was a bit strong of a word, and he didn't exactly say it to Charlotte as he said it himself as he watched Tamara slip into Christian's car.

"Why would you promise her that?"

"It seemed like the gentlemanly thing to do since you were going off with a man you hardly know to a party filled with people you don't know."

"And what on earth would you know about being gentlemanly?"

"What's that supposed to mean?"

She sighed heavily and dropped her arms back to her side. "Nothing. Just move on and let me enjoy myself."

"Right, because I can tell that's what you've been doing since you got here."

"Been watching me?"

Caught. Regrouping he reminded her, "I told you, I was keeping an eye on you for Charlotte."

"I don't need a babysitter. I'm on a date."

"Date?" Russell felt a tic beginning to twitch on his face. "Is that what you call this?"

"No, what I call this is none of your business." She narrowed her eyes and poked a finger in his chest. "Look, why don't you do us both a favor and go away? I bet if you close your eyes and give me five seconds to hide, you won't even notice I'm here. It'll be just like *Where's Waldo.* You can stay on your side of the room, and I'll stay on mine."

"What you do *is* my business."

"Since when?"

"Since the night I fucked you."

"Sorry." She gave him a blank look. "I have no idea what you're talking about."

"You don't, do you?" His left eye began to twitch.

"Nope, sorry."

"You're going to be sorry all right." Unable to help himself any longer, Russell took her upper arm in hand and pulled her out the garden doors. He had expected a bit of a fight, and although she definitely wasn't going with him willingly, she didn't cause a scene. She walked along with him, even smiling at the other party guests they passed. Once they were outside and away from witnesses, though, things swiftly changed.

"Let me go."

"When I'm good and ready."

"You're good and ready now," she said, tugging on her arm. Her movements were in vain, though, because as he told her several times previously, he was bigger and stronger than she was.

After a few unsuccessful tries on her part, she gave up, but not without letting out a long-suffering sigh beforehand, though. "Where are we going?"

"Somewhere we can have privacy."

"We don't need privacy," she muttered as she stomped alongside him. "The only thing we need is a two-by-four so I can smack you upside the head."

"Right." Russell stopped outside another set of French doors and tested the handle. When it turned, he smiled for the first time tonight. Finally, something was going his way. "In here."

"Where are we?"

Russell felt along the wall until he felt a light switch to flip. It only took a few seconds before he found and turned it on, bathing the room in a soft, ambient light. The leather furniture and massive desk could only mean one thing. "The study."

"Great. There should be something in here I can hit you with."

"If anyone gets hit tonight, sweetheart, I assure you, it won't be me." Russell locked the door behind him and released her, satisfied that she wasn't going anywhere anytime soon. There were only two doors into the room, one was at his back, and the other was across the room. Either way, Tamara had to go through him.

"You're a bully."

"And you're a brat." One he wanted to throw over his shoulder and take to bed at this very moment.

"If you don't like me, if you think I'm a brat, why the hell are you going out of your way to talk to me?"

"Because you infuriate me."

She furrowed her brow. "That makes absolutely no sense."

"It doesn't have to." He wasn't like those guys on television who wanted to talk about their feelings. In fact, he didn't want to even admit he had feelings, let alone analyze them.

"You're such a…guy."

What the fuck was that supposed to mean? "Is that supposed to be an insult?"

"No, what's insulting is you telling me about your date three seconds after you get out of my bed."

"It's not a date."

"Sure looks like one from where I'm standing."

"Then take a few steps to the left and rub your eyes, sweetheart, because you're seeing things."

"Whatever. It doesn't matter." She made a move to grab the handle, but he pushed her hand away, much to her obvious annoyance. "Damn it, move." Tamara spun around and shoved her hands against his chest, pushing him back a few steps.

"If it doesn't matter, then why are you so upset?" He wasn't going to let this go. He was going to push and push until he got an answer that held even the slightest hint of truth.

"I'm upset with myself for sleeping with you, if you must know!" she yelled.

Her answer set him back a second. It didn't make any sense, but he could tell she was being real with him. "Why?"

"Because it was a stupid thing to do. You'd think by now that I'd know better than to jump in bed with a man just because I like his looks."

"That's not the only reason you slept with me." Russell didn't like that she was comparing him to other men she'd bedded. He was nothing like them.

"Really? Because I can't think of another." She placed a hand on her hip and tilted her head to the side. "Let's not kid each other, Russell. The two of us have nothing in common."

"Except for the mad chemistry we feel for one another."

"Chemistry is just chemistry." Her voice was filled with exasperation. She shook her head slowly as if he was dim and dropped her arm back to her side. "Nothing more, nothing less."

"Why are you here?"

Tamara gave him a pointed look. "Because *you* dragged me in here." He could hear the word "Duh," even though it wasn't said.

She was missing his point on purpose. Of that he was sure. "No. This party. Why are you here?"

"Because I was invited."

Russell took a step forward. "Not good enough." The air around them vibrated with tension. They were both strong-willed people, and Russell knew that on this, neither would back down. Instead of irritating him, it intrigued him. What was it about this woman that made him want to spank and kiss her equally? "Why, Tamara?"

"What did I just say?"

"It doesn't make sense."

"It doesn't have to."

He took another step closer. "For me, it does."

"Everything isn't about you."

"True, but this is." Russell stopped a hairsbreadth away from her.

She was trapped between him and the door, with very little space between, either. Tamara looked less than thrilled about that, but Russell absolutely loved it. He had her where he wanted her. In his grasp. "I'm not going to let you intimidate me."

"I don't want you to."

"Then what the hell do you want?"

"You." Russell moved in for the kill as he covered her mouth with his, silencing her once and for all.

Chapter Eight

Tamara was a lot of things, but stupid wasn't one of them. Even though she was mad enough to do Russell some serious bodily harm, she couldn't resist the feel of him against her once more. This entire party up to this moment had been one big mistake in the making, but now that she was back in his arms, she was fine. This was where she was supposed to be, whether she liked it or not.

With a deep groan, Russell broke the kiss and nudged her to the side a few steps, then backward so she was parallel with the wall and not the door. When the flat of her back touched the solid surface, Tamara moved her hands up between them and pushed him back a bit, but not away, then turned her hand until she was holding onto his lapel. "I still don't like you."

"Dislike me all you want, just don't tell me to stop."

"I'm pissed off, not crazy."

"Pissed off. I can work with that."

As could she. Anger with one another didn't stop their bodies from responding to mutual desire. The lower half of his body was still pressed against her, and she could feel the outline of his cock.

And she could feel the moisture gathering between her folds. Had felt it since he'd strong-armed her from the ballroom, in fact. Something he'd soon discover for himself.

He dropped to his knees before her and slowly began to raise the bottom of her dress, all the while keeping his gaze firmly locked on hers. As sexy as he looked peering up at her, it was taking way too long to get to the good part. Reaching down, Tamara grabbed her dress and tugged it from his grasp and up to her waist. They didn't have time for sweet, soft, romance-type shit. Any second they could be discovered, and if she was getting kicked out of a charity ball, it was going to be for a hell of a lot more than because a boy was looking up her skirt.

Instead of commenting, Russell merely raised a brow before he lowered his gaze to view what her black dress had been covering. Which wasn't much. The black thigh-high stockings were held up by black garters that matched the lace thong panties she wasn't wearing.

"Hmm...bare." He reached out and brushed the back of his fingers against her slick nether lips.

"Yes." Freshly bikini-waxed and trimmed just for this evening, not that she'd admit anything, even at gunpoint.

"For him"—his eyes blazed with sudden anger—"or for me?"

Another question she wouldn't answer honestly at gunpoint. "For me."

"Right." Not that it mattered, because from the sudden smirk he sent her, he didn't believe her anyway. "You just keep on telling yourself that."

Before she could come back with a witty comment, he grasped her right leg, moved it over his shoulder, and moved between her parted legs. "What are you doing?"

"If you have to ask, I'll have to do some serious recon on your sexual education. Now shh...I'm busy."

Man, was he. Russell parted her folds and ran first his finger, then his tongue over her clit.

"Good Lord." Closing her eyes, Tamara entangled her hands in his hair and pressed her back into the wall, needing something solid to hold her up.

A novice he wasn't. Russell knew exactly what to do with a pussy. He lapped himself to gold in her book with his very talented tongue. His mouth teased and tormented her heated flesh. And as if his lips weren't enough, he soon added his fingers to the drive-Tamara-crazy game, plunging them into her depths as he feasted on her.

It only took a few seconds before she was flying, and if it wasn't for the grip he had on her, she was sure her orgasm would have taken her off the ground. Breathing heavily, she released her grip on his hair and dropped her arms to her sides. Damn, the man was good.

But he also wasn't done. Moving quickly, Russell spun her around until she was facing the wall, and pulled up her dress. "Open your legs," he ordered roughly.

"Bu—"

"Now." Tamara rushed to obey. His terse tone brooked no argument, and Lord knew, she didn't want him to stop for anything in the world. So not only did she open her legs, she stuck out her bottom, giving him greater access to any and everything he might have desired. "Perfect."

The crisp sound of foil ripping was the only noise in the otherwise quiet room. Her lust-clouded mind welcomed the sound of sanity. At least one of them was able to think about the ramifications of their actions. Tamara knew without a doubt that if he had pushed inside her bareback, she wouldn't have said a word, which was wrong, so very wrong. Common sense just fell to the wayside when he was around.

Maybe this whole thing was a bad idea. Here she was in some stranger's house about to get her freak on with a guy who was dating the sister of the man who had brought her. Talk about fucked up. Maybe she should call this of—The thought held no weight against the feeling of his cock brushing against her pussy lips.

Fuck those people, her body urged as she steadied her stance and prepared for his plunge.

"Ready?"

Was she ever. "Ye—"

The word didn't even have the opportunity to make its way into light, before a sharp hiss fled her lips as he held her hips in his hands and thrust deep inside her. The vigorous stroke caused her breath to halt for a good second or two, as her slick pussy stretched around his thick cock. Though it had only been a few days since he'd been buried within her, it felt much, much longer.

God, the feeling of him inside her was beyond words. Try as she might, she couldn't describe how good, how strong, how delicious his cock was. The only thought running through her mind was, "More." She wanted more. And she wanted it now.

"Fuck me," she pleaded as she arched her back to allow him even deeper penetration.

He took her at her word, plowing into her pussy. Every stroke was made as if to imprint his claim on her.

He leaned forward and spoke. His voice was hoarse and as rough as his thrusting. "You think pretty boy could give this to you?"

Was he kidding? Tamara didn't even know he was able to give this to her. She'd never been with a man so intense, so virile, in her life. "No."

"Who can?" When she didn't answer quickly enough, he took a hand off her hip and tangled it in her hair, pulling her head back toward him. "Who?"

"You, damn it. Just you." He felt so fucking good inside her, she'd risk the wrath of the gods for just one more stroke of his hard, thick cock.

"Fuck, yeah." He drove home his point as he drove home his hips.

She pressed her hands into the wall to cushion her body from the steady increase of his pistoning hips, as well as a leverage to keep her afloat. Her legs trembled, her back ached, but she wouldn't have changed any of it for the world.

Though she could hear voices out in the garden, she ignored everything except him. The feeling of his breath on her neck, his hand gripping her hip, his cock tunneling inside her.

"Fuck...ohh..." Tamara pushed back, meeting him thrust for thrust. "Yes. Yes."

"Hmm...do you feel that, baby?" His hips bumped faster and faster against her, pushing Tamara into the wall with every plunge. "Your sweet pussy is squeezing my cock so hard." He reached around and slipped his hands between her thighs, brushing her aching clit with the pad of his thumb. The fleeting sensation had her clenching down even tighter around him. "Damn, baby, it's like an inferno inside you."

"Ohhh..." Tamara didn't know that was what she needed until he did it, but it felt so fucking right. "Please, please. So close."

"Don't worry. You're going to come." He feverishly worked his thumb back and forth over her sensitive bud. "Right now. Come for me, Tamara. Flood my cock with your sweet juices."

Yes, yes, yes. She chanted the words silently as her body fought to do his bidding and reach that pinnacle. As close as she was, it wasn't enough. Then he stopped rubbing and pinched her clit hard, zooming her past close and straight to the finishing line.

It took everything out of Tamara not to scream his name as she came. Clenching her fingers closed, she bit down on her bottom lip as she trembled with her release. Despite how hard she tried, tiny moans drifted past her parched lips. But her muted sounds were nothing compared to the deep growl Russell made as he powered on. She could hear him choking back a groan seconds before he leaned forward and sank his teeth into her nape. The sharp pain was nothing compared to the overwhelming sensation of pleasure that washed over her as he gripped her tightly and came.

His groans were muffled against her skin as he leaned heavily against her, resting his shaking form against her back. Their heavy breathing was the only sound in the room for a few stark moments. Russell finally stepped back, pulling out of her body and leaving her oddly bereft at the loss. Her dress fell back into place, and she could hear him behind her adjusting his own clothing. Tamara turned slowly, using the wall for support.

"That was—"

"The best." He finished her sentence for her, and she couldn't disagree, even though she hadn't been about to say that. "Now you're coming back with me to Charlotte and Ty's."

Whoa! It was good and all, but she wasn't about to just up and bail on Christian like that. "No, I can't. I came with Christian, and he should be the one to take me home."

"You came with me as well."

Egotistical bastard. "You know what I mean."

"You're telling me you can fuck me while you're on a date with another man, but you can't ride back with me?"

"Exactly what I'm saying." She rolled her eyes as she moved away from the door. "I'll see you when I get back to their house."

"You mean you'll see me on the ride back to their house."

"I mean what I said." She spun around to face him once more. "I'm going home with Christian."

"And I mean what I'm saying. If you take one step out that door, without me at your side, I'm going to toss you over my shoulder and take you to my car. Even if it means storming through the party to do it."

"You...wouldn't. Hell, you couldn't." There was no way he could pick her up, let alone carry her across the house.

"Try me, Tamara."

Well, hell, he should have just said, "I dare you." Eyes narrowing, Tamara made a grand show of turning around and opening the doors. She glanced back over her shoulder at him, and gave a little snort, before turning back around and taking a single step.

And that's all it was, a single step, because Russell moved right behind her and swooped her up. One second Tamara was looking at the great outdoors, the next she was looking at his ass as he hauled her across the lawn, back the way they came to the ballroom.

"Russell," she shrieked, holding onto his dinner jacket for all she was worth. She wanted to be put down, but she didn't want to fall.

Loud gasps filled her ears as he strolled through a set of French doors, back into the ballroom where they had previously been. Shocked voices were mingled with sharp laughter as he walked through the room, her over his shoulder as he said he would. Embarrassed beyond belief, Tamara closed her eyes, and held on for dear life. "What are you doing?" she bit out through clenched teeth.

"Proving my point."

"What, that you're big and bad?"

"No"—he landed a sharp slap on her upturned behind—"that I can handle you."

For the first time, in a long time, Tamara had to eat her own words. And she didn't like the taste of them one bit.

Russell had been prepared for a heavyweight championship battle to get Tamara in the car. But to his surprise, the second he set her right, she silently wrenched open the car door and huffily sat down in the seat, pulling the door closed behind her.

If she didn't want to talk, that was just fine with him. They could save the argument for the house, and there was going to be an argument. And possibly a throttling as well. Oh yeah, this night would not end for the two of them until they came to an understanding of sorts. Mainly one that consisted of her calming the fuck down and admitting to him why she went on a date with that pansy. He had an excuse, unlike her, who did it out of spite.

It better have been spite, because if it was anything remotely resembling like, she was in a world of trouble. There was no way in hell he was going to let her go from his bed to Christian's. No way in hell.

The drive from the Malt's to Ty's took long enough for Russell to plan how he was going to kill Christian and punish Tamara, but not long enough for him to figure out where he was going to bury the body. The car barely came to a stop before she opened the door and got out, slamming it shut behind her. Russell was right on her heels, though. They were going to have this out tonight, even if it meant he had to hog-tie her ass down to do it.

Without bothering to lock the car, Russell hurried up the driveway, then the stairs of the porch, before storming into the house. In her haste to get away from him, Tamara left the front door open, which gave him the opportunity to catch the tail end of the conversation between her and a pajama-clad Charlotte, who wore a look of surprise on her face. Somehow, he was willing to bet this wasn't how she imagined the night ending. Good. Maybe that would teach her to interfere in his and Tamara's relationship.

"— is crazy." Anger poured from her voice in waves.

"I know you're not referring to me," he said as he slammed the front door and jumped, feet first, into the fight.

"The hell I'm not." For the first time since he carried her from the party Tamara spoke to him. Although spoke wasn't a strong enough word. It was more like yelled, which was fine with him. He was in the perfect mood for yelling.

"I'm crazy? What do you call showing up to a party—"

"With the brother of the woman you're dating?" she interjected with cold sarcasm.

"I'm not dating her!" What would he have to do to get that through her thick skull?

"Right." Her disbelief filled her words and her body language. "Excuse me. You're just fucking her."

"Not anymore."

The corner of Tamara's mouth twisted with exasperation. She didn't have to say she didn't believe him, it was written all over her face. "Since when?"

"Since the first night I fucked you."

"What the hell is going on here?" Ty bellowed from the top of the stairs. His face was a mask of fury as he took the stairs two at a time. From the way he was dressed, in pajama bottoms, Russell could only surmise that their little tussle had roused him from his bed. Good. Now the two of them could be pissed off together.

Charlotte shrugged her shoulders and raised her hands in a helpless gesture. "I have no idea." Her eyes were wide and filled with disbelief as she looked from the two of them to Ty, who quickly joined her in the foyer. "I was just—"

"Interfering," Russell said. From the sheepish look she shot him, he knew he was dead-on. "Do you know your wife set Tamara up with Christian?"

From the stern look Ty sent Charlotte's way, Russell could see he didn't. "You did what?"

"I did not."

"Right." Russell snorted.

"For your information, he got in contact with her. Not the other way around," Charlotte said.

"He did what?" Now Russell was really going to have to kill Christian.

"What, you can't believe that someone besides you might want to take a trip to the dark side?" Tamara crossed her arms over her breasts and eyed him distastefully. "Or are you surprised that someone else might want to take a trip to the fat side?"

"Dark side? Fat side?" He stared at her baffled. "What the hell are you talking about?"

"Like you don't know." Tamara shook her head in disgust and dropped her arms back to her side. "I'm going to bed. Good night."

"Good—" Like that was going to happen. "I don't think so. Get back here."

"Hey. Wait." Charlotte stepped in his path as he made to go after Tamara. A shadow of alarm fell over her face. "Maybe you should just back off and let her cool down. Tamara has a temper, and she's—"

Blood pounded in his temples. To say he was pissed off would be putting things lightly. "Used to getting her own way. A habit she's going to have to get over and soon."

"But…"

He was not in the mood for bodyguards. Annoyed, he glanced over at Ty, who was watching him with a devilish look in his eyes. "Ty."

Ty reached out and pulled Charlotte to him. "Try to keep the bloodshed to a minimum. I have to get up early in the morning."

"I'm not making any promises," Russell said over his shoulder as he headed up the stairs in a deliberate fashion. Tamara might have thought she'd won this battle, but she was in for a rude awakening. Bypassing his door, he headed directly to hers. Not bothering to even knock, knowing she'd probably just ignore him, he opened the door.

Tamara had obviously considered the conversation over and done with, because she was stepping out of her shoes as if nothing major had just occurred. How like her. "I'm not in the mood to talk, Char."

"Good, then maybe you'll shut up and listen," he said as he shut and locked the door. Standing in front of the door, he stubbornly crossed his arms over his chest.

Tamara spun around to face him, eyes wide in disbelief. "What are you doing in here?"

"Finishing our conversation." Russell tilted his head to the side and regarded her with slight amusement. "Did you really think I was just going to let you get off that easily?"

"Let! Let?" Her voice rose as she stepped closer to him. "Who the hell do you think you're talking to?"

"The biggest child I've ever seen."

"Fuck you."

"Again?" Russell slid his jacket off. "Fine with me. Just let me say, though, I don't really think this solves anything, but if you insist."

"Trust me, I don't insist. I think a lack in judgment twice is twice too many."

"And I think the only time your judgment seemed lacking was when you accepted Christian's invitation. What was that all about?"

"That was none of your business."

"You say that like you mean it."

"I do," she stated empathically. "I don't see what the big deal is. Did I say anything to you when you went on your date?" She held up a hand to halt his words. "Excuse me, nondate?"

Was she kidding? He let out a bark of laughter to cover his annoyance. "You said a lot without saying a word."

"What is that supposed to mean?"

"It means," he said slowly and clearly. "The very idea of me going out with Sandra, even as innocent as it was, upset the shit out of you, turning you into Bitchy McBitch in a blink of an eye."

"You call me one more name—"

"And you're going to do what?" He arched a brow snidely. "I think I already proved to you that strengthwise, you're no match for me."

"You've got to go to sleep sometime."

"True, but I'm stubborn enough to NoDoz myself until you see reason."

"What reason?" Now that was a good question, one he didn't have an answer to off the top of his head. When he didn't answer right away, she snorted and shook her head. "Just what I thought. You've got nothing."

"If you have such a good idea of what I'm thinking or what the hell is going on here, why don't you tell me?"

Hands on her hips she eyed him up and down. "I see another pretty boy who went slumming."

"Excuse me?"

"Come on, admit it. You wanted to know if the old saying was true."

"Which one would that be?"

"The blacker the berry, the sweeter the juice."

He shook his head in confusion. "I don't even know what that means."

"Just admit it. If we hadn't had a few drinks, you never would have touched me."

"And today, do you think I was drinking today?"

Her glare burned through him. "No, I think you were drunk on jealousy."

"And I think you're out of your mind. If you recall correctly, Tamara, it wasn't me who kicked you out of my place. That was your doing."

She dropped her hands to her sides and regarded him with cool contempt. "I just gave you an excuse to leave."

"What made you think I needed one?"

His words seemed to stop her cold for a moment, and a look of utter amazement came over her face. Russell would have given his right ball for a camera at that second. Tamara. Stunned silent. It was beautiful, and before she could recover, he barreled on. "You assumed I'm like every other guy you've fucked." Just saying that made his gut clench. "Well, I have news for you, I'm not. I didn't want to leave. And I'm not leaving now. You can't get rid of me that easily."

"Who said I was trying to?"

Okay, now that was some funny shit. "Tamara, please. You've been building a wall since the moment I met you at the wedding."

"I have not." She frowned in denial.

"The hell you haven't." Russell's anger threatened to bubble over, and he pushed it down. "We're going to have to clear something up, right here and right now. I don't lie. I don't cheat. And I don't say go left when I mean go right. If you would lower your guard, for just a second, you would realize that the only one standing in our way is you."

"There is no 'our.'"

"And that's no one's fault but your own. You can't pigeonhole me. And I refuse to allow you to put me in some tourist box. I'm not blind. I know you're not white or a size 2, yet"—Russell held his arms out wide—"here I am. I think that there is something between us, and I would love to explore it, but I'm not going to play the caveman and push myself on you." Not more than he already had anyway. "I'm just going to say this one more time. There is nothing between Sandra and me. And the only thing that ever was, was sex. It's not pretty. But it's honest."

"Definitely not pretty," she muttered. Fortunately, though, Russell noticed a lack of heat in her words and her stare. It was about time.

"But if I can pretend like you came to my bed a blushing virgin and that condom magically materialized from out of nowhere"—he sent her a pointed look—"then you can overlook my lack of judgment."

"What if I don't want to?" Her words were haughty, but her tone was anything but.

"You're acting like I'm giving you a choice."

"You're such a bully."

He stared blankly at her. "And your point would be what?"

"We'll want to kill each other in less than a week."

"But what a way to go."

Tamara shook her head as a brief smile flittered across her face. Without saying another word, she turned until she was facing the wall, then glanced over her shoulder at him. "Are you going to help me out of this dress or what?"

Not sure exactly when she'd changed her mind, Russell decided too much analysis at this point would do him no good. And if she wanted help out of her dress, he was certainly ready to do his part. Especially if it meant she'd help him out of his clothes as well. "I'd love to."

Chapter Nine

"Morning," Tamara said casually to Charlotte as she entered the kitchen. The pregnant woman was sitting at the small kitchen table picking at a piece of toast with all the interest of a kid picking at a plate of brussel sprouts. "Rough night?"

As if she'd been looking for a reason not to eat, Charlotte quickly pushed the plate away from her and turned until she was facing Tamara, bulge and all. "I should ask you."

"My night was fine." Tamara kept her back to her friend as she poured herself a cup of coffee. She knew there was no way she was going to get out of this room without spilling, but she wanted to put it off for as long as possible. "Is the intruder treating you okay?"

"No." Charlotte sent her a "duh" look. "That's why I know I'm having a boy. No woman would treat another woman like this."

"It could be a girl you know. Women are quite evil to one another."

"True."

"You know," Tamara began as she joined Charlotte at the table. "If you two would just let the doctor tell you what sex it is—"

"And where would be the fun in that?"

"We could finally come up with a name."

"I have a list."

"A list is not a name. When I get pregnant—"

"When?" Her comment seemed to amuse the other woman. "Did you say when? Sleep with a cowboy twice and now diapers and rattlers are dancing in your head."

"The hell they are. I was just trying to make a point. That the way you're doing it is lame."

"Well, when you and Russell have a baby—"

"Whoa!" Charlotte was taking this thing a bit too far. "There isn't a me and Russell."

"Right."

"There isn't."

"I think he proved quite effectively last night that there was. And I might be mistaken, but I could have sworn he slept in your room last night."

He'd stayed in her room all right, but sleep had little to do with it. They'd gone until the wee morning hours. She still wasn't sure why she hadn't just kicked him straight up in the balls after his little caveman performance last night. It more than likely had to do with the hint of truth that rang in his words. Maybe she did sort of assume he might have been looking for the fastest exit out of her apartment. And she had gone to the party on purpose just to annoy him. If all of that was sort of the truth, maybe the other things he'd said were as well.

Hell, she didn't know. All Tamara was sure about was, she was happy when she was with him. And that had to count for something. Still, she couldn't just come out and say that to

Charlotte. That would have been too much like right. "Sex has nothing to do with anything."

Charlotte tilted her head to the side and arched a brow, but she didn't utter a single word. Her look said it all. She didn't believe Tamara. Not that Tamara blamed her.

"There's nothing to tell."

"Last night didn't look like nothing to me."

"Last night was him being mad that I went out with Christian."

"Are you guys dating?"

"Since he left his letterman jacket and class ring at home, we've decided not to make it official until class on Monday."

"You know what I mean."

"Girl, please. I'm too old to be someone's girlfriend."

"So then, what are you?"

Truth be told, Tamara was confused as all hell about where she and Russell stood. She was sure about one thing, though. "We're people who have sex with each other, but don't see other people."

"And are you guys going to go out on dates? You know, catch a movie and what not."

"Maybe." They hadn't exactly crossed the t's and dotted the i's just yet. "If we want to. We are adults."

"Let me get this straight." Charlotte crossed her hands on top of her ample tummy. "You're not going to see or sleep with anyone else, and you might go out and do stuff together. But you're not dating."

"Right." Why did it sound stupid when Charlotte said it like that?

"And how exactly is that not dating."

"I don't know." She was going to give her a headache. "We're not complicating things by putting labels on them."

"Oh yeah, common sense can be pretty complicated at times."

"Who asked you?"

"Since when have I needed an invitation to have an opinion on your life?"

"I hope the intruder does a rain dance on your bladder."

"Wow, that's not nice." Russell strolled into the kitchen, stopping at the table to brush a kiss on Tamara's forehead, before heading to the sink to wash his hands.

The simple gesture felt so right, it made her yearn for more. Of course, it didn't help that Charlotte shot her a "Yeah, right, like hell there's nothing there" glance. Crap, why did he have to be so lovey-dovey right now? She had just finished saying they were basically fuck buddies. Way to blow her not-so-cleverly orchestrated cover. "I'm not nice, haven't you figured that out yet?"

"I think you can be very nice." He sent her a wink over his shoulder. "You just need the right motivation."

"I'm not sure if I'm old enough to hear this conversation," Charlotte teased.

"Shut it," Tamara warned. "How was your ride?"

"Not as good as my one last night." As Charlotte burst out laughing, all Tamara could think was how she was going to kill him. "I'm heading over to my house right now. You want to come over and check it out?"

"I was going to work on my photos."

"You can take pictures at my place."

"I could if my subject was lazy construction workers who are milking their clients for everything they have."

Russell nodded his head woefully as he pulled a paper towel off the roll. "True. Very, very true." After balling the damp towel up, he tossed it free-throw-style into the trashcan. "But you might get a few good shots of a cowboy crying as I write them yet another check."

"I want women to feel aroused by my photos, not sad."

"Ouch!" He winced. "You're right. You're not nice."

"Told you." Their playful banter seemed so natural it almost scared her. How was it that two nights of sex had turned them into *a couple*? Tamara never felt this sense of connection before, and Lord knew she'd kissed her share of frogs. "I'll see you later, though."

Russell walked over to the table and stood between the two women, resting one of his hands on the back of Tamara's chair. "Riding back with me?"

"No," she said looking up at him. "I brought my cousin's car."

He nodded as if everything made sense now. "I wondered how you got down here. What time are you leaving?" He delved his thumb through her hair and lightly began to stroke the back of her neck.

"Later this afternoon." She all but purred the answer.

"Not before I get back, though."

His caresses were making it difficult for her to think. "I might be persuaded to wait...if the offer is good enough."

"Oh, I'll make sure it's damn good." He leaned down to eye level as he spoke, his lips just a hairbreadth from hers. His masculine scent enveloped her.

"I'm going to be sick, and it has nothing to with the intruder." Charlotte's declaration, though amusing, had no effect on Russell, who continued forward until his lips brushed against her own.

Her lashes fluttered closed as she slipped under the spell he somehow managed to weave around her. Arching up toward him, she moved her hand around his nape to pull him closer, while cradling his clean-shaven jaw in the other, as she opened her lips for his gentle assault. She responded to his kiss hungrily, as if it had been weeks since their lips had last touched, and not merely hours.

After a few intense seconds, Russell slowly pulled back, dragging a distraught moan from her lips as she opened her eyes. She desperately wanted to ask him if he needed to go to his place today, but fought back the traitorous words before they could escape her now kiss-swollen lips.

"Later, love," he whispered.

It wasn't too soft, though, because the second he slipped from the room, Charlotte pounced. "Love?"

"Shut it." Her words lacked a punch due to the breathlessness of them. A fact Charlotte was too quick to pick up on.

"Not on your life."

"I need..." Tamara stood and made her way quickly to the cupboard. "A glass of water."

"Hell, I do too after that."

"Get your own." Turning her head she stuck out her tongue, even as she grabbed another glass.

"You need to explain to me why you're trying to sit on the sidelines with this man."

Tamara was going to get right on that. As soon as she could figure out the answer for herself. "It's not a big deal."

"Uh-huh."

"Look," she said as she slipped the glass under the water dispenser on the refrigerator. "I'm just going to let this ride. I'm not going to make things complicated. It is what it is." And it wasn't what it wasn't, which was easy and complicated all at the same time.

"I can't wait."

"For?" she asked, before taking a big drink from her glass.

"For you to wake up and see the truth."

"Ugggh." She groaned. Would this conversation never end? "What truth?"

"If I told you, then it wouldn't be a surprise." Charlotte held her hand out for the glass as Tamara resisted the urge to dump it all over her.

"You know what—"

In the middle of talking, Charlotte's housekeeper, Ida, walked into the room, phone in hand. "Ms. Tamara, you have a phone call."

"I do?" Her brows crinkled in confusion. Only a handful of people knew she was here.

"Yes. Mr. Christian Malt."

* * *

With phone in hand, Russell made his way down Tamara's hallway to stop quietly in front of her door. He glanced down at his watch to see what time it was, smiling in relief at the digital numbers staring up at him. Even though it was late, it wasn't insulting, booty-call late. It was only a bit after nine, allowing him the pretense of respectability for just a bit more.

Closing up shop was taking longer than he would have expected. Even after he moved out to the ranch, he would have courtroom battles to deal with. It was easier for him to quit the law than it was for him to quit his clients. Rightly so, of course. They'd made him money. The least he could do is hold their hands every now and then.

Tonight was one of those moments where a retainer had come in handy for one of his clients. They needed him, and because of that, he found himself working way past the six o'clock quitting time he normally set up for himself Monday through Thursday. Yet once he was finished, instead of making his way to his partially packed condo, Russell found himself pulling up in front of Tamara's building, wanting to see her, if only for a moment.

Though he wanted to knock on her door, sweep her into his arms, and carry her off to the bedroom, he wasn't going to. He had a plan to tame the wild filly, and it had nothing to do with sex.

He dialed her number quickly, sort of amused he knew the number by heart. Staring down at the number she'd hastily written down for him yesterday apparently paid off.

After two rings, she breathlessly picked up. "Hello." Just hearing her voice made his day better already.

"So what are you doing?" he said instead of the normal pleasantries. Russell wanted to keep her off guard and keep her on her toes.

Yesterday, he'd stood outside the kitchen listening in on her conversation with Charlotte, learning more about their relationship from Tamara's point of view than he wanted to know. Like she didn't think they were having one. Of course, that was just her take on it...for now. He was hell-bent on proving just how wrong she was. If she thought all they had was sex, then he'd take the sex away to assure her differently.

"Russell?" Her voice went from a monotone to pleased pitch. "What are you doing?"

"Talking to you. What about you?"

"Watching *House*."

Russell frowned. "What's that?"

"What's tha—" she gasped, as if the very idea of him not knowing what she was referring to was just out of the question. "It's only the best show on television."

"I don't watch a lot of TV."

"This isn't just TV." She sounded offended. "This is *House*. The hottest, limpingest white man alive."

Russell grinned at her description. "Yeah, still not ringing a bell."

"That is just sad. Next Monday, I want you here at my house by eight forty-five."

"Would you settle for here, your house, now?"

"My house?"

"Yes. I'm outside your door."

"What?" Five seconds later she'd flung open the door. "Don't you know you're supposed to play hard-to-get?" When she saw him, she smiled and clicked off her phone.

"Really?" Russell teasingly raised and lowered his brows in rapid succession as he shut his cell closed. "I thought it was my job to get hard."

"True. So very true." Crossing her arms, she leaned against the doorjamb. "What are you doing here?"

"Visiting a friend."

"What?" Her eyebrows rose. "You know someone else in this building?"

"Yes. And she's in need of a very hard spanking."

"Lucky friend."

"I think so."

Tamara dropped her arms and took a step back and to the side. "Are you going to spank from out there, or are you going to come on in?"

"Hmm"—Russell stroked his neatly trimmed goatee thoughtfully—"Decisions. Decisions."

"Very funny. Get in here." She gestured for him to come in, shutting the door and locking it once he did. She led the way to the couch and sat down, patting the cushion next to her, much to his delight.

Not one to turn down a good opportunity once it was presented to him, Russell joined her, settling next to her as the music softly came on. "So what's this show abou—"

"Shh!" Tamara elbowed him softly in his side. "You're allowed to speak during commercials."

Chuckling, Russell shook his head and pulled her in close to him. With a contented sigh, he stretched his legs out in front of them and felt his shoulders practically melt into the plush cushions on the back of her couch. Relaxed didn't fully describe him.

Even during the commercials, they didn't speak much, and Russell didn't mind at all. By the time the show was over, he was no closer to understanding what she saw in the rude lead character, but he was closer to figuring out what he saw in her.

Everything. Despite the joyful uproar that came with such a lively person as Tamara, she was somehow the peace he'd been looking for all his life.

"What did you think?" Tamara leaned forward, grabbed the remote off the coffee table, and shut the television off.

"I thought it was..." *Think.* Russell didn't catch enough of the show to form much of an opinion. "All right. His surliness reminded me of someone."

"Charlotte, right?" she said, completely missing his point. "I tell that girl she needs to watch that."

"I wasn't talking about Charlotte."

"Oh really. Then who?"

"Some girl I know. Funny, her name escapes me at the moment."

"Let me see what I can do to change that."

Tamara sat up and slung her leg over his lap, until she was straddling him, and placed her hands on his shoulders. Tilting her head, she pressed her lips to his in a soft, exploratory kiss. He wrapped his arms around her waist, holding on for a few minutes and letting her take the lead. Two seconds later, when that grew old and his caveman grunted, he took over the kiss, plunging his tongue into her mouth.

He held tightly to her waist, anchoring her to him, in the only way he knew how. Tamara was a sexy handful, in spirit as well as in shape, and he loved it. Every succulent inch of her. The longer he kissed her, the harder it was to remember what his grand plan was, especially when she cuddled into him like a cat in heat.

Hungry for more, he pulled at the bottom of her shirt, tugging it from her jeans so he could press his hands against her back. The need to feel her warm flesh under his was a desire that could not be denied or suppressed for long. His fingers, apparently under a will of their own, began to slowly make their way up her back to her bra. Reason slammed quickly back upon him, though, the second he made contact with the strap, and Russell forced his cock to calm down and his fingers to withdraw.

Tamara on the other hand took his retreat as a pause. Breaking their kiss, she pulled away and peered down at him through lowered lids. "Want to go play doctor?"

Did he ever? Russell leaned forward and brushed his lips gently across hers, then uttered the hardest words in the world. "No. I'm going to head home."

"Home." Tamara snapped her eyes open and pulled back. "What do you mean home?"

"I mean that cold, little, lonely place I pay an obscene amount of money for."

"Then stay. I promise you, you'll be neither lonely"—she undulated her hips, rubbing her sex against his rapidly increasing erection—"nor cold."

"Yes, but if I stay..." As he wanted to. "You won't get the chance to miss me." Russell lifted her and sat her back on the couch. He stood before he could change his mind and carried her to the bedroom as they both desired.

Of course, his little fireball wasn't going to be put off that easily. Pouting, in the prettiest of ways, she crossed her arms over her chest and sat back on the couch in a funk. "What makes you think I'm going to miss you?"

"Because I'll miss you."

His answer seemed to set her back a bit, but as usual, Tamara didn't stay down long. "Doesn't mean I have to like it, though."

Russell didn't, either, but he was going to stay strong and prove to her he was more than just her fuck buddy.

Chapter Ten

If it was possible to die of sexual frustration, then Tamara was hours away from being a goner. Going without sex wasn't a novelty to her. She'd had her share of dateless moments when she'd become more familiar with her own pussy than a blind person with Braille, but never had she ever had a man and *not* gotten laid. *Never, ever.* And that was just mind-numbing.

She knew for a fact it wasn't because of a lack of opportunity. Over the last couple of weeks they'd seen one another almost every night, and if they weren't able to get together, they were talking on the phone.

Despite her best attempts or words otherwise, whatever they had was turning into a relationship right before her eyes. Unfortunately, it just happened to be a relationship that didn't include sex. Which was ten times worse than being in a relationship in general.

Tamara's fight or flight sensors were buzzing off the hook. Part of her wanted to push Russell away so she didn't have to worry about falling for him too hard. The other part wanted to beat a bitch down for even looking his way when the two of them were out together. The warring emotions weren't helped at all by the buildup of sexual desires, because even though Russell wasn't giving her any, he still went out of his way to make sure her knees were weak and her panties were damp on a constant basis.

It just wasn't fair. In fact, it was so far from fair, it was borderline cruel. Enough was enough already. Despite the slow start she had, Tamara was getting the hint. Russell wanted to be more than a bed warmer.

Fine.

Good.

Now it was time to make with the loving already.

With her resolve in place, Tamara glanced once more at the secretary guarding Russell's door like a well-trained watchdog. In the last hour she'd been sitting there, Tamara had yet to see the woman let anyone past her desk. In a polite, even tone she'd informed Tamara that since she hadn't had an appointment, she wasn't going to be able to get to see Russell, but she was welcome to wait. Well, she was waiting all right; she just wasn't so sure how welcome she might be.

Tamara turned as she heard a large group entering the office. Russell was surrounded by a bunch of people, all seeming to hang on his every word. He was handing out tasks and giving orders like a general. She wondered for a moment how he could give up such a powerful position for a run-down ranch. But then she noticed the lines around his eyes and mouth and knew in an instant that this wasn't exciting to him, it was tedious.

She took in all this in a matter of moments. But her stare must have caught his attention.

Russell paused in midstep when he saw her, and smiled. "Hey, you."

"Hey." Nervous, Tamara stood and smoothed the lines out of her simple black skirt. She'd come over straight from work and was now beginning to second-guess that decision. To add fuel to the fire, she wasn't exactly sure what his reaction would be to her just showing up with no warning. "Sorry for dropping in out of the blue."

"Don't be silly. You're always welcome." To her surprise, and from the low chattering echoing through the room, everyone else's as well, Russell walked over and gave her a soft kiss on the lips. "Give me one second."

That answered that. Welcome it was. Licking her lips, she nodded mutely as he walked over to the secretary and handed her a file. They spoke in lowered voices for a minute or two while Tamara stood still and tried her best to bite back the words on her lips.

The weight of the stares from the people in the room was heavy as hell. Even though it went against every belief she held strongly, she was going to bite her tongue and not bark "boo" at the people staring at her. They were acting like they never saw a fine white man with a thick black sister before. *Damn.*

Before she could get too worked up, Russell sent the rest of the group on their way, and with a hand on her lower back, he ushered her into his office, shutting the door behind them. Tamara quickly glanced around the room. She barely registered the large space, only noting it looked professional and comfortable all at the same time. Her attention, however, was solely on him.

"You look tired."

"I feel tired." Russell began to unknot his tie, unwittingly drawing her gaze to his long fingers as he pulled the silk through the loop. *Damn.* Tamara knew her frustration levels had hit new highs when she was staring hungrily at his hands. "It's been a very long day."

Tamara clenched her hands together in an attempt to stop herself from reaching out and taking the tie from his fingers and stripping the shirt from him. She wanted to run her hands over his bare chest and down to his stomach, delving even lower. Shaking her head to dispel the images she'd evoked, she leaned against one of the chairs in what she hoped was a provocative pose.

"You want to talk about it?"

Her offer brought a smile to his lips. "Actually I'd prefer to forget about it. Friday can't come soon enough for me."

"Living for the weekend?" Tamara asked, as she eased down into the brown leather seat to the right of him. With his work schedule and her getting ready for her show, they hadn't been able to make any trips out to Charlotte's lately. It was a blessing as far as Tamara was concerned. She couldn't even began to imagine what torture it would have been to sleep beside him night after night and still have him holding out on her. Lord knew it was bad enough as it was.

"And any other time when I get to see you."

"Which is almost every night."

"Complaining?"

"Merely commenting." She only had one complaint when it came to Russell, and it had nothing to do with how often they were seeing each other. More to do with how they were spending their time together. "I think you're working too hard."

Russell bent forward and picked up her hand from her lap and gently kissed her fingertips. "Says the woman whose fingers are now permanently pruned. I could barely get you out of your darkroom last night."

That wasn't exactly how Tamara remembered it. If memory served, he was quite skilled at turning her attention from her work to him, as he carried her from the former closet turned darkroom into her bedroom and proceeded to kiss her senseless. First her lips, then her breasts, then between her thighs in the sexiest of fashions. She came twice, but neither time was he buried inside her. Nor did he allow her the same luxury of returning the favor. Russell had simply held her for a few minutes, then whispered he had to go.

Just thinking about last night was getting her hot and bothered again. Stifling a moan, Tamara pulled her hand back and jumped right to the heart of the matter. "I think I know what will make you feel better."

"What?"

"Sex." Tamara crossed her legs, edging her skirt up a bit to show off a little thigh.

Russell's chuckle made her womb clench. "You think so?"

"I know so."

"I'm not so sure," he hedged. Leaning back against the desk, he crossed his arms over his chest. "But I'll think on it."

"Think!" Tamara couldn't believe her ears. Here she was damn near propositioning him, and he was acting if she asked him if he wanted wine or beer. Fuck him! She wasn't this horny. Well, she was, but she had a vibrator she was about to bend in two. "Never mind. I have to go."

Rising to her feet, she turned on her heels, hell-bent on marching out, but was stopped cold by Russell, who pulled her back flush against him. "Damn, you're cute when you're feisty."

"I'm not feisty. I'm horny," she blurted out, sick to death of this game he was playing.

"I'm sure there's something I can do about that." Russell turned them around until she was facing his desk and bent her down until her breasts were resting against the hard wooden surface. Stepping forward, he nudged his thick erection against her upturned bottom. "I'm getting the feeling you miss my cock."

"Do not." Tamara couldn't stop her hips from pressing back, forcing his cock harder against her, nor could she stop the tremor in her voice as she lied.

"Little liar. Don't think I haven't noticed you prancing around me the last few days in little to nothing. Showing me that sexy body of yours."

Tamara pressed her hands against the desktop to brace herself. "Can't be too sexy. You're not doing anything with it."

"I wouldn't call last night nothing," he reminded her as he began to slowly push her skirt up.

The prolonged anticipation of what she hoped was to come made her body tremble with passion. This strong, all-consuming need she had for him was unbearable at best, and she'd be damned if he didn't know it. "It wasn't sex."

"Everything isn't always about sex," he whispered close to her ear.

"I know, but that doesn't mean I don't want it."

"There's no doubt in my mind you want sex. The only question is, is that all you want?"

Tamara was tired of this. What did he want from her? "If I say yes..." She left the words hanging in the air between them, waiting to see what he would say.

"Then we'll fuck, and you can go on your way, and I'll go on mine. And whenever one of us gets an itch, we'll scratch it with one another or maybe someone else."

Despite her protest of not wanting a relationship, she couldn't help but feel revulsion for what he was suggesting. Just the idea of him with another woman was enough to make her see red. "I don't think so." Her words were clipped and her frown fierce as she glared over her shoulder at him.

In the face of her anger, Russell merely grinned."The idea of me fucking someone else doesn't sit well with you."

"What do you think?"

Russell grabbed her by the arms and pulled her up a bit, then drew her arms straight back before lowering her gently to the desk once more."I think you need a reminder of just what it is you want."

"What's that?" If she didn't know, how in the world could he?

"Me." Before Tamara could utter another word, Russell brought her wrists together and looped his tie around them, pulling it tight as he bound her hands behind her back.

"What the hell are you doing?"

"Giving you exactly what you've been begging for."

Good. It was about damned time.

Amusement warred with arousal inside Russell. There wasn't any doubt in his mind, holding back from Tamara had been a good thing. Unfortunately, it had also been very painful as well, especially after last night. His cock was in a permanent semihard state. Ready to perform after the abstinence at the drop of a...well, drop of a zipper. It had taken everything out of him to keep his end goal in mind.

Yes, he could have fucked her numerous times. And yes, it would have been great, but it wouldn't have gotten him any closer to her than he had been when they'd met a month ago. Now he could honestly say he knew what she was like in and out of the bedroom, and he liked them both just fine.

"I might have been a bit remiss in my thinking." The sight of her full, rounded ass, framed by the sexy, cream-colored boy shorts, had his cock aching to delve deep into the warmth of her body. "I can't believe I was out of this"—Russell rubbed his hand against her bared flesh—"for so long. Part your legs a bit, baby."

He watched patiently as she did as he bade, before reaching out gently and taking hold of the edges of her underwear. He drew them over the curve of her buttocks and down the length of her long legs, before allowing them to pool on the floor at her foot. "Step out."

His two-word sentence garnished him quick results, leaving Tamara looking sexy as all get-out, in thigh-high stockings, with her skirt resting around her waist. Stepping back a bit, he feasted his eyes on the treasure he'd uncovered. Lord, was she beautiful like this, tied up and tempting. The heady aroma of her arousal teased his senses as no other had before. Russell wanted to drop to his knees and devour her whole, but something told him that today was a "strickly dickly" day.

It was more than obvious Tamara was way past foreplay. A sentiment he could definitely relate to. She wasn't the only person on edge from their lack of intercourse. She was just the first to break. Speaking of breaks, Russell's gaze drifted to his closed, yet unlocked door. He needed to take one before they got too wrapped up in their afternoon delight. "Perfect. Now stay still. I'll be back."

"Back?" Tamara raised her head up and made to move, but Russell put a stop to that real quick. Flattening his hand on her back, he held her in place. "What did I just say?"

"Stay still."

He fired off a single, sharp smack to her bare flesh. The noise echoed and resonated throughout the room, along with the sound of her surprised gasp. The palm of his hand stung. "Then that's what I mean."

"But...where are you going?"

"To handle something. Now don't move again, or I'll make that last smack seem like a love tap."

"Bastard."

Despite cursing, she didn't move an inch, a fact that wasn't lost on Russell. So his brat could mind. Damn. He'd been really looking forward to teaching her a lesson. With a quickness in his step, he made his way back over to his office door and locked it. Russell didn't want anything to interrupt them. This would be the first time he'd had an office rendezvous, so he wanted to make sure he did it right. If he was lucky, the memory of the two of them together in here would last him until his dying day.

As he walked back to the desk, he unbuckled and unbuttoned his pants, leaving the zipper in place for now. He stopped directly behind her once more and licked his lips as he looked her over. "Decisions. Decisions."

"What's there to decide? Stick it in and fuck me."

"Stick it in, huh?" Pulling her up, Russell spun her around, then picked her up to sit her on the edge of his desk. "You're such a romantic, baby."

"You want romance, fuck a Hallmark card."

Russell winced. "No, that might hurt."

"You are such a tease." Tamara's frustration was more than evident in her blazing gaze. "When I get free, I'm going to make you pay."

Instead of feeling threatened, as he imagined she was intending, he felt turned on. Tamara mad, naked, and aroused. It could be fun as was most things with her. "I like you like this."

"Frustrated?"

"No, bound for my pleasure. We're going to have to do this again."

"I agree. But reversed."

"We'll see." He laughed, knowing good and well that it would be a cold day in hell before he allowed her to tie him up. Starting at the top, Russell began to unbutton her white blouse, stopping when he neared the bottom to pull the edges open, bringing her cream-colored bra into view.

The sexy lace was like artwork against her skin; unfortunately, it was an obscuring one, keeping him away from what he wanted. But since he was unwilling to untie her and risk her wrath before he could fuck her, he pushed the stretchy cups down until her nipples were exposed. The bra was still covering the bottom half of her large breasts, but now, instead of restricting his view, it was holding them up to him like a sacrifical offering.

One he couldn't resist. His hands brushed over the exposed tips, causing her to gasp. Then leaning down, he captured her lips.

They drank hungrily from one another, their tongues dueling in a ritualistic move. Her sweet taste blinded him to everything around him, but she was something he was becoming quickly accustomed to.

Before he became too drunk on her essence, he lifted his mouth from Tamara's, and he lowered his lips to her breasts. Her answering moan was all the go-ahead he needed; he took one of her beaded nipples between his lips. She moaned softly as his tongue circled the hard peak before drawing it into his mouth.

While his lips were busy with her breasts, his hand slid between their bodies and moved down quickly to her pussy. With his fingers he parted her nether lips and plunged two fingers into the tight, wet abyss of her sex.

Moaning, Tamara gyrated her hips forward, wordlessly begging him as he tried to open her moist center. Their two weeks apart was very telling. Her pussy was so tight, he could barely scissor his fingers inside her, a fact that only made him want to fuck her more.

He wanted to shove his cock into her pussy and give her the pounding they both wanted so desperately, but he refrained. If it killed him, he was going to take his time with her, pleasuring her over and over until she went mad with it. It was the least he owed her for the way he'd tormented her the last few weeks.

Hungrier now than he'd been before, Russell slipped his fingers out of her wet body, and reached for his wallet and the protection he'd pocketed within it days ago. He made quick work of his zipper, shoving his pants past his ass in his haste to enter her.

After sheathing himself for their protection, he stepped up and gripped his cock tightly, centering it on her moist opening. "Lean back, baby."

Without saying a word, Tamara leaned back a bit, resting her upper body on top of her bound hands on the desk for leverage. "Perfect."

And she was.

With his gaze firmly centered on her passion-filled eyes, Russell took his time and entered her slowly, sinking only half his cock on the first thrust. Biting back a groan, he retracted his length until only the head remained before plunging forth once more.

She bit out a sharp cry as he buried himself balls-deep inside her. It was a tight fit, but well worth the effort. Exquisite torture of the best kind. He could feel the walls of her sex stretching to take all of him. The heady sensation caused him to groan as the heat of her pussy surrounded him. He paused for a moment to allow her to become reaccustomed to him, before he pulled out, then forcefully thrust back in. "Why did we wait so long to do this again?"

"Because of you."

"Oh yeah." Russell gripped her hips in his hands and used them as leverage to pull her farther onto his cock. "That was stupid."

"You're preaching to the...choir."

"Wrap your legs around my hips. I want to fuck you as deep as humanly possible. I want you to feel me for days after this."

"I feel you." She moaned.

"No"—Russell held tightly to her hips, as he powered deep within her—"but you will. Then you'll remember exactly who you belong to."

"I belong to—"

He didn't even let her finish. "Me."

Tamara bit down on her bottom lip, stifling the moans bubbling up from within her. His woman wasn't a quiet lover, and unfortunately, the last two times they'd made love, counting this one, were in places where she couldn't open up and let loose. He was going to have to rectify that as soon as humanly possible because he wanted her to be as wild and as loud as she wanted. Untamed, like a woman in the throes of passion should be.

"I can't get enough of your tight pussy." Her pussy clenched around him, welcoming him back home. It was like heaven. It was like hell. He was perfect. She was perfect.

"So tight. So good." Russell glanced down between them and watched in wonder as his pale shaft penetrated her dark sheath. The erotic sight was a mosaic masterpiece in the making. "So pretty."

"Yes, yes, yes." Tamara closed her eyes and dropped her head back, pumping her hips up to meet him thrust for thrust.

"Look at me." He paused in midstroke to give his command. Moaning, Tamara looked up at him. Her dark eyes were filled with passion. Her face was a road map of pleasure. "Better. Much, much better."

Russell couldn't put a damper on the need he had to ensure Tamara knew he was the only one for her. In her life. In her bed. In her heart. She was his. Just as he was hers.

"Yes...yes...fuck me," she pleaded."Fuck. Fuck."

Her breasts bounced in rhythm to his quickening thrusts. It was a far cry from a smooth, subtle ride. It was wild, fierce, and all-consuming.

He could see the struggle within her to close her eyes, but like the fighter she was, Tamara battled it, meeting him thrust for thrust, while drowning him in the stormy seas of her eyes.

Her legs tightened around him as her breathing became a ragged, jagged symphony of erotic sounds. The more he thrust, the louder she became, making him want to pound her even harder. But common sense won out, forcing him to mutter, "Shhh" despite his own personal desires.

But quieting Tamara was like trying to hold back a typhoon. "Please." Her body began to shake. Her nipples pebbled to hard little stones, and her pussy gushed with evidence of her impending release. "Please, Russell…"

As if he could ever turn down a request like that. Russell bore down on her, grinding his pelvis against her pearl with every downward stroke. He pumped his hips wildly until her eyes grew glassy and her breath short.

She strained against him for a few seconds, then broke, letting out a deep moan as she reached her pinnacle. Russell quickly covered her mouth with his when she came, swallowing the heady cries down as he neared his own release. Her body convulsed and shivered, making the liplock almost impossible to keep, but he kept at it, kissing her through her orgasm, as if the very breath from her soul fueled his own.

All the while, he fucked her, fighting her contracting muscles with everything inside him. Her sweet pussy was milking his cock, squeezing it so tight he knew he wouldn't last much longer. Not long at all.

He broke their kiss, more concerned with his balls tightening. His heart pounded. He felt light-headed and drunk. With all his might, he pulled her onto him as he pushed deep within her, coming inside her hot, pulsing body. He took her peaked nipple into his mouth to mute his own deep groans. His savage suction had Tamara gasping and arching up to him, as he rode out the waves of his release.

Her body was limp beneath him. The only thing holding her upright were her bound hands behind her. She was a sexy, panting mess of loving, and she'd never looked more beautiful to him.

Struggling, Russell eased out of her battered sex and pulled her up to him. He worked quickly to release her hands, then tossed the tie down on the floor as she slumped back down to lay flat on his desk. She looked exhausted. A feeling Russell could well relate to.

Too tired to care about much, he opened his top desk drawer and yanked out a tissue, cleaning himself quickly before dropping into his chair. As soon as he had energy, he would offer to do the same for her, but right now, he had to sit, before his tired legs gave out.

Breathing heavily, Tamara turned her head in his direction and smiled softly. It wasn't just the look of a well-satisfied sex partner. It was the look of a well-satisfied lover. "Sex strike over?"

"Is your denial over?"

She chuckled and rose shakily to a seated position. To his disappointment, she began to right her appearance. "Do you always have to have the last word?"

"When it comes to you...yes."

"Why?"

Russell scooted his chair forward, then pulled her down from the desk to his lap. She gasped aloud at the sudden movement, but made no attempt to rise; instead, she cuddled close to him. "Because you need a man to stand up for you and to you."

His comment brought her head up, and she faced him with a cocky grin on her pretty face. "And you think you're the man for the job?"

"No. I know I am," he replied, utterly and completely serious.

"Stubborn." The words were said with lack of heat, and maybe just a hint of wonder in her eyes.

"And you love it." Probably as much as he was beginning to love her.

Chapter Eleven

"Are you nervous?"

"Nervous me? What do I have to be nervous about?" Tamara pressed the phone tighter to her ear as she paced back and forth in the women's restroom. "Other than the slight chance my photos could suck, not sell, and cause the critics to laugh uproariously and flay me alive in the press."

"Your photos are wonderful."

"Says the biased best friend."

"Please. Would I lie to you?"

"You better," she muttered nervously.

"Come on, you can do this. I'm going to talk you through it."

"A virtual hand-holding."

"Yes." Charlotte sighed heavily. "I'm so upset I'm not there tonight."

"Woman, you're seconds away from bursting." Charlotte was officially on bedrest now. The last three weeks had been filled with false contractions and a slew of late-night phone calls. Just thinking about her friend took Tamara's mind off her show. She was more nervous for the petite woman than she ever could be about this stupid show. "Even if Ty said you could come, I would have put my foot down. You should be in a hospital."

"I should be with you bragging about how talented my best friend is."

"Who would you brag to?" Tamara asked looking around the empty room. "There's no one in the bathroom."

"Are you still in there." Charlotte's exasperation was loud and clear over the phone line. "Girl, get out of there and go face your adoring public."

"I'm too nervous." Despite her words, Tamara made her way over to the entrance. Even though she knew it was stupid, she cracked the door and peeked her head out to see if anyone was laughing and pointing in the direction of the five pieces she had hanging up.

So far so good.

If attendance was anything to go by, she'd say the show was a big sucess. She was one of six other photographers who had their work on display at the Inner Eye, but other than the few family members she'd invited and the owner of the gallery, Tamara didn't know a soul. Like the big stupid that she was, she'd made her mother and cousins promise not to come near her during the exhibit, too afraid she would use them as a shield to avoid talking to people. She could see the error of her ways now that she was hiding in the bathroom like a big loser.

Get a hold of yourself, she said to her inner coward. This wasn't the first time she had work on display, but it was the first time it'd been as personal to her.

The five photos she selected featured Russell prominently in three of them. One of him on a horse in the corral. Another she'd selected from the photos taken from the first night in her apartment. The last one was a shot of Russell sleeping. She'd woken up one morning before him and just so happened to catch a glimpse of him sleeping face down, with one arm dangling off the edge of the bed and the sheet barely covering the gentle rise of his buttocks. Acting quickly, Tamara climbed from the bed and grabbed his cowboy hat and her camera. She postioned the hat to lean against the bed near his hand, and snapped several frames before the sleeping man awoke.

As soon as he did, though, they quickly put the camera right back to work. Taking pictures of the two of them that Tamara would never let leave the sanctuary of her darkroom. Still...it was fun. Almost as fun as every other thing they'd been doing together in the last three weeks.

Since that evening in his office they'd grown even closer. Tamara still wasn't willing to discuss their relationship outside of sexual torture, but she was happy. A first for her.

"Come on, this is ridiculous. Where's your momma?"

"Probably out there embarrassing me," she whispered into the receiver as she took a tentative step outside the door. Dinah, her mother, was very proud of Tamara, and she didn't care who knew it. It was as endearing as it was embarrassing, but it was a mom thing, so Tamara understood.

"And Russell?"

"He's on his way," she said as she walked farther into the room.

At least she hadn't made him promise to stay away from her. Although she did try to make him promise to avoid her mother. That didn't work so well, though. He'd already said he was going to make a point of introducing himself to her mother, despite what Tamara said. She knew her mother was going to love him once she met him. Dinah would love anyone Tamara cared about, and she cared about Russell, no matter how hard she tried not to. Somehow, someway, he'd wormed his way inside her heart, and she was having a hard time disliking it or much of anything he did. He was endearing that way, damn him.

"Good. At least one of us is there with you tonight."

Maybe once he showed up, she'd grow a backbone and face her fear of failure. "True but…" Tamara's words drifted away as she caught sight of the man in question. "Good goobaleegoo."

"What? What?"

Tamara watched in awe as Russell made his way over to her through the crowded gallery. "Remember that moment you had when Ty walked into your office party?"

"Oh yeah." Charlotte had a faint quality to her voice that by all rights no very pregnant woman happily married to a big strapping man should have when it came to her best friend's man. "Russell show up?"

"Yes."

"Is he dressed nice?"

Nice wasn't even remotely close to how fine he looked. Over the last three weeks she had several opportunities to see him in work wear, but she'd never seen him like this. The tailored, black, four-button suit fit his muscular frame as if was made especially for him. "Black suit and tie."

"Tell me…is he wearing a Stetson?"

"Oh yeah." And he looked every inch like the yummy, elegant cowboy she'd come to know and lo—no, like. Strongly like.

"Damn."

"Oh yeah," she repeated, unable to say much more. All of a sudden, the butterflies that had been fluttering frantically in her stomach from nerves began to dance for a completely different reason. Her heart sped up as he approached her with a welcoming, soft smile on his face. And suddenly she knew without a single doubt that no matter what happened tonight, she was going to be just fine. "I'll talk to you later."

"Uh-huh. You don't need me now, do you?"

"Bye, Charlotte," Tamara said, avoiding her friend's question like the plague.

"Bye."

She clicked the phone off just as he reached her side. "Sorry I'm late." Russell leaned forward and brushed his lips across her own. The fleeting kiss was much too tame and short for the way she was feeling right now, but common sense and the last shred of dignity she had kept her in place and not on top of him as she truly wanted.

"You're late?" Tamara hadn't even noticed the time.

"A few minutes. How are you doing? Nervous?" Russell took her hand into his and caressed the back of it with the pad of his thumb.

"Please," she bluffed. "I'm fine."

"Good." Russell turned so he was standing by her side and able to view the many people circling about. "This is exciting."

"It's all right." Tamara downplayed her emotions as she peered around. "Lots of people."

"Which means sales for you?"

"Only if someone outside of my mother and boyfriend buy them."

"Boyfriend?" Russell glanced back at her, eyebrow raised.

The teasing tone in his voice caused her to flush. She'd never called him that before, and if he kept this up, she wouldn't again. "Shut up."

"Uh-huh." From the laughter swimming in his eyes, she could tell she hadn't intimidated him at all. Only fueled his amusement more. "Either way, your photos will sell," he said confidently. "How could they not, with me as your subject?"

His bravado caused her to laugh. "Of course. What was I thinking?"

"I have no idea."

Their bantering was interrupted by the arrival of a whirling dervish.

"I've been looking for you everywhere," Lilith Zorg gushed as she pulled Tamara into an impromptu embrace. The gallery owner and self-appointed bohemian princess was as gregarious as she was outlandish, but she was also well respected for launching the careers of several artists. "Do you know what you are?"

"A nervous wreck."

"No, you're a nervous wreck who just sold her first photo."

"I did?"

"Yes, *Slumber.*"

Tamara's eyes widened in wonder as she tamped down the need she had to jump up and down and squeal like a little girl. "*Slumber.* Really?" The photo of Russell sleeping was one of her favorites. "I can't believe it."

"Believe it, girl." Lilith brushed her violet bangs from out of her eyes, pushing them back against her otherwise ebony hair. "They're also looking at *The Dance,* but they want me to cut them a deal."

"And?"

"And I'm letting them sweat it out for a second."

"Don't let them sweat too long." Tamara was fine with a deal. The sticker prices were way beyond anything she would have charged in the first place.

"That's my job, girl." Lilith turned her rapt attention from Tamara to Russell and extended her hand to his. The many silver bracelets she wore clanked and banged against one another as she did, making the movement as musical as it was fluid. Tamara had seen her do that so often that it hardly registered any more. It was just one of those things Lilith did that made her stand out, as was the colorful muumuu she wore. "If it isn't the muse in the flesh."

Russell took her hand and shook it. "I wouldn't go that far."

"Oh, I would." Tamara was clueless until she came across him in the corral. Whether he saw it that way or not, he was the inspiration behind her photos. "You are a big part of this."

"I'd say big all right." Lilith's gaze roved boldly over him as he released her hand. "*Underneath It All* is one of my favorite photos tonight. I wasn't sure if I should hang it on my bedroom wall or out here. That photo has garnished a lot of interest tonight from the *Brokeback Mountain* crowd."

"The what?" Russell's smile dimmed as he furrowed his brows in confusion.

"Them, honey." Lilith pointed to a group of men standing in front of the photo taken in Tamara's apartment that featured Russell with his shirt and pants opened. It focused less on his face and more on his body, every hard inch of it. "The group is getting bigger by the second." Lilith smiled secretively at Tamara. "I think your photo is outing a few people tonight."

"Outing." Russell paled. "I think I need to see this picture."

"You haven't seen them yet?" Lilith's voice rose, as if in surprise.

"No."

Lilith gasped dramatically as if she'd been caught off guard.

"I wanted it to be a surprise." Tamara didn't show anyone the photos before framing them.

"It's a surprise all right." And from the tone in his voice she could tell he wasn't sure if it was a good one or not.

"Then allow me to be your tour guide, but I warn you"— Lilith looped her arm around his and tugged him toward her— "you might need to bring a pen to autograph a few chests tonight."

"Lord, have mercy," Russell muttered as he walked with Lilith over to the photos and the small group of admirers standing in front of it.

While Russell was busy with Lilith, Tamara went in search of her mother, to tell her the good news about the sale. It took a good fifteen minutes of hugging to satisfy her mother, who looked close to tears. Once she quieted the ecstatic woman, she motioned for her cousin to come and get her to take her home. Tamara's nerves couldn't have handled a minute more of the loving exchange. After saying good-bye to them, which took another five minutes, she went to find Russell. With the crowd around her photos, it took a few minutes, but she managed to worm her way next to him and slip her hand through his.

To her utter surprise, though, he didn't take it like she assumed he would. Instead he took a step back and shoved his hands in his pants pockets. His abrupt movement caused her to step back herself in wonder. Was he really that upset over the photos she picked of him to hang? "Everything all right?"

"Of course." His voice and eyes said otherwise, though. "I was just checking out the photos you hung."

"Okay," she said hesitantly. "Did you not like the ones I chose?"

"The photograph of Ty with his head on Charlotte's belly is amazing."

"Thank you."

"And the ones of me"—he paused for a second—"are great. It was a bit daunting to see myself up there like that, but I'm amazed at what you were able to capture. You're very talented."

Now she was more confused than ever. "Then what's the problem?"

"There's not a problem, per se. I'm just a bit confused."

"About?"

"When exactly you took this picture?" Russell turned to face the picture hanging on the wall in front of them. The picture of Christian. As soon as Tamara saw the photo of the man practicing roping, she froze. Damn. In the midst of everything she forgot to mention a few things to him.

"Oh."

"Yeah. Oh. When did you take this?"

"I—" Before she could answer, her cell phone rang. She quickly grabbed it and answered it. "Hello."

"Hey." Charlotte's voice sounded a bit thready.

"I can't talk right now. Let me call you back."

"I might be a little busy later. My water just broke."

* * *

Even though Russell wanted nothing more than to talk to Tamara about the picture, they weren't able to. The drive out to the Dollar for the first time in almost two months would be done in separate cars. Tamara's vehicle was up and running now, and she insisted on driving her own vehicle out to the ranch. Part of Russell believed it was just her way of avoiding an argument. But it wasn't going to work. They were going to have this conversation. It was only a matter of when.

The two-hour drive to Moreno Valley where the hospital was located seemed even longer, thanks to the rapid thoughts racing through his head. But by the time they pulled up to the hospital, he was calmer than he'd been in the gallery.

It also helped that Tamara was bouncing around like Tigger before he could even get the car in park. The woman had driven like a manaic, with him following. From the way she'd driven, he wasn't surprised her car had been in the shop for engine repair. She was as enthusiastic on the gas pedal as she was in the bedroom.

Russell smiled at that thought as he turned off the car and exited his vehicle. "What's up?"

"She had the baby." Tamara was practically beaming with pleasure.

"Already?" Russell glanced down at his watch in surprise. "Aren't these things supposed to take like hours, days even?" What he knew about childbirth wouldn't even fill his hat.

"Sometimes, but she had a C-section. That only takes like an hour, tops." Tamara grabbed his hand and began walking toward the entrance of the hospital. The bright lights inside the starchy white room seemed a bit like overkill to Russell, but then again, he'd been in a dark car for a couple of hours.

"What did she have?"

"Ty won't say. He told me to come in and see for myself." She growled in mock outrage. "This secret thing is getting beyond old."

"Then let's go unravel it." Russell pulled her into the open elevator and pressed the button to the floor for maternity. On the short ride up, he watched Tamara. She looked so alive and excited, and it made him wonder how she'd look pregnant with their child. The thought stopped him cold. *Their child?* He'd never imagined a woman carrying his baby before. This was a first, as was the right feeling he had growing inside him at the thought.

When they exited the elevator they saw Ty standing outside a room, talking excitedly into the phone. He looked up and spotted them, waving them over as he finished his conversation.

The tired lines around his eyes were nothing compared to the joy radiating from his gaze and the large smile he was beaming.

"Well...?" Tamara demanded the second they neared him.

Ty closed the phone and smiled. "Why don't you go on in and meet your goddaughter."

"Goddaughter." Tamara gasped, her eyes welling with tears. "It's a girl."

"I hope so, or the thing I cut off was definitely not the umbilical cord."

"Oh my God." Tamara rushed through the open doorway leaving the two men alone.

"Daughter."

"Yep."

"Are we stocking up on guns and ammo now?"

"Who do you think I was on the phone with?"

"Congratulations, man." Russell pulled his friend in for a hug, slapping him on the back as he did.

"Thanks," Ty said as he stepped back. "Good thing your house is finally done. I'm going to need help keeping those randy boys away."

"We can do bad cop, worse cop like our dads used to do with my sister."

"Not that it ever worked."

"Don't remind me."

The two men chatted for a few moments longer, allowing their women to have some alone time together with the new arrival.

"So are you ready to meet my darling Candace?"

Ty pushed open the door to the hospital room, and Russell followed him inside. Instead of Charlotte holding the baby, though, Tamara was sitting next to her on the bed with the infant in her arms. He couldn't see much of little Candace, but the sight of Tamara blew him away.

She looked like the quintessential earth mother. And those earlier thoughts crept back once again. What if this was him coming to visit his woman and child? As if sensing his gaze on her, Tamara looked up and smiled. "Isn't she the most beautiful thing in the world?"

To be honest, she looks like a little old man, Russell thought, but the woman holding her was definitely beautiful.

"Of course she is," Ty answered. "She's my baby, isn't she?"

Charlotte smiled and rolled her eyes. "I did contribute a little something too."

The baby began to fuss, and Charlotte announced it was time for Candace's dinner. Tamara handed her back, hugging and kissing her friend before rising from the bed. She gave Ty a big bear hug as well.

Russell ran his hand through his hair, his tiredness finally catching up with him. He'd spent the entire day working before meeting Tamara at her show. Add to that the frantic two-hour drive out here, and he was ready to crash. It seemed as if Tamara was feeling the same way. Although still looking quite happy, he could see her weariness as she walked over to him.

"Lord, I'm tired."

"I bet. Are you ready to go home?"

"No. I think I might crash at Charlotte's tonight. That's an awful long drive to make right now."

"I meant to my house."

"It's finally all done?"

Though the construction part of the house had been finished for about two weeks now, it had taken the interior designer this long to get it painted and prepared for him. He'd planned on bringing Tamara out tomorrow to see it, but it looked as if fate was stepping in and taking over as usual. "The last of the furniture was delivered today. You can be the first person to get the grand tour."

"I'd love to."

They rode down together in the elevator, and he walked her out to her car. He resisted his urge to lean down and kiss her when she got in, and instead, shut the door firmly after telling her to follow him out to the ranch. When they finally arrived, he watched as she exited her car and stared up in rapt fascination.

"I can't believe how different it looks. The last time it was just wood and brick, and now, it's a home."

She captured exactly how he felt about the place as well. "Come on in and I'll show you around."

They toured the first floor, stopping in each room to see the finished results of Russell's labor of love. When they reached the gourmet kitchen, she looked around in question. "Why did you spend so much in here? You don't even cook."

"I can hire someone to cook. Besides, it's good for resale." Not that he ever planned to sell the place. He had a dream of making this ranch something that would be passed on from generation to generation.

"You've done a great job down here. Is the upstairs just as nice?"

"Why don't you judge for yourself?"

After he finished the tour, he led her to the master bedroom, which had been painted in warm tones and outfitted with sturdy yet comfortable furniture.

"I'm exhausted."

"I'm not surprised." He massaged her shoulders. "It's not every day a woman becomes an aunt and a famous photographer."

"That's true." She laughed lightly.

"But since we're on the subject of your photos…"

"What's my chance of this not being made into a big deal?"

"Slim to none."

"That's what I thought." Tamara shrugged to remove his hands from her shoulders. Russell let her go without a word and waited until she turned around and faced him before speaking. "Yell away."

"Yell." Russell shook his head. "I'm not going to yell. This is going to be a calm and rational discussion."

"Really…so that means two other people are going to have it, then."

Her comment caused him to chuckle. "No. You and I are."

"Calm. This will be a first."

"Of many to come." Russell sat down on the bench in front of the bed and began to pull off his boots. "It might have taken me a while, but I finally figured out that fighting with you is like ramming my head into the wall. It's annoying and gives me a terrible headache."

"Fine, let's try it your way."

The anger Russell had felt earlier was gone. Besides, he knew that coming off like a jackass, all possessive and upset, would get him nowhere with her. He was just going to keep things simple and get straight to the point. "I just have one question."

"Shoot."

"Why?"

She furrowed her brow. "Why what?"

"Why you didn't tell me you were seeing him?"

"Seeing him?"

"Yes."

"I wasn't seeing him."

He removed his socks and threw them down next to his boots. "What would you call it?"

"Photographing him," she said sharply.

"Right." There was more to it than that, and they both knew it.

"See, this is why I didn't tell you. I knew you would jump to conclusions and automatically assume I was fucking him behind your back."

"I don't believe that for a second."

His words deflated her quickly, causing her to go from looking angry to confused in two seconds flat. "You don't."

"No." And the sad thing was that he had to tell her that.

"Then what's the problem?"

Russell stared at her blankly. Was she kidding him, or herself? "The fact that you kept it from me."

"Why? I didn't think you'd be too pleased about it."

"I'm more displeased you hid it. That you felt the need to hide it." And that she didn't see it as a problem.

"I didn't hide it. I don't have a reason to. You're not my father."

It was time for some straight facts. "No, but I'm your man. Or haven't you figured that out by now?"

"I realize that." She squared her shoulders.

"Do you? I think we have enough working against us without you unconsciously sabotaging us as well." From the way she gaped at him, he could tell his words caught her off guard.

"I am not."

"I believe you're not doing it on purpose, but I definitely think you're testing me."

"Testing you. For what?"

"To see if I'm going to break. To see if I'll stand up to you, or if I'm just going to let you ride roughshod over me. But let me tell you something. I don't play that way. I care for you, Tamara, probably more than you're ready to hear right now, but if you're waiting for me to fuck up to prove I'm fallible, stop," he said bluntly. "I'm not perfect, but I'm perfect for you, and the sooner you realize it, the better we both will be."

"That's not the way it went down," she insisted. "It was business and nothing more."

He rose, cutting her words off. "Fine, justify it all you want, but think on this, seriously. If the situation was reversed and you found me hanging out with, let's say Sandra, behind your back, would you let it go? Would you trust me, like I trust you?"

When she didn't reply right away, Russell knew he had his answer. "I'm going to hop in the shower." And just to prove he wasn't holding a grudge, he walked over to her and took her chin in his hand, using it to tilt her face up. "By the way, it was a beautiful picture."

Leaning down he brushed his lips over hers while she stood there in mute shock. Then he turned and walked into the bathroom, closing the door behind him.

Chapter Twelve

This wasn't exactly the way Tamara imagined spending the night. Even though they technically didn't go to bed mad, things hadn't been hunky-dory, either. She could tell he was still upset with her, and it bothered her, more than she cared to admit. Damn it to hell, this having feelings for someone definitely came with low points. His feelings were important to her, and his silence weighed heavily on her shoulders.

Sighing, Tamara turned on her bedside lamp, then rolled over in bed until she was facing him. From the sounds of the gentle snoring he was making, Russell, unlike her, didn't have a problem sleeping. Then again, he wasn't the one with the loud conscience.

Unfortunately, she only knew one way to shut her conscience up, and that was to appease her man as well as herself. Tamara snuggled up behind Russell, and slipped her hand between his side and his arm. Closing her eyes, she leaned into him and slowly ran her hand down his chest to his flat stomach, before brushing her fingers against his flaccid cock. Even in this state, it was still an impressive piece of equipment. What impressed her more, though, was the way he quickly began to stir to life.

Opening her eyes, she raised her head up a bit and kissed his shoulder, loving the feel of his warm flesh under her lips as she began to stroke his cock in a lazy rhythm. Slowly but steadily she caressed him, moving her hand up and down his thick erection with the patience of a woman who had all the time in the world.

The sensation of him in her hand, warm and alive, made her own body respond in so many delicious ways. The feel of him growing harder and longer, his flesh hot and thick, pulsating between her fingers, fed her ego like nothing else. By the time she'd pumped him to full mast, she was no longer the only one awake.

Reaching behind him, Russell grabbed her hip and pulled her in close to him. "As a lawyer, I feel the need to let you know this is illegal in almost all fifty states."

"Only if you press charges."

"Good point." His voice, though filled with humor, held traces of sleep in it still. "What time is it?"

"Time for an apology."

Russell stilled, then chuckled. "Damn, I'm dreaming."

Tamara smiled. "Tell me if this feels like a dream." She released him and sat up, then scooted over to give him some room to maneuver. "Roll onto your back for me."

"If you insist," he said, before doing as requested.

"Oh, I do." She leaned over him and took his cock in hand once more. "Feel free to go back to sleep, if you want."

"As if I could."

Without saying another word, she leaned forward and bathed the crown of his cock with her tongue. His slit trickled a bit of precum that she lapped up greedily before taking him deep into her mouth. The salty yet pleasing flavor peppered her senses. She kept going until the tip of his cock grazed the back of her throat, then slowly came back up, until only the head remained before plunging down once more. His impressive length prevented her from deep throating him like she wanted, but she wasn't going to allow something as simple as that to keep her from having a good time.

His answering groan was the only sign of approval she needed as she began to skillfully pleasure him. She used her hand as much as she used her mouth, stroking and sucking him at the same time, and from the way he was moaning and moving, she was doing something right. Tamara wished she could watch as she sucked him. His face was so expressive when they made love, she could only imagine what he looked like now.

"Fuck, baby."

With a guttural groan, Russell gripped the sheets and arched up toward her. His excitement fueled her own, moistening her pussy as if their positions were reversed, and it was he who was pleasuring her instead of the other way around.

He moaned as he moved his hand down to her head and gripped a fistful of hair. He gave a sharp tug that did little more than get her attention, before murmuring hoarsely, "Stop."

Following his lead, Tamara reluctantly came up and off his cock. She had been so into it that it felt weird to suddenly quit, especially since she didn't want to stop. There was nothing she wanted more than to have him come undone in her mouth. "What if I don't want to?"

"This is makeup sex right?"

"Something like that." Even though she wasn't sucking him, she kept her hand moving up and down his shaft. She wanted him on the edge, ready to come at any second.

"Then we're going to have to get to the actual sex before we can make up."

"Oral sex doesn't count?"

"Not to me." Russell took hold of her arm and pulled her up to him until she was staring deep into his eyes. "Your mouth could never compare to your pussy, as delightful as it is."

"Ahh, baby, you're such a sweet talker."

"I try."

Smiling, Tamara leaned forward and playfully nipped at his bottom lip. "So, does this mean you forgive me?"

"I still haven't decided." His twinkling eyes said otherwise, though.

"Is there anything I can do that might help you decide?" If he wanted to play, she was more than willing.

"Yes. Get on all fours."

She liked the sound of that. "Am I going to need a saddle, cowboy?"

"No, but I might need a riding crop."

Even better. "Kinky."

"You haven't seen anything yet."

If that was the case, she was going to have to make him mad more often.

He reached over to the nightstand and withdrew a condom from the top drawer. He knew that once things got started, he wouldn't want to stop and get it out. Better now than later, when he'd be too far gone to care about protection.

Running his hand over her upturned cheeks, Russell wondered why they'd skipped this position. Her full, sexy ass beckoned him to do all sorts of naughty things to it. From spanking, to fucking, to flogging, there was a wealth of possibilities he couldn't wait to explore one day.

Then again, there was no time like the present.

Leaning forward, he nipped at her rounded bottom and laughed to himself when she cried out in mock pain. He planned that her cries would soon be those of pleasure. Placing his hands on her full ass, Russell slipped his thumbs between the crease of her buttocks and separated her cheeks. The sexy sight of her brown, puckered hole had his mouth watering.

"Wha—"

Russell leaned forward and swiped his tongue across her rosette, dragging a hiss from Tamara. "Russell."

He wanted to tell her to just sit back and enjoy, but that would require him moving away, and he wasn't ready to do that just yet. Instead, he continued on his oral exploration of her bottom, kissing and frenching as she writhed in what he could only describe as pure enjoyment.

But as content as he was to pleasure her this way, it wasn't the only thing he wanted to do. Russell moved one of his hands between her legs to search out her other treasure. When his fingers found the puddle of moisture covering her nether lips, he grinned. No doubt about it, his girl definitely liked his tongue on her. "Is this for me, baby?" he asked, as he dipped two fingers into her wet pussy.

"Hmmm," she moaned, instead of replying, much to his delight. The needy little noises she emitted made him want to fuck her all the more, but first he was going to explore her body a bit further.

Rising up once again, Russell withdrew his juice-slicked fingers from her wet pussy and pressed one against her rosette carefully. Tamara stiffened and moved forward a bit, but he followed her with his hand, refusing to allow her to escape that easily. "Where are you going?"

Tamara glanced over her shoulder at him. "Shouldn't I be asking *you* that?"

"I think it's pretty obvious where I'm going." Without removing his finger from her ass, he placed his other hand between her legs and brushed his fingers against her hardened bud. His new movements brought forth a welcoming sound of pleasure from her lips, and when she didn't move away from him again, he increased the pressure against her rosette.

"Russell," she said breathlessly. "I don't think I'm this sorry."

"Are you sure?" He pushed harder until his finger popped through the resistant ring and sank knuckle-deep inside her.

"Hmm..."

"Thought so." He chuckled as he moved his finger slowly in and out. "I'm not going to fuck you here tonight. But it will happen, sweetheart, and you'll love it as much as I will."

"I've never done that before."

"Which makes it all the sweeter for me." Russell added a second finger into her tight hole and twisted it as he pumped it in and out of her. Hard and aching, his cock strained from the need to come. Russell looked forward to the day when he would fuck her ass. He would fill her as no other man had before, possessing her, claiming every inch of her body and proving to her once and for all that she belonged solely to him.

As he frigged her clit, he fucked her ass with his fingers, steadily increasing the depth and the pressure until she began to pump back against him. From the way she cried out as she gyrated against his hand, Russell could tell that the day he fucked her ass would be sooner rather than later.

"You like that, don't you, baby?"

"God..."

"You like my fingers buried deep in your ass. You wish it was my cock, though, don't you, baby, fucking you long and deep?" Russell could tell from her heady noises and motions that she was getting close to coming. "Tell me and I'll let you come."

"Yes," she groaned. "Yes. I want you to fuck my ass. Happy?"

"Almost."

His fingers continued to play her body like a finely tuned instrument, until she stiffened, then screamed her long-awaited release. Aroused now more than ever, Russell pulled his fingers out of her body. He quickly sheathed his cock, then gripped her hip with one hand and positioned himself at her opening with the other. His mind shouted one word, *Mine*, as he thrust inside her, seating himself balls-deep on the first stroke.

Tamara cried out as he filled her, echoing the need coursing through his own blood. This would not be a slow and drawn-out fuck. He was feeling too primal for that. Russell had an almost innate need to possess her as surely as she did him, and if he had to do it one stroke at a time, he would. Succumbing to his desire to dominate her, Russell began to fuck her in earnest.

Tamara pushed back with his every thrust, her own enthusiasm more than apparent. It never ceased to amaze him that no matter how many times he took her, her pussy was still as tight and juicy as the first time. In all his life, he'd never felt anything as good as her pussy. "Fuck, baby, you make my cock so hard."

"I can feel it. Every single inch of it. Filling me. Filling me so good."

"That's right, baby, filling you and only you."

"Mine."

"Fuck, yeah." He grunted. "And you belong to—"

"You. Always you." She arched into the curve of his body, thrusting back against him, forcing his cock to slam against her ass with every pump. Their lewd noises filled the room. Rough, loud, and wild. Sex just didn't get better than this.

"Please," she begged. "Don't stop. Never stop."

"I won't, baby. I'm going to fuck you forever. You belong to me." His voice was rough and urgent and almost unrecognizable to his own ears. The harder he fucked her, the harder he wanted to fuck her. And if the glass-shattering noises coming from Tamara were anything to go by, his method more than met with her approval.

Her breathing quickened, her body shook, and her pussy clenched around his cock like a vise. "Ohhhh…" she groaned. She reached out blindly and grabbed hold of the comforter, digging her nails into the thick material. "Good."

"That's right, baby, come."

She whimpered and bucked, trembling around his cock as she came. The intensity of her savage release triggered his own. With one long, guttural groan, he dug his nails into her hips and came, flooding the condom with his seed.

Tamara's legs gave out, and she collapsed forward on the bed. Russell reacted quickly and pulled out. He steadied himself on his knees to prevent himself from falling on top of her. Panting, he worked on catching his breath as he removed the condom, dropping it carelessly on the nightstand. It wasn't pretty, but he'd just worry about the mess tomorrow. Exhausted, he lay down beside Tamara, a bit light-headed. His heart was pounding rapidly, and his head was spinning, but it was totally worth it.

"Your pussy is going to be the death of me."

Chuckling, Tamara rolled over to her side so that she was facing him. "So, do you forgive me?"

"If I tell you no, can we do it again?"

"Yes."

"Then no."

"Liar." She laughed softly and moved closer to him, resting her head on his shoulder.

The contentment he felt at this moment was like no other. Finally, he understood why Ty could smile from just thinking Charlotte's name. Russell didn't know much about love, he only knew he'd never felt this way about a woman in his life.

Chapter Thirteen

Tamara whistled as she walked into Charlotte's hospital room, feeling much better than she had this morning. She might have been a complete failure in Girlfriend 101 last night, but this morning she'd earned some serious brownie points. The power of the blowjob was remarkable.

"Hey, Momma."

Charlotte turned to look at her and smiled. For someone who'd given birth less than twenty-four hours ago, she looked great. Motherhood suited Charlotte, just as Tamara knew it would. "Hey. I didn't know you were coming back so soon."

"Are you too tired for company?" Tamara stood at the foot of the bed, willing to go if need be.

"Heck, no." Charlotte hit a button on her remote control to raise the bed. She winced when she came to a forty-five-degree angle, but then smiled. "I'm bored out of my mind."

"Where's Ty?"

"He went home to shower, then bring me back something to eat."

Tamara sat down in the chair closest to the bed. "He stayed all night?"

"Yes, despite the fact the nurses asked him to go." Charlotte grinned.

"They didn't make him?"

"Have you met my husband?"

Tamara grinned. "Enough said. Where's the princess?"

"She was sleeping, so I let them take her. She should be back soon, though. They want me feeding every two hours."

Tamara eyed her friend's breasts. They didn't seem any larger than normal. "You packing yet?"

"No, my milk's not in yet, but the colostrum is."

Tamara crinkled her nose in disgust. "Okay, I don't know what that is, but we're going to pretend like I do."

"You'll learn soon enough."

"Not too soon, thank you."

"Uh-huh," Charlotte teased. "I've seen that look in Russell's eyes. You'll be wedded and bedded before long."

"Well, the bedded part for sure." Russell hadn't made any mention of weddings, which was fine as far as Tamara was concerned. She could only handle so much change at one time.

"So how did the show go?"

"It went well. I received a call this morning. Lilith said she sold all the pictures. Even one of a certain someone heavy with child," she said referring to the picture she took of a close-up of Charlotte's belly. As soon as she had heard it sold, she knew exactly who'd bought it. "I thought I told you I would make you a copy of it."

"I didn't want a copy, I wanted that one. Besides, when you're famous, I can say I knew you when."

"You guys didn't have to do that." But it touched her that they had.

"Of course we did. Keep in mind, we only bought one photo. That means you sold four more all on your own."

"I did, didn't I?" Tamara puffed her chest with pride.

"Yes, you did."

"Lilith was pretty impressed with my debut. She wants more of my work. I think I might need to get an agent."

Charlotte's eyes widened in wonder. "Serious?"

"Yes."

"Wow."

Their one-word exchange made Tamara chuckle. "I know. It's hard to believe, even though it's happening to me."

"So yesterday was the best day ever."

"Well, almost." Tamara crinkled her nose at the thought of how bad it could have been.

"Almost?"

"Yes, I nearly screwed things up with Russell."

"Impossible." Charlotte waved her hand as if she could erase Tamara's words. "You could coldcock that man's momma and he'd forgive you. Of course, you probably wouldn't be able to sit down for a month."

"I'm not so sure about that."

"Well, what did you do?"

"Nothing in my book. At first, anyway."

"What about his?"

That was a completely different story. "I never told him about the pictures I took of Christian, and it upset him."

"You didn't?" The censure in Charlotte's voice made her wince.

"I didn't do it on purpose, really, I didn't."

"You accidentally kept it from him?" Sarcasm dripped from Charlotte's words.

"Okay, see, when you say it like that it sounds stupid."

"Probably as stupid as when you said it."

"Ouch." Tamara let out a deep sigh. "You know, this having someone to answer to isn't all it's cracked up to be."

"It has its perks."

"Yeah, but the downsides are a killer." Tamara grimaced. "Can you believe that I actually felt bad? Me?"

"Guilt is a bitch, isn't it?"

"Yes, it is, stinky guilt."

"Welcome to the world of relationships."

"Lucky me." Tamara frowned. "You know what I don't get."

"Men?"

That was a given. "Besides that."

"No, what?"

"It's only been two months. Two. Why in the world do I give a flying fuck about what he thinks or feels, and I'm not just talking about this incident. I think about him all the time, not just what he's doing, but how's he doing. The other night, he sounded really tired and wasn't going to come over, so I took a cab to his house to see him."

"Aww…that's so sweet."

"That's my point. Since when have you ever known me to be sweet?"

"I've always thought you were sweet."

"Well, to my family and friends, maybe, but to a guy I was just sleeping with, never that."

"Maybe because he's not just some guy you're sleeping with."

"Tell me about it," she said putting all the confusion she felt in her voice. "When did that happen?"

"What?'

"When he did slip under my fuck-buddy barriers and become someone I care about?"

"I don't know."

"Me, either, but let me tell you something, sister, I don't like. Not one bit."

"Why?"

"Did you miss the point when I said two months?"

"What's time have to do with anything?"

"Everything." Tamara fumed more to herself than to Charlotte. "It doesn't make sense for me to care for him deeply. Other than the two of you, we have nothing in common. He's a cowboy, for goodness' sake."

"Yet you love him."

"Yes...wait...no." Charlotte burst out laughing much to Tamara's irritation. "What's so funny?"

"You are. You sound just like me when I fell for Ty. So let me do you a favor and save you a whole lot of heartache. You love him, Tamara. I know you do. He probably knows you do, and if you're honest with yourself, you know you do. So just admit it."

"I will admit no such thing. Two months, Charlotte."

"Love, Tamara, doesn't care about race, religion, gender, or time. It's a gift, and if you're lucky enough to find someone who cares for you back, then embrace it and thank the good Lord, because not everyone is so blessed to receive that gift."

Tamara opened her mouth, although for the life of her she had no idea what she was going to say. There was no doubt in her mind she'd fallen for him. His opinion of her wouldn't matter so much if she hadn't. She just didn't know how to say it or prove it, without doing something outlandish like saying the "L" word.

To make matters worse, Charlotte's arguments actually made sense, even though she didn't want to admit it. She was thankfully stopped from having to confess that sad fact, however, when the nurse pushed open the door with little Candace in her arms.

"This one has been asking for her momma."

"Saved by the bell," Charlotte muttered as she smiled and took the baby into her arms.

Tamara couldn't have agreed more. "And what a beautiful belle she is." She smiled over at her godchild while Charlotte got the mewling girl settled at her breast. It took a few tries before the pale-skinned beauty latched on correctly and quieted down to a homemade meal.

Charlotte winced at first, but soon the grimace melted into a content smile. She lovingly caressed the nearly hairless head of her daughter and cooed softly to her as Tamara looked on with envy.

If she had a child with Russell, chances were that he or she would be this lovely, but theirs. All theirs. Her heart flipped like a somersault in her chest, not just at the thought of having a beautiful baby, but also at the thought of having Russell's baby, which in itself was scary and yet somehow exciting at the same time. She waited until after the nurse left before speaking again. "Do you still get stupid stares and backhanded comments?"

"Every day and twice on Sunday," Charlotte answered without looking up.

"You might want to consider changing churches, then."

Laughing, Charlotte looked back up. "You know what I mean, goof."

"I do." Tamara let out a heavy sigh.

"But you didn't ask me the biggie."

"What's that?"

"If it's worth it."

"Is it?" she asked, even though she already knew the answer.

"Absolutely."

* * *

After seeing the interior designer out, Russell did a solo walk through his house, pleased with what he saw. Everything he'd hoped for was alive in the rooms before him. Now all he needed to bring his dream to life was a family to fill the house. Lucky for him, he had the perfect candidate in mind for the job.

Despite all the obstacles that might come, he knew without a shadow of a doubt Tamara was the woman for him. And for a man who just two months ago had shuddered at the thought of matrimony, that was a huge admission. They weren't going to get married tomorrow, heck, maybe not this year, but it was going to happen. Of this he was sure.

In fact, while his checkbook was still at the ready, he figured he might as well give the contractor a call. It couldn't possibly take that long to add a darkroom onto the house.

Smiling at the thought, Russell started back down the stairs, crinkling his brow when the doorbell rang. He could have sworn Tamara took a set of house keys with her.

"Back already?" he asked as he swung the door open. "I was sure you were going to stay at the hos—" Russell's words died out as he spotted Sandra standing on the other side of the door. She smiled brightly at him as he stared down at her, partly in shock, partly in irritation. She had no business being here, a fact he was apparently going to have reiterate to her once more.

"You thought I was going to do what?"

"I thought you were someone else," he said in a flat and uninterested tone.

"Really? Who?"

"Tamara." Russell wasn't going to mince words with Sandra. After the party, he'd been straight up with her, letting her know in no uncertain terms just where they stood with one another. Nowhere.

"She's still around?" She said it as calmly as if she was talking about a stray cat.

Russell ground his teeth together and counted to ten silently before answering. "Yes. She is."

"Interesting."

"No, what's interesting is you showing up." Russell crossed his arms over his chest. "What do you want, Sandra?"

"I heard through the grapevine that the house was done. I wanted to get a tour."

"I don't think so."

Her smile dimmed. "Come on, Russell, for old time's sake."

"No." His curt answer caused her smile to drop altogether.

She looked shocked, the first real emotion he'd thought he'd ever seen on her face. "Can I at least come in? I need to talk to you."

"About?"

"It's private."

Russell made a show of looking behind her. "We're in the middle of nowhere, Sandra; it doesn't get more private than this."

"Don't make me beg, Russell."

He was a fool, and he knew it. "Ten minutes." Russell moved back and let her enter, even though his common sense told him to do otherwise.

Russell led the way to the living room, refusing to detour to any other room. He even went as far as to stand while she took a seat on the couch, in hopes of cutting her stay even shorter. This wasn't a social visit, and he wanted to get it over with as quickly as possible.

Sandra, of course, could never do things the easy way. Instead of sitting back like most people would have, she sat stiffly, crossing her legs at the ankle and her hands at the wrist on top of her lap.

The classy look, which was what he assumed she was going for, did nothing for him.

"Well." He hoped he sounded as bored as he felt.

Her lower trembled and her voice shook. "Where did we go wrong?"

"Probably about the time you thought we were a we."

"How can you be so cruel?"

"Because kindness didn't work." Russell didn't like being put into the role of the bad guy. It, along with their fictitious relationship, wasn't something he'd signed up for. "Sandra, there is nothing and there has never been anything of substance between us. We weren't even exclusive."

"What do you mean?"

Russell regarded her with cold disdain. "You don't think your extra outings were a secret, did you? In a town this small, you really should know better."

"I only went out with those other guys to make you jealous." As if on cue, crocodile tears began to make a slow trek down her pale checks.

"Did you fuck them for me too?"

She gasped. "I never—"

"Oh please." This was growing old. "Don't mistake my silence for ignorance. I condoned it because I didn't care. I still don't."

"Did you ever care for me?"

"As a friend, but nothing more." He wasn't a cruel man. Having this conversation with her wasn't something he was enjoying, but he wasn't going to be manipulated by her. "It's inevitable that we're going to run into each other from time to time. I'd prefer we were able to chat amicably when we do."

"Amicably." Her voice took on a shrill like quality. "I love you, Russell."

"I'm with Tamara now."

"What about me?"

Russell wanted so badly to say, "What about you?" but he held it back. "You'll be fine. You always are."

"Maybe I'm tired of being fine." Sandra rose quickly and walked over to him, dropping down on her knees before him. "I want you, and I'm willing to do anything to prove it."

There were so many places Russell would have preferred to be at that exact moment in time, and none of them was where he was at. Of all the many times Russell had seen Sandra on her knees before him, this was by far his least favorite and the most annoying.

"Get up, Sandra."

"Not until you listen to reason."

"What you're saying isn't reason. It's foolishness."

"You're calling my love for you foolishness?"

"No, I'm calling this act you're doing foolish. You don't love me, any more than I love you."

"How can you say that?"

"By moving my lips." Russell ran his hand through his hair and cursed the fates for his stupidity. What on earth had he ever seen in her? "You need to leave."

"You'll have to throw me out."

"You're being overly dramatic." That was putting it mildly. "I know you have more pride than this. Act like it."

"You can't seriously tell me you want her instead of me."

"Should I try jokingly, then, because it's obvious the way I'm doing it isn't getting through to you. I'm with Tamara. I care for Tamara." Maybe if he spelled it out for her she'd finally understand.

"Oh for goodness' sake." Russell grabbed her hands and yanked her to feet. The swift movement sent her sprawling against

his chest as a cheerful voice called out, "I'm back. Russell, where—
"

"Fuck." Russell cursed under his breath. With a disgusted sigh, he pushed Sandra away from him and looked at Tamara who was standing in the doorway with a surprised look on her face.

Her confused gaze ran from Sandra, then back to Russell. "Am I interrupting?"

"Yes, you are," Sandra said triumphantly as he shook his head.

"No, you aren't." Today was definitely not going the way he planned. "As trite as it sounds, this isn't the way it seems."

"Isn't it?" Sandra interrupted. "I think she can see for herself what's really going on here."

"You're right, I can." Then to his surprise, Tamara looked at him and smiled. "I have an answer to your question, Russell."

"You do?" He had no idea what she was talking about, but she didn't look pissed off. That had to be a good thing.

"The situation is reversed, and I absolutely trust you."

"You do?"

"Yes. I'm going to put the groceries up and let you two get back to your conversation."

Russell watched in amazement as Tamara calmly walked from the room. He'd been expecting...hell, a reaction like one he'd get from Sandra, screaming and tears or running away. He should have known better. Tamara was so far away from Sandra, it was as if they were night and day.

If he'd been surprised, Sandra was completely flabbergasted. But she didn't stay down for long. Turning on her heel, she marched after Tamara. As much as he wanted to go defend his woman, he knew better. She didn't need him to fight her battles; she was more than capable of taking care of herself, but that didn't mean he didn't want to watch her do it.

Chapter Fourteen

Tamara was very proud of herself. Despite what she saw, she hadn't lost her mind. She didn't go crazy or ghetto and go off on a Jerry Springer-like tirade on Sandra. Instead she looked with more than her eyes. She looked with her heart, and saw the truth. Russell didn't want Sandra, he wanted her, and Tamara would be all kinds of stupid to allow the other woman's pathetic ploy to get to her. She knew better. Hell, she *was* better than that.

Energized and confident, she walked into the kitchen to begin to putting away the groceries she'd bought. Tonight, she was going to put Russell's new kitchen to good use and make him an old-fashioned southern recipe. Her mother would be so proud, she thought with a grin, of her newfound domestic streak.

But before she could even get the first bag unpacked, Sandra stormed into the kitchen. Gone was the classy, well-put-together woman she'd met not so long ago, and in her place was someone who looked a bit deranged.

"Are you really that naive?" Sandra's eyes were filled with fury. "Don't you see what's going on before your very eyes?"

"I do." Despite what the other woman was attempting to do, Tamara couldn't find it in herself to work up even the slightest bit of rage. She was too filled with pity to do that. "You'll find someone else one day."

"One day." Sandra was apparently not a woman used to being pitied. "I have someone now. It's you who's the outsider. In more than one way, I'd like to add."

The pity began to diminish a bit. "Are you seriously going to try to play the race card? Come on. Aren't we both a little too old for childish games like that? This is the new millennium, honey. You're going to have to come up with something a bit more original than that to get me upset."

"I'm not trying to upset you. Just trying to save you from yourself. Girls like you always end up getting hurt. Russell's out of your league, sugar. I think you'd be happier with someone more your style."

"Funny thing is, Russell is my type. Who would have thunk it, right? Besides, Sandra, the truth of the matter is, you don't know me. Not at all, especially if you think your pathetic little play of power is going to send me running for the hills. I'm not some weak-willed female who is easily spooked. I'm. Not. Going. Anywhere."

Tamara could see from the surprised look in the other woman's eyes that this was exactly what she'd thought would happen. *Good Lord, does she think this is some cheesy Regency romance novel?* Still she had to admire the other woman's determination; even now she wouldn't back down. "I may not know you, but I know men."

"And?" Tamara asked a bit intrigued where Sandra was going with this new line of attack. Because Lord knew, she didn't know a thing about men.

"And I know Russell will never be happy with"—she ran her heated gaze over Tamara—"someone like you."

"He already is."

"But for how long? Do you really think you'll be able to help him in business? Be the perfect hostess he needs at dinner parties, the beauty on his arm at meetings."

Tamara couldn't help but smile. Sandra was just regurgitating a revamped hostile version of the same exact thing Tamara had said to Charlotte. It was amusing, now that the shoe was on the other foot, how stupid that speech was. Listening to Sandra say it only made Tamara realize how unimportant those things were. "I think Russell can handle the running of his own business. He doesn't need me for that."

"He doesn't need you for anything."

"Yes, he does." And she was finally getting it. "To make him happy."

"He was happy before. With me."

"Honey"—Tamara tilted her head and shook it sadly—"he was never with you."

"Is that what he told you? Because if so, he lied. We had sex countless times."

"Yes, but you probably never made love."

"How would you know?"

"Because if you had, he wouldn't be with me." It was that simple as far as Tamara was concerned.

"It won't last. This infatuation of his. He's always done everything Ty's done. He'll get over that."

"But he'll never get over me." She'd tried to be nice, but it just wasn't working. "Look, Sandra, you're fighting a losing battle with an unmotivated opponent. I'm not threatened by you or by what you think you used to have with Russell. Whatever it *was* is of no importance to me, because it's his past. And I'm his future."

"So you finally figured that out, did you?" Russell spoke from behind them, drawing both women's attention in his direction.

Tamara wasn't sure how long he'd been standing there, and it didn't matter. She would have said what she had whether he'd been in the room or not. Now there was only one more thing he needed to hear. And that was a little bit of down-home honesty. "I'm a bit slow, at times."

His lips twitched. "I'd say." Russell walked around the island until he was standing beside her and slipped his arm around her waist, before turning his attention toward their unwanted visitor. "Sandra, I think it's time you left."

"Long past." Fury radiated from the other woman in waves. "When you're ready for a real woman, Russell, you'll know where to find me."

"Like I told you already, Sandra, I have one."

Russell was disappointed it had to end this way. He'd always been very clear that his and Sandra's was a mutually beneficial relationship only, with no strings attached. And for a while, it seemed to work for both of them. But he was no longer that man, not since he'd gotten together with Tamara. And by the look on her face, Sandra had expectations he'd never known.

The sound of the front door slamming echoed throughout the room and signaled not only Sandra leaving, but hopefully the start of a whole new chapter in Russell's life, with Tamara being the central character of each chapter.

He looked down at the woman in his arms, grateful more and more each day that he'd taken a chance on her and she on him. Sighing, Tamara rested her head on Russell's shoulder and snuggled close. "Talk about someone being ad-dick-ted."

"I wish I could take credit for her bizarre behavior, but I sincerely doubt it has anything to do with my prowess in the bedroom."

"What do you think it is?"

"Probably a combination of a lot things. Sandra isn't one to give up on something when she's set her mind to it. Plus, I heard a rumor a few weeks back about her father making a couple of bad investments. He tied up the bulk of their money into some real estate that, thanks to the economy right now, is taking a big nosedive."

"You think the fear of having to paint her own toenails now is what has her marching in the loony parade?"

Russell shrugged. "It might. Mr. Malt is a smart man, though. I'm sure he'll rebound soon. Sandra probably just wanted to hedge her bets."

Tamara pulled back, her eyebrow arched. "Well, people in hell want ice water. Doesn't mean they're going to get it."

"If I didn't know better, Tamara, I'd think you'd fight for me or something." If this is what it took to get her to finally admit her feelings for him, he could only thank Sandra.

"If it came down to a battle of the babes, which team would you have rooted for?"

As if she had to ask. "I'm not dumb, I know a ringer when I see one."

"You know, from the way you were speaking to her when I arrived, well, it might give someone the wrong impressions about your feelings for me."

"Really?"

"Yeah, someone might think you were in serious like with me."

Serious like? Okay, he could play this game. "Then maybe I should clear it up so *someone* doesn't get the wrong idea. I'm in deep, serious, heart-aching, cock-hardening, head-in-the-clouds, cheesy-eighties-power-ballads *like* with you."

"Damn, you had to break out the power ballads."

"I only speak from the heart, baby."

"That's some kind of *like*."

"I think so. And since we're putting this all out there, the way you proudly declared yourself my woman might make a different someone think you maybe like me back."

"Declared myself? I don't recall all that."

"I recall it enough for the both of us."

"Then, cowboy counselor, I can't argue with that or dispute that I am in some serious, doodling your name on paper, sighing when I hear the old Jets jams on the radio station because their songs make me think of you, *like* with you as well."

His woman had a way with words. "Your paper doodling *like* trumps my power ballads like."

"Then we're agreed. We're in *like* with one another."

"Yes." Russell nodded. "We're also in love with another, but we have time to get into that later."

"We have plenty of time for that," she agreed with a soft smile.

"Speaking of being addicted. I think I feel the shakes coming on."

Tamara's eyes sparkled with laughter as she shook her head and made a *tsk, tsk* noise. "Not again."

"Oh yeah. It's been like ten hours since my last fix. I need a taste." Russell picked Tamara up and sat her on the kitchen island. "I need a taste. Bad."

Tamara wrapped her hands around his neck and toyed with the back of his hair. "Don't say I didn't warn you."

"You did." She just hadn't warned him it would be a lifelong addiction he'd never want to be free of.

"The power of the black vagina strikes again."

"I think it's white man's kryptonite. Able to bring a cowboy to his knees with a single thrust."

"Think we should alert the media?"

"Nah, let them find out on their own." He pushed her legs apart and stepped between them, bringing him closer to the object of his desire. "So is there a cure for this?"

"Yes, and if you're lucky, I just might give it to you in forty or fifty years."

"You thinking long-term here?" Because he certainly was.

"Maybe."

"I like maybes." He was sure he'd be able to turn that maybe into a definitely with no problem.

"By the way, I got a call the other day. My temp job is officially over."

"It is?"

"Yes."

"Any ideas to what you might want to do next?" He had a few suggestions if need be.

"I was thinking of taking a break from temping and trying the photography thing full time for a bit."

"That's wonderful." And more than coincided with what he had in mind.

"Yeah. Thought I might possibly rope a cowboy into marriage—in a few years, mind you—and maybe even shoot out a few kids or so."

"Shoot 'em out?"

"Yeah. If Charlotte can do it in four hours, then I can do it in three. I'm thinking twins. You know—bam, bam. Get 'em in and get 'em out."

Russell's lip twitched as he tried to hold back his amusement. "Twins."

"Yes. You know how competitive I am."

"Yes, I do. But twins?"

"It's negotiable."

"Good to know." His hands grasped her hips, pulling her forward until the seam of her jeans was pressed against him. "Any particular cowboy in mind?"

"I was thinking I'd see if Christian had any plans for the fall." Russell snorted in lieu of commenting. "But then I thought, if he was busy, I'd give you a go."

"Well, I do have room to build a darkroom out here. It would be a shame if I just allowed the space to go to waste." He'd built this ranch to be the start of his legacy. He couldn't think of anything better than to have Tamara with him along for the ride.

"Waste not, want not. That's what I always say." She wrapped her legs around his waist.

Russell tightened his hold on her and picked her up. "You know I'm going to tell our kids you proposed to me, right?"

"Just like you know I'll deny it."

"Who do you think they'll believe?" he asked as he headed toward the stairs. If they were going to be negotiating babies, he knew the perfect place for the talks to take place.

"I guess we'll just have to find out."

He was looking forward to it.

THE END

Lena Matthews

Lena Matthews spends her days dreaming about handsome heroes and her nights with her own personal hero. Married to her college sweetheart, she is the proud mother of two children, three evil dogs, and a mess of ants that she can't seem to get rid of.

When not writing she can be found reading, watching movies, lifting up the cushions on the couch to look for batteries for the remote control, and plotting different ways to bring Buffy back on the air.

TITLES AVAILABLE In Print from Loose Id®

A GUARDIAN'S DESIRE
Mya

CROSSING BORDERS
Z. A. Maxfield

DINAH'S DARK DESIRE
Mechele Armstrong

FORGOTTEN SONG
Ally Blue

GEORGINA'S DRAGON
Willa Okati

HARD CANDY
Angela Knight, Morgan Hawke and Sheri Gilmore

HEAVEN SENT: HELL & PURGATORY
Jet Mykles

ROMANCE AT THE EDGE: In Other Worlds
MaryJanice Davidson, Angela Knight and Camille Anthony

SETTLER'S MINE 1: THE RIVALS
Mechele Armstrong

SOMETHING MORE
Amanda Young

STRENGTH IN NUMBERS
Rachel Bo

THE ASSIGNMENT
Evangeline Anderson

THEIR ONE AND ONLY
Trista Ann Michaels

TRY A LITTLE TENDERNESS
Roslyn Hardy Holcomb

WILD WISHES
Stephanie Burke, Lena Matthews, and Eve Vaughn

Publisher's Note: The print titles listed above were previously released in e-book format by Loose Id®.

Non-Fiction by *ANGELA KNIGHT*
PASSIONATE INK: A GUIDE TO WRITING EROTIC ROMANCE

LaVergne, TN USA
15 September 2010
197187LV00003B/61/P